"Green makeup. Wow. Sallow people of the world, beware."

Buffy was not impressed with Willow's story of the theater gremlins. "Nobody's gotten hurt yet, have they?"

"Well, no. But what about the invisible oil on the floor?"

Giles frowned. "Now, that, I admit, does sound a trifle odd."

"It could be a spell," Buffy said, shrugging. "Somebody playing a practical joke."

"But—" *But what about the whispers*, Willow started to protest, but looking around at the faces of her friends, she let a breath go and smiled. None of them was taking her seriously. Not even Tara. "Sure. No big. Just some practical joker."

"Besides, if there ever was anything demonic in the theater, it was probably Anouilh," Giles muttered darkly. "What that man did to *Antigone* . . ."

Buffy the Vampire Slayer™

Available from POCKET BOOKS

These Our Actors

Ashley McConnell and
Dori Koogler

**An original novel based on the hit television series
by Joss Whedon**

POCKET
BOOKS

NEW YORK LONDON TORONTO SYDNEY SINGAPORE

First Pocket Books edition October 2002

™ and © 2002 Twentieth Century Fox Film Corporation.
All rights reserved.

POCKET BOOKS
An imprint of Simon & Schuster
Africa House
64–78 Kingsway
London WC2B 6AH
www.simonsays.co.uk

The text of this book was set in Times.
2 4 6 8 10 9 7 5 3 1
A CIP catalogue record for this book is available from
the British Library
ISBN 0-7434-5034-5

Printed and bound by Cox & Wyman Ltd, Reading, Berkshire

Acknowledgments

Ashley McConnell would particularly like to acknowledge the friendship and support of her friends during the writing of this book, especially Judy Tarr who provided a refuge from escalating stress; the Deming Fire Department Emergency Medical Service for talking her into getting her head examined; Mimbres Memorial Hospital staff for making sure she was more or less in one piece; Kim Brown and Nanette Morton who dropped everything and sallied forth on no notice on a successful four-hundred-mile round trip rescue expedition; Max, Cream, Mouse, Freya, and Isis for not walking on, bumping into, or otherwise jarring the fragile human; and very definitely, the blackhanky crew for desperately needed support. You all gave a stiff-necked Irishwoman a reason to unbend. And, of course, my co-author, who also deserves my thanks, but she knows all that, right? I am delighted to have my name on a book cover with yours, Dori Koogler.

Dori Koogler would like to thank:

The Diving Board Gang—Kay, Beth, Becky, Linda, Doris, Jennifer, Ann, Debra, Keith, Mimi, Katie, Marina, Sue, eluki, Michelle, Sherri, and especially Badger, who can kick butt harder than *any* of them. I wouldn't have got here without your encouragement.

JP, my net home and Fount of Wisdom. This is for Pat.

The Spike-list Troika—BTVS-TabulaRasa, Spike's Salvation, and The Gutter. Told y'all I'd deal with That Creature.

My children, Will and Francis, for putting up with all the craziness of a Writing Mom.

And of course, Sam, Fraser, and Ashley, without whose encouragement and support—and NAGGING—I wouldn't have written this book. I love you guys.

Chapter One

Attic peninsula, b.p.e.

Thousands of years before the present era, men gather on the slopes of a natural amphitheater, a small basin rimmed by olive trees. The floor of the basin is bare earth, a soft white powder scuffed by many bare feet. One edge of this floor is defined by a simple wooden wall with openings, doorways, at each end. The audience can see through the doorways to the slope rising upward on the other side; the wall encloses nothing.

It is early evening. Orange and gold are beginning to fade from the skies, and shades of deep blue are forming over the wild mountains on the near horizon. The brightest stars, the gods themselves, are beginning to appear in the sky.

The audience observes, intent, fascinated, as a smaller group of men enter the basin floor through the doorways and cluster below, facing them. The small group is chanting a prayer in a ragged chorus. They are dressed in white chitons and wear no sandals; laurel wreaths are bound around their brows.

The audience seats itself on rocks, fallen logs, and the grassy slope itself, and falls absolutely silent. Men are on the lower slopes. Women are separate, higher, seeing the ritual from a sharper angle.

The words gather power as the voices meld together, match rhythms. The olive leaves shiver, though there is no breeze. Doves shake themselves from sleep in protest.

The voices deepen. The chant echoes the sound of booted feet on the deck of a ship, marching back and forth; the sound of waves crashing against a shore, as they crash against the shore not far from this place.

The audience leans forward.

The cluster of men below are a circle now, moving, stamping their feet with the rhythm of the chant: One and *two* and one and *two* and one and *three* and . . .

The audience holds its breath as the circle stops. It moves into itself, into a knot of men. Spreads apart into a semicircle—leaving one figure alone in the middle.

A single figure. Alone.

Never before has a single figure stood alone before gods and men in the ritual contests.

And this one, this one stands taller than a human man, on sandals built up the span of a hand or more. And it wears a face that is not a human face but a mask, a terrible mask of grief that covers not only a human face but half a body.

The voice that comes from this figure is not the voice of a chorus, but the voice of a single person. It does not speak to the gods in the voice of the people using the voice of the people, *We implore thee, O Immortal Ones!*

It speaks for itself.

I, King that was, spoke to the gods . . .

The chorus answers, giving voice now not to prayers but to the thoughts of the audience, that watches amazed at the new thing that is created before them. *Men who speak to the gods beware; the gods may be pleased to answer . . .*

The actor—the first actor—speaks again, with more courage as the audience tenses, leans forward and listens intently.

The power finds focus.

And afterward, when the stars have faded, and the chorus has gone, and the first actor drinks wine with his fellow poets and rubs his feet and jokes that he near lost his balance as well as his bladder for fear that Dionysus would strike him dead for his daring, when men of the audience have left the little basin but babble still at what they have seen this night, a shadow sits and looks around him and marvels that he is all alone.

Not for long, the power assures him. *They'll come back. Creators, audience—they'll all be back.*

Sunnydale, California, Fall semester, 2000
"Welcome to Introduction to Drama," said the tall

man standing in the middle of the stage. "I am Doctor Addams. This class will meet every Tuesday and Thursday afternoon here in the theater, except when technical rehearsals require the afternoons."

A hand shot up from one side of the auditorium. "What's a technical rehearsal?" someone demanded.

Willow Rosenberg sighed.

"That is one of the things you'll learn in this class," Addams responded, "if you remain in it." He didn't look as if he thought many of them would.

Ooh, ominous, Willow thought, amused. Another prof with a low opinion of students. Well, if that was an example, she couldn't really blame him. She leaned back against the worn leather of the seat and looked around. This class was actually being held in the theater auditorium, and she'd never taken a class here before.

The theater was one of the older buildings on the UC Sunnydale campus, dating from the sixties. The lobby was nice, a wide, bright room with a rotating stainless-steel sculpture of the Earth holding pride of place in the middle. Several doors led variously to the restrooms, the auditorium, the hallway that led to classrooms, and the stairway to the technical booth upstairs. One wall was lined with huge windows overlooking the outside bank of rosemary and the sidewalk, the other with posters under glass of various productions dating back from the very first show ever done on its main stage, *Oklahoma!*. Willow didn't much like that particular poster; it reminded her too much of a dream she'd had once of Riley, Buffy's boyfriend, wearing a cowboy hat. She much preferred the more recent posters, for *Tiny Alice, Rosencrantz and Guildenstern Are Dead,* or *A Russian in the Woods.* (Not that they'd actually done *Russian,* but someone in the department clearly had hopes.)

In fact, after that dream she might have dropped Drama if it weren't for the fact that she'd already registered for the class and thought Buffy was taking it with her. The idea of being on stage for the very first class—

Willow shivered, hating the dream-memory that everyone was staring at her and she wasn't prepared, wasn't ready, didn't know what they all *expected* of her. And besides, that awful dress . . . ick.

But Buffy had dropped, and here she was by herself after all. Not fair.

Willow frowned. Talk about not being fair . . .

Buffy had her hands full with Dawn and being the Slayer and training and everything. She couldn't be there all the time. After all, Buffy wasn't taking advanced physics, either, and that was all right.

Overhead, a net of steel catwalks supported banks of lights. Willow twisted in her seat to see the blank window set high in the wall behind her where the sound and light crews watched the action on stage for their cues. The class was scattered throughout the auditorium; she estimated about two hundred students were present, most of their number clumped up in the front. The theater seated more than twice that many. Willow, seated several rows from the front, was pleased to have empty seats on either side to park her extra books.

Notes for this class, she decided, would definitely

be in purple, except the history part; that would be in black as always, of course. And if there was anything really *interesting,* well, she always had a red pen for magickal notes.

"This class will present an overview of the history of the theater, the development of drama from its roots in Greek religious ritual to today's postexperimental theater," the professor went on. "You will also be exposed to the concepts of stagecraft, makeup, costuming, lighting, and all the other elements that create the gestalt that is a play.

"There will be—yes, young lady?"

The same eager beaver as before had her hand up and was waving it frantically. At least this time she had the sense not to blurt out her question without invitation.

"Tests? Papers?"

Professor Addams sighed gently, clasping his hands behind his back, and looked down for a moment before responding. He was a tall, lean man of indeterminate age, clean-shaven, with neatly trimmed graying brown hair and wire-rimmed glasses. The stage lights reflected in those glasses, making it impossible to see his eyes. Watching him, Willow had the sudden impression that he enjoyed being on the stage, enjoyed the theatrical pause before answering the question, even enjoyed the fact that the students couldn't see his eyes. His voice was perfectly modulated to reach the very last row in the back.

"Don't interrupt me again, young lady," he said at last. "Learn patience, and all will be revealed." It was a gentle, almost humorous rebuke, but Willow made a small face and a note to herself: *Cranky prof.*

Addams waited until the student wilted, then turned back to the rest of his audience. He was standing at the center of the stage, framed by the proscenium arch, in the center of a spotlight. Even with the house lights and the rest of the stage lights up, Willow could see the outline of the spot as if it were a white aura surrounding him.

"Drama is an ancient form of human expression, dating from before recorded history. One theory is that it arose from ritual supplications to the gods. Participation in the ritual was essential to the health of the community.

"In that spirit, your participation in this class will include both tests on the material and a choice of a research paper or support for other students in the advanced acting and directing classes." He smiled thinly. "That support will consist of a minimum of fifteen hours of work in the theater, building sets, running lines, making costumes, or in any capacity the upperclassmen may find you useful. You may stay after this class, or, if you have a prior appointment, you may come to the theater sometime this week and speak to the stage manager. I'm certain she'll find something for you to do." He spoke as if *theater* was spelled the British way, *t-r-e,* not *t-e-r,* with a veddy upper-class English accent. He sounded like Giles, only as if he'd been in the States a little longer. British, but willing to drink coffee occasionally as well as tea. The accent went well with his tweed jacket and gangly build. He didn't wear a tie, but if he did, she was sure it would be "old school."

Willow took automatic notes, including a query to herself about finding out whether she could do both support *and* a research paper for extra credit. Addams was still talking, describing the tests, and her pen moved over the lined paper of the notebook. *Ritual supplications to the gods,* she thought. Riley in a cowboy hat was a ritual supplication to the gods? She tried to imagine a pantheon featuring Roy Rogers and Dale Evans. Well, maybe. There *might* be a cowboy dimension out there. If there was one without shrimp, there'd almost have to be.

This class could be even more interesting than she'd thought. And if she built sets, or did makeup—she wasn't quite sure what "running lines" meant—then she wouldn't be standing on that stage, would she? And there wouldn't be a spotlight on Willow Rosenberg.

And she could be Research Girl, too. That was good. Willow bounced a little with satisfaction. She was *really* good at being Research Girl.

"It's really different," she told Xander later that evening over the heavy bass line of the music at the Bronze, where the gang had gathered to compare notes on the first day of classes. "So I stayed after to see about the theater work stuff, and they had all these flats—scenery things—and they had this whole crew just splatting paint at them."

"Painting them?" Buffy, bearing a tray of drinks, set it down on the low table and handed Willow a steaming mug of chai.

"Nope, not painting exactly." Willow accepted the

cup in both hands, and sipped carefully at the scalding liquid. "Splatting. Sort of Jackson Pollacking. But when you stand in the audience, far away from it, it looks really cool."

"So are you going to sign up for it?" Buffy passed beers to Xander and Anya. She was reaching for Tara's Coke when Willow waved a hand and the drink floated up off the tray. Tara snagged it out of the air, frowning slightly.

Willow sipped again. "It's only fifteen hours. And tonight I already got an hour and a half in. It was fun. If you were taking the class you could come too." She smiled at Tara, and then looked pointedly at Buffy, widening her eyes and biting her bottom lip.

Buffy laughed. "Oh, no, Will," she said. "I am so not falling for that kicked-puppy routine. Responsibilities, remember?" She gave Willow a mock frown, and Willow sighed.

"I know, I know," Willow said. "I just wish . . ."

"How many people were there?" Tara said.

"Ten, I think," Willow replied "The guys building the sets, and there were a couple of seniors from the acting class practicing a scene, and three people up in the lighting booth. It was funny; they were all doing things for the same play—" She paused to sip again, and bit her lip as if momentarily lost in thought.

"What?" Xander put in, when Willow didn't continue.

"Oh. Sorry." Willow smiled apologetically. "It's just that, there were people doing all these different things, totally separate things that don't seem to have anything to do with each other, but it's all going to come together."

"Like elements of a spell," Tara suggested.

"Yes, exactly." Willow nodded enthusiastically. "Like the actors are the words, the painters are the candles, the lighting guys are the . . . the incense maybe. Or not," she added, at the expression of laughter on Tara's face. "But it is, really. You've got to come and see."

"I think I'll take your word for it," Tara said.

"They're so focused," Willow went on, as if she hadn't heard her. "They're creating something and it's amazing." The band segued into a slow song and several of the dancers came off the floor, headed for tables or the bar or the relative isolation of the space behind the stairs. The music dimmed underneath the sudden buzz of conversations and clinking glassware from the bar.

"It's almost like . . ." Willow set the empty teacup back on the tray and snuggled against Tara's side. Tara put her arm around Willow's shoulder. "Almost like Scoobystuff. You know, only without the fangs and demonyness. They're all so intent."

"Wow," Buffy said. "Scoobystuff without demonyness. What a concept. I could so get used to that."

Xander chuckled. "Me too," he said.

Anya frowned. "But, Xander," she said, "you're always talking about how much you love fighting demons. Besides, the sex is always more satisfying after a patrol where we have to fight."

Xander closed his eyes for a split second. "Ahn, honey . . ."

Anya huffed out a sigh. "I know, I know, too much sharing again, right?" She crossed her arms over her chest and slumped back in her seat. "I don't see what's so wrong about telling people that you're good in bed."

Xander repressed a wince. "How about we dance, honey?" he said, not looking at Buffy or Willow as he pulled Anya to her feet. Anya cocked her head, listening to the new, slow song the band was starting up.

"Well, all right," Anya said. "Pressing up against your body is almost as good as having sex."

"I don't think I'll ever get used to that," Buffy said shaking her head when the couple had disappeared into the dancing crowd. "Thank God Giles isn't here. He'd have polished his glasses right out of the rims."

Tara giggled. "I dunno," she said with a sly glance at Willow. "I kinda think Anya had a point." One corner of her mouth quirked up and she lifted an eyebrow at Willow, who blushed faintly but smiled back.

Buffy rolled her eyes theatrically. "Okay, enough with the arch looks. Just get out on the dance floor already. I'll watch the drinks."

Willow felt a momentary flicker of guilt that Buffy was all alone, but the feel of Tara's hand in hers snuffed it out. She let Tara pull her onto the dance floor and into her arms.

"You know," Willow said as she rested her head on Tara's shoulder, "I wonder if maybe it really does have to do with the ritual stuff."

"Anya and Xander's sex life?"

Willow lifted her head to find Tara laughing down

at her. "No, silly. The theater." She put her head back down, nuzzling into Tara's soft throat. "Doctor Addams said the whole drama thing started with invocations. I wonder if there's leftover magic in the theater."

"When they're Pollocking the sets?" Tara teased gently, sliding her hand down Willow's spine to rest on her hip. "Or when they're figuring out who gets the spotlight?"

"They want to be stars, every one of them," Willow said, smiling as Tara's fingers traced a sigil of possession on her thigh. "They like the idea of being up there with people staring at them. It's weird." The two witches shared a shudder of distaste at the idea. Neither one had ever been Popular-with-a-capital-P, and they were just as well pleased not to be.

Willow thought of Harmony, who had been Popular and was now a vampire. She shifted her head slightly and looked at Buffy, sitting all alone on the sofa, fiddling with the drink in her hands and staring at nothing. She had been Popular too, back before she came to Sunnydale, but now she was the Slayer. And Cordelia, who had epitomized Popular, was off in Los Angeles with Angel, helping the helpless and sacrificing her social life.

Willow sighed and turned her face back into Tara's neck. "Popular" and fighting demons didn't seem to be mutually compatible. But at least she wasn't all alone. She had her friends, and, most importantly, she had Tara. She pressed a kiss into Tara's throat. Tara made a small, happy sound, and her arms tightened around Willow. They were too occupied with each other to notice when their feet left the dance floor, nor did they see when all eyes in the Bronze turned toward them, swaying in midair to the music.

Weird it had certainly been. Willow and a handful of other students from the class—a mix of freshmen and sophomores—had remained in the theater after the lecture to talk to the professor, or someone, about the work option, while the rest of the students had packed up books and papers and lunged out of their seats as if they couldn't wait to get outside for a cigarette or simply to escape. Addams had looked the remaining few over, sniffed, and disappeared without another word, apparently not caring whether they chose heavy labor or not. As soon as he was gone, however, strangers appeared from out of the wings. Most of the strangers didn't bother to do more than glance at them. They proceeded to pull large, wobbly frames out from between pairs of curtains, or shove furniture around, or kneel down on the stage to stripe it with masking tape.

But one, a woman in her early twenties with long brown hair tied back in a ponytail so long that it looped back upon itself and still hung halfway down to her waist, marched to the edge of the stage and looked down at them. Waiting until all of the Intro students were looking up at her, she said, "I'm Laurie. I'm the graduate stage manager. Are you the Intro students planning to sign up for backstage work to get out of writing a paper for Addams?" Her voice was hoarse, as if she spent a lot of time yelling or she'd injured her vocal cords at some time.Or maybe both.

The students nodded, and one of them, the clueless

one who'd wanted to know what a technical rehearsal was, said, "What's backstage?"

Laurie rolled her eyes. "Give me strength. You're gonna find out.

"Okay, here's the deal. There's a signup sheet in the back. You've got to report to a crew head, that's me, or Lew"—she pointed to a young bearded man with a hammer who paused long enough in a battle with a giant canvas frame to raise a hand and wave— "or Marcie, who's up in costumes, or Alan in sound and lights, every time you show up, and we'll sign you in and out and mark your time. You put in fifteen honest hours and you're done. We're doing a lot of different stuff this semester—the senior directing class is doing scenes from Shakespeare, we've got a couple of Albee one-acts, children's theater is doing *Beauty and the Beast,* and reader's theater's doing *Spoon River.* Plus the orchestra thinks this building was built for *them* for some reason. We need a lot of warm bodies to do props, paint scenery, make costumes, strike sets, the whole nine yards. I don't suppose there are any actual drama majors among you?"

Nobody raised a hand. Laurie sighed and lowered herself to sit on the edge of the stage, blue-jeaned legs kicking restlessly. "Of course not. That would be too *easy.* Okay. Now listen. The first rule in this theater is: if somebody tells you to stop what you're doing . . . Stop. What. You're. Doing. *Instantly.* You got that? We're dealing with electricity, hammers, power tools, some dangerous stuff, and nobody's going to get hurt if I can help it."

"Has anybody really gotten hurt here?" Clueless asked, on cue.

"Only really stupid people," Laurie said, smiling through gritted teeth. "Are you *sure* you don't want to do a paper instead?"

But Clueless persevered, so Laurie took down all the Intro students' names and made a note of the time and turned them all over to Lew for their very first lessons in the creation of theatrical illusions, which, as Willow informed Tara later, consisted of how to paint "flats," the scenery that looked to the audience like walls and trees but was really only canvas and wood and paint. Clueless promptly knocked over a (fortunately nearly empty) paint bucket. Lew sent her up to Alan in the lighting booth. As punishment, for the next half an hour the battery of lights over their heads flickered on and off like strobes in the Bronze while Alan demonstrated the different spotlights and follow spots and gels and dimmer switches to his new recruit.

Lew had growled and moved his painting crew into the shops. *Xander would love this place,* Willow thought. Table saws and jigsaws and hammers and all kinds of buildy things, like shop class, only—no, actually; it was just like shop class. Only, she'd never actually taken shop class, so she was merely speculating, but she was willing to bet it was just like shop class. And the funny thing was, once they were all back in the shop, even with the saws and stuff running, it seemed quieter somehow. She wasn't always listening. Out on the stage she always felt like somebody was saying something to her that she wasn't quite catching.

"But you said there were rehearsals going on," Tara pointed out quite reasonably later that day. "You were probably trying to hear them. It drives me crazy when I can't quite hear something somebody's saying. I always think they're talking to me."

"Yeah, that was probably it." Willow bit her lip, thinking back, trying to remember everything that had been going on. "Yeah. Probably."

Chapter Two

London, England, 1880

The orchestra had just finished the overture when William slipped into his seat. It had been a trick, getting the money for the ticket without Mother knowing, but it was worth it, and so were all those dreary hours he'd spent chatting up the appallingly stupid ticket girl. Cecily—the name alone was perfection; of course, she was the most perfect woman in the entire world—was seated in the row in front of him, just to his right, and they were close enough to the stage that the lights just spilled onto her face, but not his. He could watch her for hours, and she'd never know. It would be better, of course, if she did know; if she turned, recognized him despite the darkness, gave him a look that promised Heaven . . .

But he was getting ahead of himself. First he would woo her with his words, beguile her with his brilliance, entice her with his . . . with his . . . *Botheration, what begins with e?*

He sighed. He was wasting time composing when he could be watching Cecily.

Her hair was different today, swept up in a new style with one lone curl resting on her white neck, just where it met the graceful curve of her shoulder. *Someday I will kiss her just there,* he thought, and blushed at his own audacity. It was most decidedly improper to be thinking such things about a pure, innocent girl, he told himself, but the thought would not go away, and he found himself imagining how such a circumstance might come about.

They would be dancing, perhaps, and she would be flushed with the exertion. She'd ask him to step outside for a breath of cool air, and they would find themselves in a deserted corner of the garden, the scent of roses surrounding them, and she would rest her head upon his chest. He would stroke her hair, brush it away from her shoulder, and then, gently, tenderly, he would kiss her. Her skin would taste of roses, and when he touched it she would sigh . . .

A swell of music from the orchestra and applause around him shattered the thought, and he gave a guilty start, but it was only the scene change. It was suddenly too warm, and his clothing too tight. He shifted in his seat and pulled at his collar as the orchestra finished the entr'acte music and the curtains opened.

The audience gasped as Puck appeared on the

stage, as though from nowhere. William sat forward in his seat, amazed, and adjusted his wire-rimmed spectacles. Where had he come from? He had not yet figured it out when he heard another gasp, close to hand, at Oberon's entrance. William was dismayed to note that Cecily leaned forward, her eyes wide and her lips parted on a sigh at the sight of the Fairy King. Brows knit, he glanced at the stage. The fellow was handsome enough, he supposed, if one liked that sort of Edwin Booth look, but not handsome enough to elicit such a response, surely. And yet . . . William looked at the women in nearby seats; they all had the same rapt expression as Cecily. Frowning, William turned back to the stage, determined to figure out why they were all so taken with the bloke. Bond, the programme said the actor's name was. Hamish Bond. A Scot; William stifled a groan.

The reason for their fascination became apparent when Bond—Oberon—spoke. His voice—deep, velvety, without a hint of barbarous burr—was enough to thaw a heart of ice, warm and seductive, and William was spellbound in spite of himself. Though he had read the play several times, the words seemed different somehow when performed, and before the second act was done, he had forgotten that Cecily was sitting so near him. He was caught up in the story and noticed nothing else.

When the final curtain fell and the house lights came up, William stayed in his seat, his head spinning. It was only when a fat dowager in a particularly horrid shade of purple rapped him on the knee with her lorgnette and spoke sharply to him that he realized he ought to be leaving with the rest of the audience.

He stood, mumbling an apology to the glowering woman, and shuffled his way to the aisle. The words, the poetry of the play, whirled inside his head until he was giddy with them, and he stumbled, knocking into the woman ahead of him. She gave a small shriek as she tottered on her feet, and he grabbed her around the waist to steady her. "I beg your pardon . . . ," he began, horrified.

"I beg your pardon!" she said at the same time, and then they both went stiff. She turned to face him, sliding out of his grasp.

It was Cecily.

He'd just had his hands around Cecily's waist.

"Er . . ." He stammered, blushing and averting his eyes. Behind him, he heard masculine snickers. The crowd flowed around the two of them, grumbling at being blocked.

"I do beg your pardon for being so clumsy," William said. He looked up and gave Cecily an earnest glance.

"Think nothing of it, William," she said coldly. Then, a bit more politely, "I didn't know you liked the theater?"

"Oh, I . . ." He couldn't tell her that he'd come just to be near her. Not out loud. He could write reams about it, but speak the words? What a horrifying thought. "I've been longing to see Shakespeare's work on the stage," he said instead. "Wasn't it wonderful?" His eyes shone, and for a moment he forgot to be awed by Cecily's beauty. "Bond was amazing!" For a split second he thought he saw a flicker of interest in her face, but it vanished when Cyril Lasher stepped around him and took her arm.

"My dear fellow," Lasher drawled, "one might almost think you were as struck by that Scot as the ladies were. The next thing you know, you'll be writing a poem about the fellow." The smirk on his lips left no doubt about what he was implying. His friends tittered, and William noted with sorrow that Cecily, too much the lady to laugh out loud, suppressed a smile. Though of course she could not possibly know what that boor Lasher was implying. His shoulders fell, and he took a step backward.

"Forgive me," he said, looking only at Cecily. "I see that I'm detaining you." He nodded to her, then joined the stream of people going up the aisle, fixing his gaze firmly on the feet of the person ahead of him and reciting the Kings of England from Elizabeth onward to drown out the jokes Cecily's friends were making at his expense.

It was only when the pair of shoes he'd been blindly following disappeared through a door, and then there were no more shoes at all, that he realized that he was finally alone. He looked up, surprised, and stopped.

This part of the theater was quite shabby. The wallpaper was peeling in spots, and the doors had cards tacked to them, each with three or four names on it. The carpet was worn and faded and stained, though well-swept, and the air was stale and chilly. He gave a sigh; this wasn't the first time his concentration on his thoughts had led him astray.

He looked up and down the hall and had just decided that the way back to the lobby was to his right, when one of the doors opened and a babble of feminine voices poured out. The girl who'd opened the door gave a little squeak of startlement, and so did William, for she was clad only in her chemise and corset, with an open wrapper over them. He hastily averted his eyes.

The girl made another sound that might have been a laugh, and William heard the rustle of the wrapper as she pulled it tightly around herself.

"There, guv," she said, "You can look now. I'm proper covered." There was a trace of amusement in her voice.

He looked up. She was indeed decently covered, but still he felt the heat rising in his face. She saw it and smiled.

"Here, now," she said, "have you come to see one of the girls?" She stepped back a bit, motioning through the open door to where three other girls, in various states of undress, were removing greasepaint or combing out their hair.

"Er, no, um, I'm . . . I've taken a wrong turn," he answered, giving a quick glance at the half-naked girls before fixing his eyes resolutely on her face. "Can you direct me to the lobby, please?"

The girl looked at him, one eyebrow lifted. "Cor," she said, "we don't get many proper gentlemen back here." She stepped into the hallway, pulling the door closed behind her. "Go that way," she said, pointing to her left, "and then right at the end of the corridor. When you get to the big mirror, turn right again. That should do you." She took a step nearer to him. "Unless, of course, you'd like to stay and . . . chat a while." She hooked her fingers underneath his lapel and gave a slight tug.

He felt his blush deepening, and his glasses slipped on his nose. "Ah," he began, pushing them up, and she laughed.

"A shy gentleman," she said, smoothing his lapel. "Don't worry, ducks. I won't bite." She took another step, so that she was close enough for him to feel her breath on his face. It smelled of whiskey. "Unless you ask nice. . . ."

He stumbled backward, holding up a hand to fend her off. "Er, no, thank you. That is, I . . ." She laughed again, and pinched his cheek.

"All right, love. It's your loss." She turned him around so that he was facing in the right direction. "Go along then," she said, and swatted him on the derrière.

He gave a small, undignified squeak and hurried down the corridor. Behind him, he heard the door opening and her laughing through her words, "Blimey, girls, you'll never guess . . . ," before it shut again.

When he got to the large mirror at the end of the second corridor, he couldn't remember whether the girl had told him to turn right or left. He looked first one way, then the other, and finally chose left. After a few steps the air grew chillier, and he began to suspect that he'd made the wrong choice, but he saw what looked to be an exit—it had a large bolt on it, at any rate—and made for that. It did indeed lead to the outside, but William was dismayed to find himself in an alley after he'd gone through it.

The air was sharp, and he shrugged into his overcoat. He trudged through the refuse toward the street, but a cry from behind him made him turn around.

"Who's there?" he said, peering into the gloom. He took several cautious steps back into the alley; the cry had sounded as though someone were in trouble. He hesitated for a moment, unsure of what to do. Then there was a scuffling sound, and another, louder, cry, as of someone in pain. That decided him, and he strode deeper into the shadows.

Just past the door he'd come out of, he came upon a couple that apparently did not need help; the man was leaning back against the wall of the building, his face hidden in shadow. The woman was standing between his splayed legs with her face buried in the man's neck. One hand was tangled in his hair. His hands hung limply at his sides, and he made a sound equal parts pain and pleasure as he moved under the woman's touch.

Suddenly the man gasped and clutched at the woman, pulling her closer to him, and William, repelled and fascinated at the same time, turned away, afraid of what he might see next. His foot caught in a drift of the debris that seemed always to collect in alleys. He tried to catch himself on a haphazard stack of wooden boxes, but they crashed to the ground with a horrid racket, and he fell to one knee on the filthy cobblestone. He hissed in a breath at the bruising impact, then swore a mild oath as he felt his trousers rip. Mother would give him holy hell for that—she hated paying for mending.

The noise of the falling crates startled the couple, and they broke apart. The man let out a stream of invective, including some words that William had never heard before, and took a threatening step forward, shoving the woman roughly behind him.

"Here," he said, his fist upraised. "What do you . . . ?" He broke off when he saw William. "Who the devil are you, boy? I know you."

William's eyes widened. The man was Cecily's father.

"I'm, er, I'm a . . ." *Good Lord no, mustn't say I'm a friend of his daughter's!* He held up his hands. "I'm most dreadfully sorry, didn't mean to disturb you, I was . . . I heard a noise . . ." He paused, took a deep breath. "I thought someone was hurt."

The tall man scowled at him. "Well, nobody is hurt," he growled, but he was plainly lying; there was a stain on his collar where fresh blood was seeping from a hidden wound in his neck.

William's eyes narrowed, and the other man, seeing it, put his hand to his throat, pulling his overcoat up around his collar. "Well," he said gruffly, "I appreciate your concern, lad." It was quite plain that he was far from appreciative of being interrupted, but William let the comment pass as the token courtesy it was. "We're perfectly fine here," he went on, "so you can be on your way."

The woman put her hand on her customer's arm. "Bertie," she said, her impatience plain, "we're not finished, here, pet." She stepped forward, looking up at him with a frown, her clothing awry, the buttons done up wrong. She curled her fingers around his arm, and tugged him back toward the shadows.

"Yes," William said, swallowing. "Er, right, then, I'll just be off. . . ." The woman leaned forward and . . . growled at him. The change in her face was startling; for a second she looked very dangerous, though she was quite small.

He felt the hair on the back of his neck lift, and took a step back. He would have sworn that for an instant her eyes blazed yellow, but when he blinked, they were a normal dark color. He touched his hat brim and turned, banging his injured knee into the crates in his hurry to be gone.

He hardly drew breath until he was safely on the street again.

Despite Lasher's insinuation, William was at the theater again the next night, this time to see the play and not Cecily. Once again, he was enthralled by the performances. At the interval, he made his way to the gentlemen's smoking room, but came to an abrupt halt when he saw, once again, Cecily's father before him. Addams was talking to two other men of his own age, and he appeared to be quite put out about something.

"Dammit, Reed," he said to the shorter of his companions, who shushed him frantically, though it did no good, "we're on to something here, we can't just throw over the effort. I'm sure that there's a clue in this play. There are definite references to the incantations here. If Moreham wins the bet, you'll both be—"

Reed laid his hand roughly on his arm. "For God's sake, man, think where you are!" he whispered fiercely; and as if the words had finally penetrated, the taller man gave a start and darted glances around him. When he saw William, his face turned an alarming shade of red and his eyes widened.

"Yes, yes, Reed, Denbigh," he said, shaking off the other man's hand, "you're quite right." He gave William a hard stare, then turned and with a jerk of his head indicated that his friends should follow him.

William stood as the crowd shifted about him. Cecily's father had given him the cut direct. His heart sank; even if he managed to impress the woman of his dreams, his perfect lady, now there was no hope for them if her father cut him dead. Unless they ran away, like Hero and Lysander . . .

He spent the remainder of the interval in a club chair in the far corner of the room, drinking sarsaparilla, thinking of how he would pour his love for Cecily into his poetry. She would see how deep and true his feelings for her were, and she'd declare her love for him. Then they would sneak away in the middle of the night across the Scottish border to Gretna Green, in defiance of her father, and after they were married they would make a grand tour of the Continent. Her father would relent then, surely, at the prospect of a grand-child . . .

He shook himself out of his daydream. It could not

be proper for him to be thinking of Cecily in that way, even if he were imagining them married. He put the thought firmly from his mind, but when the interval was over and he was back in his seat, he noticed how much the actress playing Hero resembled Cecily. That naturally led to imagining himself as Lysander, and he spent the rest of the play trying to keep his mind on the plot, shifting in his seat until the woman next to him gave him a queer look and asked if he were all right. After that he sat still, though he was mightily uncomfortable by the time the curtains closed.

He spent the next afternoon paying calls—discussing the weather, the latest gossip, and, of course, the play he'd seen. He was determined to see it yet again, to try to capture some of the magic of those words for his own work—although of course he acknowledged humbly to himself that he could never come close to the mastery of the Bard.

Several of his set had seen it too, and the girls were especially eager to talk about Bond. As he'd known he would, he eventually ran into Cecily, since Thursday was her day for calling. In the course of discussing the play, one of the young ladies who had also seen it the night before mentioned having seen Cecily's father there as well.

Cecily's mouth pinched in and she sighed. "Yes," she said, when Millie Cranshaw expressed surprise. "He's been to the same play every night this week. He's going again tonight." She sighed again and leaned forward, whispering to Millie behind her fan. "I begin to suspect that he's developed a *tendresse* for one of the actresses. Why, William, whatever is the matter?"

William, struggling not to spit out the tea he was choking on, thumped his chest and swallowed. "Went down wrong," he managed to gasp before the coughing spell set in. Sally Trumble snatched his teacup before he could crush it, and Cyril Lasher pounded him hard on the back. At length the spasm subsided—no thanks to Lasher—and he managed to sip some of the water that the Cranshaw's butler had brought. As soon as he'd finished the water, he made his excuses and left, heading straight for the Aldwyn Theatre to see if he could get into that night's performance.

That night, he stood in the theater lobby, scanning the crowd for Addams. He spotted the older man going into the theater just as the orchestra struck up the overture, but lost him when a gaggle of fortyish matrons, chatting excitedly about Hamish Bond and his astounding blue eyes, swept between them. There was no way to get to the man now without being seen; the orchestra was dashing toward the last bit of the overture.

William went reluctantly to his seat and found, much to his chagrin, that he was just in front of the group of women. He was a little scandalized at their whispered comments. Some of them were old enough to be his mother; they shouldn't be interested in an actor's bare chest, much less his bare . . . anything else! He sank down in his seat and tried to concentrate on the purity of the words, ignoring the vulgar giggling of the matrons in the row behind him.

Eager to escape the distraction, he was out of his seat as the curtain closed for the interval and headed for the relative safety of the gentlemen's smoking room. He took a chair in the farthest corner, picked up a newspaper, and pretended to be absorbed in reading it. One of the headlines, about a gruesome murder the night before, caught his attention, and he began to read it in spite of himself. He was so caught up in the ghastly story that was startled nearly out of his wits to hear a familiar voice nearby. He looked up and discovered Cecily's father and the same two men who'd been with him the night before. What *was* the man up to? William held his paper up a little higher and peered around the edge.

The three men managed to find chairs as far from the bulk of the crowd as possible, which luckily put them fairly close to William, and they sat with their heads together, murmuring and casting withering glances at any fellow who approached them too closely. William twisted awkwardly behind his newspaper, trying to hear what they were saying, but he could make out very little. They seemed to be talking about the same thing he'd overheard the previous night—incantations and bets and plays. William shook his head; none of it made any sense to him.

Liveried waiters brought out trays of whiskey, and Addams and his friends took glasses. Addams knocked his back in one stiff-armed toss and reached for another before the waiter got away. William winced. He'd never learned to like the taste of the stuff himself.

The whiskey seemed to loosen their tongues, for

their conversation grew louder. William could make out something about ancient play texts and more about an incantation and a bet, and they were angry about someone named Moreham and how far ahead of them he was in his research. The smaller of the three, his carefully combed salt-and-pepper side whiskers shaking, demanded to know what Cecily's father was doing to remedy the situation, and William heard a disgusted snort. A familiar voice grew just a fraction louder.

"You know bloody well what I'm doing, Reed. I have a . . . a source in the cast."

Reed gave a short bray of laughter. "A source. Is that what you call her?" The other man leaned back in his chair, his hand over his mouth.

"Really, Bertie," Reed said, laughter bubbling in his voice. "The only thing she's liable to be a source for is the clap." The other fellow gave up trying to hide his smile at that and began to giggle.

William risked a glance over the top of the financial section. "Bertie" was glaring from one of his companions to the other. "Think you know all about her, do you?" he said acidly. "Well, actually, you're right about one thing: She is a whore. And she does have . . . special talents. She's one of Peggy Dover's girls." He gave the other two men a grin that showed far too many teeth to be entirely friendly.

William's newspaper rattled as his hands convulsed on the edges. Oh, this was far worse than he had thought. He knew that the woman he'd seen with the man was most likely a prostitute, but gentlemen did not boast about having to patronize those sorts of women. At least no gentleman he'd ever known, which, granted, was a far-from-large sample. But still, how would Cecily feel? What horrible pain would it cause her to know this? Well, she should never know it from his lips.

Both Reed and the taller man gaped. "My God, Bertie," said the taller one, rising to his feet. "You don't mean to say that you're seeing one of . . . *those* girls?"

"Quiet, Denbigh, you bloody idiot," the man hissed, and jerked on Denbigh's sleeve. Denbigh sat down with a plop on the leather chair and looked at Reed, who swallowed hard.

"Peggy . . . Peggy Dover?" Reed said, his voice shaky. "I knew a man once who went to Peggy Dover's . . ." He licked his lips and passed a trembling hand over his side whiskers. His eyes were wide, the pupils large and dark, and he blinked several times but said nothing more.

"You can't be serious, Bertie," Denbigh said. "You know what those . . . girls are capable of!"

"Yes, I bloody well do know, you moron," Cecily's father hissed. "I also know that I've gotten more information from those *girls* than you've gotten from your sources. I've gotten more information than anyone but Moreham, and I may well get ahead of him tonight."

Just then the bell announcing the end of the interval sounded, and the men began to put out their cigars and drain the last of their whiskies. William was one of the last to leave the room; he watched as the three men strolled toward the door, then folded his newspaper neatly and got up from his chair. When he turned, however, he found "Bertie" standing in the doorway, giving him a hard stare. William swallowed, and then, amazed at his own brazenness, he walked right past him, giving a slight nod.

"Good evening, sir," he said. "This play is most incredible, isn't it? I should like to be able to see it three more times. . . ."

With that, he was past the man. He kept his shoulders stiff until he was back in his seat again, and it took almost an entire scene for his heart to stop pounding in his ears.

When it finally did, and he could concentrate again, he tried to make sense of what the three cronies had said, but eventually gave up the effort as hopeless. The only thing he knew for certain was that Cecily's father was involved with a woman of exceptionally . . . unsavory reputation and that it would devastate Cecily if she knew. He resolved once again not to let her hear the shameful thing from him. He couldn't help imagining, though, how he would comfort her if by some mischance she did find out. He'd put his arms around her and let her sob it out on his manly chest, pet her hair, perhaps kiss her forehead, and she'd look up at him with tear-stained cheeks and . . .

He was quite surprised when the curtain closed; he'd completely missed the end of the play.

Chapter Three

Sunnydale, California, Fall semester, 2000

Weird or not, Willow couldn't suppress a certain excitement as she reported to the theater the next Thursday afternoon. The construction crew was in the workshop, stretching canvas over a set of tree-shaped frames that could double, eventually, for Burnham Wood or the Beast's Forest.

"All you have to do," one of the seniors was explaining to another one of the Intro draftees, "is draw some lines in black, like this, and from the audience it'll look just like the bole of a tree. Really."

"Don't you have to paint it, like, brown?" Willow recognized one of her classmates and winced. Clueless. If Alan from the lighting booth had given up on her and sent her back down, maybe Pollocking again so soon wasn't such a good idea. She'd already done that, after all. Maybe she could try something different this time. Stepping back into the hallway, she looked up and down the shabby carpeted aisle that ran the length of backstage.

To her left were the costume storage rooms and the women's dressing room; to her right were the props room and the men's dressing room. She could hear the voices of the upperclassmen from the directing class rehearsing onstage, working with a stage fighting instructor. Not something she wanted to stick around and watch, she decided. She'd seen fighting, and she knew fighting, and this wasn't fighting. For one thing, nobody was exploding into dust, and for another, all the gore was red. How could it be real fighting when you had only monochrome gore? Where was the pustulant yellow, the bilious green, the eerie blue? She wandered over and checked out the stage blood. Nope. Red. Red, red, and more red. Bo-ring.

Makeup, though. That might be interesting.

The women's dressing room was long and narrow and smelled of sweat and anxiety and cold concrete. Along one side a table was set against the wall, with a mirror running the length of the room and a row of round lightbulbs glowing softly along the top. The table was marked with stains and smears of old makeup, but the mirror was polished clean, without as much as a finger smudge to mark its clarity. Flat boxes were carefully lined up at the base of the mirror, waiting for their owners.

Willow couldn't resist sneaking a peek at one. It

was just over a foot long, perhaps eight inches wide and three inches deep, divided into compartments of varying sizes containing makeup brushes, a small pot of extremely white foundation and several shades of tinted, heavy grease pencils in red and black and lipsticks in a variety of colors, as well as lipliners, mascara, and a small Ziploc bag of Q-tips. She tried to imagine gunking her face up with the contents of the box and failed miserably.

Behind her, metal racks held the costumes in use for the plays currently in rehearsal. She looked them over too, particularly fascinated by one white brocaded lace blouse that almost looked like a wedding cake, if a wedding cake had underwires. She had no idea what on earth the seniors were rehearsing that called for this costume, but it looked intriguing.

"Can I help you with something?"

Willow turned to find Laurie standing in the doorway watching her. The graduate stage manager, dressed in the drama students' unofficial uniform of jeans and show T-shirt, stood with arms full of costumes.

"Oh. Hi. I'm sorry." The other woman's direct gray gaze was flustering her. "I'm one of Doctor Addams's Intro students. I'm supposed to be working, and I guess I was just exploring."

"Have you signed in yet? What's your name?" Laurie Gray-eyes didn't sound very welcoming. "You shouldn't be wandering around by yourself, you know." She moved around Willow and started hanging up the costumes.

"Uh, not yet. I'm Willow. I didn't know I was

doing anything wrong." Impulsively, Willow took an armful from the other woman and started helping, burrowing through the crowded racks for hangers. With both of them working, they managed to get the dresses sorted out quickly.

Once they were finished, Laurie studied her a moment longer, then seemed to decide that Willow wasn't all that suspicious-looking after all. "You're not, really. Doing anything wrong, I mean. It's just that—"

"Dammit!" The roar from the stage sounded all too surprised and sincere to be part of a play. Both women jumped, and Laurie said sharply, "Come on."

Willow followed her through the hallway and the backstage area, through the wing, and suddenly found herself once again on the stage itself. Three young men were clustered in the middle of the stage area, one halfsitting, half-lying on the floor, with the other two standing over him wringing their hands. Stage swords, rapiers, lay not far from them, their silvery coating glistening in the lights.

"What happened?" Laurie asked.

The recumbent actor was too busy cursing to answer. One of the others ran his toe over the boards on the stage floor, following a yellow strip. Instead of the wooden planks Willow expected to see, the stage had been covered with panels of plywood, painted matte black, with cryptic stripes and squares marked with various colors of masking tape and occasionally bright yellow duct tape. Willow remembered the marks, but the plywood hadn't really registered before. It wasn't *supposed* to stand out, after all, she realized.

The black surface showed dozens of scuff marks, trails of sawdust, and a few spots where someone had spilled some water near the wings. But the actors were stage center. "Somebody oiled the floor," said one of the men, kneeling beside the other. "Mikey hit his mark and went ass-over-teakettle."

"He could have put my eye out," the other man, still on his feet, said indignantly.

"I *twisted* my *goddamn ankle,*" Mikey said.

"Let me see," Laurie said, and moved the two men out of the way. "Willow? Give me a hand here." As she knelt beside the infuriated Mikey, Laurie hit an oily spot too and went down harder on one knee than she intended to. "Ouch! What is this stuff? You can't even see it."

Willow, settling beside her a little more cautiously, ran her hands over the floor. She could feel the sudden slickness of oil, but to her surprise, the dry, dusty part of the plywood flooring and the slippery part looked exactly alike. She had to define the affected area solely by touch. "It looks like it's just here by this stripe," she said. Turning her attention to Mikey, she examined his ankle. The injury didn't look terribly serious, but then she was used to more than the average amount of blood and bruising. She'd graduated from Sunnydale High, after all. "I think you'll be okay," she said, giving Mikey a quick smile.

"Are you sure?" he asked, biting his lip. "It could be broken."

She rolled down his sock to expose the swelling ankle, and taking his Reebok-shod foot in her hand, tried carefully rotating. He gasped. "I don't think it's broken," Willow said. "You should have somebody look at it though."

"Damn," one of the other men said. He had collected the stage foils and was examining the ends of the blades. "You really could have put an eye out, Mike; there aren't any tips on these swords. Did they come off when we dropped them?"

"Can you stand up?" Laurie asked. Mikey assented reluctantly, and Laurie and Willow helped him get to his feet. He refused to put weight on the injured ankle.

"You're going to have to go over to student medical," Laurie said. "And if they write you up, I'm going to have to replace you in the production."

This gave Mikey pause. "Well, maybe it isn't *that* bad," he said at last, gingerly placing his injured foot flat on the floor. He winced. "Hey, no problem," he announced through gritted teeth. "I'm doing fine."

Willow frowned. He didn't really look "fine" to her. On the other hand, it wasn't exactly life-threatening, either. She decided to let Mikey take care of himself, and looked around the floor, trying to see where other slippery spots might be. Maybe there was a spell for that—that would be a useful thing to have.

"Laurie," one of the other men said, "I can't find the buttons for these things anywhere."

"They were there when you got them out of the prop room, right?"

The two uninjured men looked at each other. "Uh, I didn't check. Did you check?"

"No, I thought you checked. Besides, the swords always have buttons."

"What's a button?" Willow piped up.

"It's a knob thingy on the pointy end of the sword," Laurie said. "Covers the sharp."

The two men rolled their eyes, but said nothing.

"You know," Laurie said evenly, "I'm really getting sick and tired of this. It's bad enough when somebody sews zippers shut in between acts. But slippery floors, well, somebody could get hurt."

"Yeah," Mikey said heroically. Then he remembered that he was doing Not Really Injured, and added, "Somebody could, even if I didn't."

"Whoever's doing this stuff had better stop it." She shot Willow a look, and Willow realized why—Laurie was suspicious about finding her alone in the women's dressing room. She hoped there weren't any nasty surprises lying in wait there. Evidently Laurie had decided Willow looked like the innocent type, but Willow had the feeling that decision could be reversed really fast if evidence turned up otherwise. "We're going to have to move rehearsals to the construction room until we're sure the stage floor is safe. And Lew, I want you to check the prop weapons. Willow, you can help him out."

"Okay." *More weapons?* she thought. *Oh, well. At least these are weapons that aren't supposed to kill things. Maybe.*

Someone else said something she didn't quite catch, but by the time she looked around, whoever it was wasn't talking anymore. Nobody responded, so it couldn't have been that important.

"Does this happen a lot?" she asked Lew a few

minutes later, as they moved flats and boxes out of the way to get to the racks on the wall at the back of the prop room. "Practical jokes, I mean?"

"Oh, we get our share, but this term we seem to be having more than usual. It's driving poor Laurie to distraction. I don't envy her."

"Is Laurie in charge of everything?"

"Kind of," Lew said. "The stage-manager job is the only paid student job in the theater, and she really takes it seriously. She's by God gonna *manage,* if you know what I mean. Not that it doesn't need it," he added gloomily, replacing the foils and wrapping a red ribbon around the hilts. "That's so nobody will use them before we can find the buttons," he told Willow.

The redheaded witch looked up at the rack of assorted edged mayhem on the wall: foils, more rapiers, broadswords, halberds, axes. Several of them had red ribbons wound through or around the hilts. "Looks like you're kinda running out of swords," she observed.

"Yeah, the gremlins have been having a really good time at our expense this semester." Lew hung the rapier up with the rest of the swords and chose two more, carefully checking to make sure the buttons on the end were intact.

"Gremlins?"

"Theater gremlins. Ghosties and goblins. Every theater has 'em. You mean you haven't taken Theater Superstitions 101 yet?" Lew gave her a quick smile, and Willow found herself smiling back. He really was a nice guy.

"No, didn't see that one in the course catalog. Tell me about them."

"Well," Lew said, leading her back out to the stage area, "let's see. You know the green room?"

"No, what's that?"

"That's where you wait for your cues," one of the weapon-deprived actors broke in smoothly, taking one of the new swords. "It's hardly ever green, so it's not surprising you haven't found it yet."

"Green's bad luck," Lew added.

"Never whistle backstage," Mikey, the other actor, said, taking the other foil and scuffing warily at the floor. His ankle was still hurting him, but Willow could see that even in that short a time he was doing much better. "Bad luck. If you do, you have to leave, turn around three times, spit over your left shoulder, and then knock on the actors' door and ask permission to come back in."

"No peacock feathers in the theater. The evil eyes will make you sick during a performance."

"No hats on the bed onstage—someone will go up on their lines."

"No, a hat on the bed means somebody's going to die," Mikey contradicted.

"Never look in a mirror over somebody's shoulder—you'll take their spotlight."

"Never wish an actor good luck—always tell them to 'break a leg.'"

"Then there's the Scottish play. . . ." The three men all nodded somberly, apparently depressed by the mere mention of the production.

"Aren't there any good things?" Willow asked uncertainly.

"Black cats," Mikey said. "Black cats are good."

"Yeah, every theater needs a black cat. They're lucky."

Willow looked from one to another of them, not at all certain whether they were teasing her or not, but they all seemed to be perfectly serious. "If green's bad luck," she said cautiously, "why do you wait for your cues in the green room?"

"Uh . . ." Lew shrugged. "Maybe so we can forget our lines in there and remember them out here?"

"Sounds good to me," said the first swordsman. "Hey, can you feel any slippery spots?"

"Nope," Mikey said. "Shall we run through that scene again?"

"Laurie said to use the construction room," Lew reminded them. "You'd better do it. She's probably going to make me rip up every piece of plywood on the stage and do it over again just to make sure it's safe before we put the set up."

"There isn't enough room in the construction shop," Mikey sulked. "You can't move around in there."

"Then you'll just have to do more *corps à corps* before you're a corpse," his partner retorted.

"What are you guys waiting for?" It was Laurie, marching determinedly down the aisle through the auditorium toward them. "Lew, pull up that flooring and replace it. But don't rip it up—we'll have to use the good stuff again. Mikey, Steffo, I told you to take it to the construction shop. Come on, we've got a show to put on here."

"Told you so," Lew said to Willow, grinning. "How are you at pulling nails?"

Willow grinned back, rolling her eyes. A few minutes later she was learning the fine art of removing plywood from a stage floor, working on her hands and knees next to Laurie, with Lew and a couple of the other seniors from his crew on the other side of the stage.

After sweat and effort and nearly bouncing the business end of the hammer into her nose a couple of times, Willow was ready to resign from the stage crew and go back to being Research Girl. But she could see out of the corner of her eye that Laurie was working just as hard at it as she was and getting just as many splinters, and besides, she liked the theater majors. So instead of quitting, she shifted her position slightly, eyed a particularly recalcitrant nail with resolute determination, and murmured under her breath, "Loosen!"

Rather to her surprise, the nail popped obediently out of plywood, stage floor, and all, and hung in the air six inches in front of her face. She blinked and grabbed it, looking around quickly to make sure nobody else had seen.

Nobody had. Working her fingers under the sheet of plywood, she lifted it, looking for the next nail, which was cleverly disguised by the layers of paint the flooring had received in however many productions it had seen since being laid down. She grinned. Setting down the hammer, she began magicking the nails out of the wood.

"Willow, don't just yank up the plywood—we have to use it again!"

Startled, she looked around to find Laurie looking down at her, Willow's abandoned hammer dangling from one hand.

"It's, it's . . ." She stammered, not sure if the other woman had seen the spell working.

But Laurie didn't have that what-the-hell-have-I-just-seen? look on her face—just twin lines of exasperation between her eyebrows.

"I think the plywood's okay," Willow said meekly. "I didn't tear it or anything." *Can you tear wood?* she wondered. Shuffling on her knees, she made space for Laurie to inspect the clean edges she had just pulled up.

"Good grief," Laurie remarked. "You did that with just your hands? And you're not bleeding?"

Willow checked her hands. No blood.

"Nope."

"You're lucky."

"Guess I fit right in, then," she chirped. "Maybe I can be your black cat."

"Huh?" Laurie was kneeling beside her by this time, hooking the claws of the hammer over the edge of the plywood beside the next nail. "What do you mean?"

"Oh, the guys were telling me about the gremlins and stuff. Green rooms and black cats and Scottish plays and—"

"Oh, gawd," Laurie groaned. "All that superstitious crap. I wish they wouldn't feed it to every class of freshmen that comes in here. Half of them decide the place is haunted and drop out before midterms, just because some practical joker can't resist telling ghost stories."

"So you don't believe in ghosts?"

Laurie snorted. "Never met one. Worked on plays since I was in the sixth grade. You'd think I'd have come across one if they existed."

"Yeah, you'd think," Willow said softly. It never ceased to amaze her that people could live in Sunnydale for any period of time and still make a comment like that. She'd seen more than one ghost in her day. Heck, she'd *been* a ghost once. She sat back and looked out across the stage, past the footlights, to the broad cone-shaped rise of empty auditorium seating staring down at the half-stripped stage floor.

Earlier that day, a substantial number of those seats had been filled with students juggling books and papers and day planners and pens and backpacks.

The night before, all the seats had been filled by an audience for the University Chamber Chorale. Willow and Tara and Giles had attended. They'd been sitting right over there—stage left, she'd learned that was called. Orientation in the theater was defined from the point of view of the actor on the stage.

Now it was absolutely empty, the seats tilted up against the seat backs, but it didn't feel empty. She tilted her head, trying to figure out exactly how it did feel. Waiting?

Downstage right, Lew stood up, wobbling a slab of plywood taller than he was on its edge. "Laurie? Honest, I think this is dry. Do you really want us to move it out and replace it?"

"Wouldn't it make more sense to just check the floor instead of pulling everything up?" Another one of Lew's team, a skinny blond kid whom Willow recognized as one of her classmates from Dr. Addams's course, was examining a broken fingernail with extreme disgust.

I could probably do a spell, Willow thought. *An oil-finding spell—that might come in really handy in someplace oily, like Texas, but . . .* She wasn't sure what it would take to create an oil-finding spell on the spur of the moment.

Come to think of it she wasn't absolutely sure it *was* oil. If she could grab a piece of the slippery ply-wood, maybe she could ask Giles about it.

Laurie was sitting back, cross-legged, rubbing her eyes. "If you can see what's slippery and what isn't, fine. Go ahead. Leave it down. Mikey will be really happy with you, I'm sure."

Lew flexed the wood back and forth, yelped, and sucked frantically at the web between thumb and index finger of his right hand. "Damn splinters!"

Laurie sighed deeply.

A pair of students ventured heads one above the other, images out of a Marx Brothers movie, through the curtains at the back of the stage. "Lew? The saber saw is jammed again," the top head said.

"And Mikey and Steffo are fencing back there and keep bumping into us," the bottom head added.

"And we've run out of brown paint," the top head

pronounced with the air of someone laying down a trump. The two heads vanished.

Lew marched to the middle of the stage, faced the empty auditorium, spread his arms wide, and roared at the top of his lungs, *"Will no one rid me of this troublesome priest?"*

Laurie sighed again and buried her face in her hands. Willow could barely hear her murmuring, as if in prayer or in chant:

> *"Either I mistake your shape and making quite,*
> *Or else you are that shrewd and knavish sprite*
> *Call'd Robin Goodfellow. . ."*

An echoing scream came from backstage. *"Dammit, who dyed all the clown-white green?"*

Chapter Four

London, England, 1880

William was delighted to find, in the next morning's post, an invitation to a musicale at Cecily's. Despite her father cutting him dead, despite his dreadful faux pas at the theater two days before—the palms of his hands still burned at the memory of her slender waist—still she forgave him, still she welcomed him into her home.

He took extra care with his coat, brushed his soft golden-brown curls until they shone. He blinked earnestly into the mirror, trying to make certain his tie was just right, wishing she would look into his meek blue eyes and see the utter devotion that was hers for the taking. He might be sitting in a corner yet again all evening, but still, he would be there, basking in her warmth. If she only knew. If she only saw. . . .

When at last he came downstairs, Mother was waiting for him in the parlor. She knew, of course, how he
felt about Cecily—how could any mother not know?—
and she knew what a specific social invitation, as
opposed to a simple afternoon call, meant to him.

"Well," she said, a proud smile on her face, "you
look quite handsome, my dear."

William felt a blush creep up his neck. "Thank
you, ma'am," he said, ducking his head slightly.

"Now," she said, and gave him a kiss on the cheek,
"go along. I will be out myself tonight, so you must tell
me all about it tomorrow. I want to hear all the latest
gossip." She gave him a cheeky grin, and he laughed.

"I'll make it a point to ferret out the juiciest scan-
dals just for you," he said.

"Off with you, now," she said, giving him a slight
push toward the door. "And remember, I'll be expecting you to tell all tomorrow."

With a light heart, William stepped out his front
door, not knowing it would be the last time he would
see his mother with living eyes.

There was already a crowd when William arrived.
The butler let him in and directed him to the music
room, where Sally Trumble sat at the pianoforte, playing something melancholy. William greeted Cecily,
who was receiving her guests just inside the room.

"William," she said, "how good of you to come."
There was the proper amount of enthusiasm appropriate to greeting a guest, of course—Cecily was always

quite proper about manners—but she seemed a little distracted as she gave the fingers of his offered hand a tiny squeeze.

"It was good of you to invite me," he said, trying hard not to stumble over the words at the feel of her warm skin. She looked over his shoulder, and he realized that there were others waiting to greet her. He let go of her hand, gave her a slight bow, and stepped into the room. Besides the pianoforte, a harp and a violin were set up at one end of the room, and he stifled a wince, hoping that whoever was playing the violin had some skill.

A number of chairs and benches and sofas had been arranged through the room, with little tables beside them convenient for refreshments. Despite the fact that someone was performing, most of the young people present seemed more interested in nibbling at the sandwiches and cakes and talking to one another than they were in listening. *Of course,* William thought. *They probably wouldn't appreciate fine music anyway.* And the invitation had not specified a guest musician. This was merely another social occasion.

But what of that? It was an opportunity to see a—*the*—jewel among women, and in the setting of her own home. What more could he possibly ask?

Sally finished her piece and stood up from the piano, laughing a little at the raucous applause from Charles Gladham, who had been dramatically mooning over her for half the season, and waved to indicate that someone else should have a turn. One of the younger girls stepped up, and, settling herself on the bench, struck up a slightly risqué popular song that startled a laugh from the entire room.

With a sudden start of panic, William hoped that he would not be asked to play. He had had lessons on the pianoforte, but he poured all his energies—no, he corrected himself sternly, he *placed all his worship*— at the feet of the muse of poetry, not music.

All the seats far away from the instruments were already taken, and William was just looking for a likely place to lean when he felt a hand on his shoulder. He turned and, to his surprise, found himself face to face with Cecily's father.

The tall man was smiling at him, but his eyes were hard. "Young . . . William, is it?" he said. "Might I have a word?" He gave a slight push on William's shoulder and jerked his chin toward the door. The strength of the man's grip brooked no denial, and William found himself marched out of the music room, across the foyer, and into the library. He glanced enviously at all the volumes, but had no time to admire them properly; his host shut the door and turned to him.

"Look here," the older man said brusquely. "About what you saw at the theater the other night. We're men of the world, you and I. We understand how things are." He reached into his pocket and pulled out an envelope.

William's eyes widened. Surely the man wasn't going to offer him *money* to keep silent about that disturbing evening?

Apparently he was. "I've a hundred pounds here. Take it. We'll forget the whole thing happened."

William made no move to take the envelope, and Addams lifted it with a slight nod. William shook his head.

"No, sir," he said firmly. "I'll not take that. There's no need for it. What I saw that night—" He swallowed at the thunderous look that came over the other man's face. "What I saw was none of my business, sir, and I shan't tell anyone about it. It would get back to Cecily, and hurt her, and I would never do anything to hurt your daughter." He knew he was blushing, that he'd given away his feelings, and to Cecily's father of all people, but he didn't care. He'd be damned to eternal hell before he'd purposely do anything that would cause Cecily grief, and perhaps it was best that her father knew that. He squared his shoulders, lifted his chin, and pushed his glasses up on his nose, looking the other man straight in the eye.

Addams stared back at him, eyes narrowed, and then slowly put the envelope back into his pocket. For long seconds he said nothing, his gaze fixed on William, weighing his words, and then he smiled. Something about that smile sent a chill slithering down William's spine. "I'm glad to hear that," he said. "Quite glad." His smile broadened into something more friendly. "Shall we go back in, then, now that that's settled?" He gestured to the door, stepping back so that William could pass by.

William stepped forward, turning slightly so that he kept his face to Addams. For some reason, the thought of turning his back on the man sent the chill down his spine again. He reached out to open the door.

A hard hand clamped onto his wrist and gave a bone-crunching squeeze. William gave a sharp cry of pain and pulled back, but the pressure increased. "If you know what's good for you, you'll see that you keep to your word, my boy," the older man said softly. There was a gleam of something dangerous in his eyes, and William nodded, his heart nearly pounding out of his chest. Addams held him for a moment more, then with a vicious smile, tossed William's hand aside and opened the door himself.

As he followed Addams into the foyer, he was startled to see the butler, a trim middle-aged man named Clermont, open the door to what appeared to be a pair of police persons. Certainly they were not guests for the musicale. The master of the house stepped over to see what was the matter.

Curious, William lingered a moment, drawn by the music yet dearly wishing to know what was going on.

One of the newcomers showed Addams a piece of paper. William could not hear what was said next, until Cecily's father raised his voice in exasperation. "God, I should have known that bloody fool Denbigh would do something this stupid. The man was a complete and utter dolt who didn't have the sense God gave cheese."

At that moment, Cecily and a few of her friends came out of the music room. She blinked when she saw William, but nodded to him. Several of the young men migrated over to her father and the police. Cecily looked clearly annoyed to have lost her court and turned to William instead. He was delighted at her choice.

"Shall I bring you something to drink?" He was determined to do something for her, but she put her hand on his arm.

"No, William. Thank you, but I'm quite all right," she said. She smiled absently at him and turned back to the music room, looking over the rest of her guests.

She still hadn't taken her hand from his arm, and he held very still, so that perhaps she wouldn't notice. "Are you sure?" he said. "It's no trouble, really."

She shook her head. "No, I'm fine," she said. "I really should get back to my guests." She lifted her hand from his arm. "Please excuse me." Not looking at him, she swept past and back into the music room.

She had put her hand on his arm. She had touched him. He could still feel the heat from her fingers lingering on his skin, and his heart felt as though it would burst through his chest at any moment. He found an empty chair in the corner of the music room and reached into a pocket for the notebook and the pen he always carried with him and began to try to catch the feeling in words, not paying attention when Lasher and Charles Gladham came back in and started an animated conversation, with Cecily, of course, in the middle of it. Someone was playing the harp now, but naturally no one was paying attention.

"The nerve of them," Gladham was sputtering, "coming to your own home, Cecily. How dare they?"

"I mean to point out," Cyril said, obviously trying to appear even-handed, "it's something of a mystery, and the police must follow all avenues of inquiry."

William studied the words on his pages. Pitifully

inadequate, as always. Perhaps if he had some punch? As he passed the little clique, casting a longing eye at Cecily, knowing she would never know of the courageous sacrifice he himself had made for her not half an hour past, Cyril stopped him.

"Ah, William! Favor us with your opinion. What do you make of this rash of disappearances sweeping through our town? Animals? Or thieves?"

Disappearances? he wondered, confused. What on earth was the man going on about? *Oh. That must be what the conversation in the foyer had been about.* He recalled hearing Mother gossiping with one of her friends about something in one of the less reputable newspapers about such things. "I prefer not to think of such dark, ugly business at all. That's what the police are for." How abominable to think it should be discussed in this house! He looked at Cecily. The poor, lovely darling. First that her father should be such a . . . and then that the police should come to her very door . . . ! "I prefer placing my energies into creating things of beauty."

Gladham laughed, leaned over, and snatched the forgotten pages from his hand. "I see. Well, don't withhold, William."

Lasher nodded. "Rescue us from a dreary topic!"

Flustered, William made an ineffectual effort to take the pages back, but Gladham held them out of reach. "Careful—the inks are still wet. Please—it's not finished—"

"Oh, don't be shy." Gladham skimmed the hastily scratched words, then raised his voice to declaim. A small audience gathered, abandoning the harpist. "'My heart expands. 'Tis grown a bulge in it, inspired by your beauty, effulgent.' *Effulgent?*"

"And that's actually one of his *better* compositions!" Lasher proclaimed to the crowd, which giggled.

"Have you heard?" James Gillings interjected. "They call him William the Bloody because of his bloody awful poetry!"

He felt as though he would sink straight through the floor. They were all staring at him, laughing.

"It suits him," Lasher sneered, looking William in the eye as he referred to him in the third person, as if he wasn't even there, taking the pages from Gladham and shoving them back into his nerveless hands. "I'd rather have a railroad spike through my head than listen to that awful stuff."

He could barely manage to see, barely manage to smile thinly as if acknowledging the joke—one must always pretend to laugh with the fellows, after all. One must preserve one's dignity at all costs. It was the sight of Cecily's sudden flush that hurt the most. She left the group quite suddenly and absented herself from the room for quite some time.

He himself, of course, had to stay. One could not be seen to run away, not if one ever wished to appear in public ever again. Fortunately he had only writ those few lines this evening, so they had to find something else to seize upon and mock, the vultures.

He wanted rather desperately to write about the horrible experience—everything being grist for the writer's mill, after all—but the paper was rumpled past use, and besides, he didn't quite dare.

After a while there was music again, and conversation turned elsewhere, and he happened to see Cecily circulating among her guests, her face pale and her head held high as a queen's. When she finally settled, alone, upon a sofa in an alcove, he plucked up his courage to approach her. She was staring blankly out the window into the gloom.

"Cecily?" he said hesitantly, wanting desperately to apologize for the scene he hadn't caused.

She sighed. Perhaps she rolled her eyes as well; he wasn't sure. "Oh. You. Leave me alone, William."

She meant Gillings and Gladham and Lasher, surely. "Oh, they're vulgarians. They're not like you and me."

"You and me?" She looked up at him, and he felt as if she had never really seen him before—as if she really *saw* him, his fine features and softly curling hair and glasses and painfully perfect tie and almost new evening dress suit, and he swallowed hard.

"William," she went on, "I'm going to ask you a very personal question, and I demand an honest answer. Do you understand?"

He nodded, unable to speak past the lump in his throat.

"Your poetry. It's—they're—not written about *me*, are they?"

He thought he might faint from dizziness, from joy. She knew! She *knew*! "Every syllable," he said firmly.

"Oh, God," she said, turning back to the window.

"Oh, I know," he stammered, "it's sudden, and, please, if they're no good, they're only words, but—the *feeling* behind them—I *love* you, Cecily!"

"Please, stop," she groaned.

Stop? No— "I know I'm a bad poet"—oh God, it hurt to say it, but it was the truth, and he could never say anything but the truth to her; it wasn't in him to say anything but the truth to someone he loved so desperately— "but I'm a good man, and all I ask is that . . . that you try to *see* me—"

With that, she turned to look at him again, with the same open eyes. Only this time there was no mistaking her expression. No pretending it was something else. No lying to himself. "I *do* see you. That's the problem. You're nothing to me, William. You're"—she shook her head, seeking the proper words and, alas, finding them— "*beneath* me." And with that she rose from the sofa, avoiding even the touch of his outstretched, loathsome hand, and went back to the guests who *were* her friends, who laughed at him.

This time he didn't care who saw him as he fled the house, weeping. The cost had been too high. He had no dignity, no anything to protect anymore.

The hired cab drew up before the Explorers' Club. The footman came and opened the door, and Albert Addams stepped down. He thrust a coin at the driver, whose eyes opened wide.

"Lor', sir," the man said, "I ain't got enough to change this."

"Keep it, keep it, man, and be on your way," Addams growled, waving impatiently at the driver. The driver swallowed hard.

"Blimey, sir, thank you, thank you so—"

"I said be on your way." Addams looked at the man, and there was something so fierce in his expression that the driver paled and drove away hastily. Addams turned to the footman.

"Have the others arrived?"

The footman, unperturbed by the older man's obvious agitation, nodded. "They've gathered in the reading room, sir," he said. "They're awaiting you."

Addams stalked up the steps to the ornately carved door of the club. "Good," he said, handing his hat and coat to the footman, who had opened the door for him, and marched into the foyer and straight up the stairs.

The reading room was in an uproar when he opened the door. Nearly all the members of the Explorers' Club were gathered there, and they'd all obviously heard about Denbigh's death, for many of them looked frightened, and all of them were speculating about what exactly had happened to the poor chap. Most of them were standing; a few of the older members were slumped into the leather club chairs. Formally dressed waiters moved about the room, offering brandy and cigars and, sometimes, other substances, their shoes silent on the thick oriental carpet. The waiters all wore their typical stoic, I-won't-remember-this-when-I'm-out-of-the-room faces, but their auras were just as agitated as the club members' were.

Addams spotted Reed near the fireplace, talking to Patrick Spencer. He went over to them and pulled Reed aside.

"What the devil did that idiot do?" he said roughly.

"Bertie! Thank God!" Reed seemed not to have heard the question. He ran a hand through his hair, obviously not for the first time that night. "This is ghastly."

"Reed," Addams said, clapping a hand to the other man's shoulder. "What happened to Denbigh?"

Reed shook his head. "He . . . he thought he could get information from one of Peggy Dover's girls."

"He was a fool." Jack Moreham looked up at the two men. Moreham was short and brown and rather reminded Addams of a weasel. He was swirling brandy in a large snifter and grinning.

"He certainly was." Reed's eyebrows flew up into sharp angles, and Moreham's grin grew wider.

"Why, Bertie," drawled Moreham, "I do believe this is the first time in years you've agreed with me about anything."

"Don't get used to it," Addams replied. "I must say, Jack, you don't seem too broken up by poor Denbigh's death."

Moreham took a sip of his brandy. "Why should I? If he'd gotten what he wanted, we'd all be cursing him for getting ahead of us in the search for that damned incantation."

"Ah." Addams smiled, but there was no humor in it. "You just can't abide to lose a bet, can you, Jack?"

Moreham was about to reply when a tall, thin man

with a large nose stepped between them. It was Charlie Mopps, the unofficial president of the club. He looked to be in his late twenties—exactly the same as he had when Addams had joined the Explorers' Club twenty years before. Some of the older members said that he'd been the leader of the group for sixty years or more, and there were whispers about dark magicks, powerful spells that kept him from growing any older. Judging from the looks of some of the longer-lived members of the club, Mopps wasn't the only one to benefit from such spells.

"Gentlemen," Mopps said, "we have more pressing matters than who wins a bet. We've lost one of our members, and we must see that his killer is punished." His voice was mild, but there was steel in it, and Addams and Moreham gave each other one last glare, then nodded.

Mopps smiled. "Good," he said. "I'm glad to see that we're of one mind on this."

He turned to the rest of the group. "Gentlemen," he said, never raising his voice, but nonetheless the heated conversations stopped immediately and all eyes turned to Mopps.

"I believe we have some business to attend to."

Chapter Five

Sunnydale, California, Fall semester, 2000

"Clown-white is supposed to be white," Willow explained later. "It's white makeup. Really *white* white makeup."

"Like clowns wear," Tara nodded. "Got it. So they were doing a clown show?" Tara was sitting at her desk, studying art history—or at least she had been before taking a very welcome break to discuss Willow's latest Adventures in Drama. As opposed, she pointed out, to Dramatic Adventures, which on the whole was definitely a Good Thing, since Dramatic Adventures had more of a tendency to end up with Ouch and sometimes Die. So far there had been minimal Ouch and no Die, even though the swords and slickness could have been Bad.

"No, they use it for highlights and lots of stuff. We haven't gotten to that part of the class yet. There's a whole semester for makeup. But the point is, somebody turned it all green and icky. I mean, I've seen better looking demon blood than that stuff." Willow was licking at a cherry ice-cream cone. She paused to look at it, shrugged, and took another lick.

"It sounds like a real mess. Are you sure you want to keep working there?"

"Yeah. Besides, maybe Giles would like to look at this." She pulled a scrap of wood out of her backpack. "This was the slippery stuff."

Tara examined it curiously, turning it over in her hands. It was painted black on one side, with a bit of yellow masking tape in one corner, and raw pressed plywood on the other. "It's not slippery now." She rubbed it with her fingertips. "Dry as anything."

"Nope. But when it was on the floor of the stage, whoops, slip-slidin' away. Laurie had us pull up the whole floor to make sure it was safe, but then it was all dry. So I'm wondering, maybe it's magick or something. I mean, they've got all those superstitions— there's got to be some reason for it. You don't find superstitions in a physics lab."

"Maybe physics majors are more likely to get work?"

Willow considered this and nodded. "I still feel like I'm hearing things," she added, taking a delicate bite out of the rim of the cone. "I can't quite understand them yet. I wonder if maybe there's a poltergeist." Her eyes narrowed, and she crunched through the rest of the cone in a businesslike fashion, brushed the crumbs away, and headed for her computer. Tara smiled and shook her head. When Hacker Willow showed up, she might as well settle in for a good evening's studying, because her partner was going to be thoroughly involved in chasing down every scrap of information available in electronic form. It was a good thing they'd already had dinner.

The next day, after classes, Willow headed to the Magic Box. It was where she usually met Tara after classes, and now that Giles had bought the place, all the Scoobies ended up congregating there.

Even if she had never been introduced to the study of magick, never met Tara, Willow thought she would probably have been drawn to the Magic Box. There was something wonderful about the store. It was almost like the smell of paper and ink when you walked into a bookstore, when you knew there were all kinds of new stories to read that you had never read before. The Magic Box had books, of course, hundreds of books in English and Latin and Greek and languages in alphabets she was only beginning to puzzle out. It had incense, too, and smelled of patchouli and jasmine and new and mysterious scents every day. One whole wall was full of candles and herbs used for spells. There were charms and waxes and amulets and figurines and crystals and beads and little statues, some of them doing things so complicated that when she finally figured it out she couldn't stop blushing for days. There was eye of newt and toe of frog and dragon's blood and demon's earwax and scrying balls and sunflower seeds in case you got the munchies in the middle of spellcasting. There were drawers full of chalk for drawing spell circles and athamé blanks and tons of semiprecious stones, each one with its own particular virtue for protection or attraction or power or whatever. There was stuff upstairs and stuff downstairs in the basement, and the inventory kept changing. She despaired, sometimes, of ever learning it all. Anya, Xander's girlfriend, now *she* knew it all backward and forward, but then she *was* a demon, or at least she used to be. Willow paused at the sight of Giles standing on a ladder, reading dusty labels off of dusty jars on a very high shelf, while Anya stood at the bottom of the ladder and made busy notes in a notebook, with running economic commentary. If either of them heard the bell jangle when she opened the door, they gave no sign of it.

"K'dath demon scales," Giles said, squinting at the faded brown lettering on a label peeling from a brown jar. "How interesting. I haven't seen any since . . ." He trailed off, and there was something in his voice that made Willow shiver.

Giles was dear and fusty and tweedy and always polishing his glasses, and every once in a very long while something else looked out of his eyes and you could tell that inside that British librarian was someone tougher than the average middle-aged British librarian. Much, much tougher. And not just because he knew spells from books, either.

"Fifty cents a dozen. Fifty cents? That's insane! Ten dollars is more like it. K'dath demons shed only once in two hundred years. Whoever priced that must have gotten them wholesale last shedding season. Either that or they're fake Mishui lizard knockoffs. Either way, they're underpriced. Ten dollars." Anya scribbled on the ledger.

Giles looked down at her, sighed, and replaced the jar with an air of a man who had had this argument far too often to want to repeat it.

"Hi, guys!" Willow said brightly. "Giles, can I ask you a question?"

"Oh, hello!" Giles looked genuinely glad of the interruption. Anya scowled. Anya didn't like anything that interfered with the important things in life, defined primarily as money and the acquisition thereof. Tara's theory was that Anya's real role as a vengeance demon had been to make Karl Marx's life hell. Since she'd gotten sidetracked, she was taking it out on everyone else.

Willow set her backpack on the counter, and Giles started down the ladder.

"We're not finished," Anya pointed out.

"Surely we can take a small break," Giles responded. "We've been at it now all morning."

"Only three hours," Anya said. "And we've barely touched the inventory behind the counter. We haven't even started the upstairs yet, and as for downstairs—"

"Please, Anya," Giles said, rubbing the bridge of his nose. His tone brooked no further argument. "A cup of tea for my nerves. Why don't you heat something up, while I talk to Willow?"

"And maybe I can help," Willow offered.

"Well—we can't pay you," Anya warned her.

Giles lifted an eyebrow. "'We'?" Anya gave him a mutinous look.

"All right, 'Giles,'" she said, with just the hint of a pout. "Giles, we're never going to get finished with this inventory if you keep taking breaks for tea and conversation."

Having won her point, Anya trotted away, happily toting up numbers and profit margins. Giles watched her go, shaking his head, and then led Willow over to an open area at one end of the store where a table had been set up. Nearby, a plate of cookies, a hot plate, and teapot stood ready, and he busied himself with the familiar ritual of making tea for the two of them. Willow watched him fondly.

He turned in time to catch the smile on her face and smiled in return. "A bit of a habit, isn't it? So what is it this time? Nothing dire, I trust?" He handed her a mug of tea and seated himself across the table from her, pushing several thick volumes out of the way.

"Oh no. I was just wondering—I'm taking this class, and I was wondering if you knew anything about ghosts and theaters."

"Ghosts and theaters?" His eyebrows rose above the wire-rimmed glasses. "Do you have reason to think a theater is haunted?" His sharp gaze touched the textbooks she had neatly placed within comforting arm's reach. "UC Sunnydale's, for instance?"

"Well, not really. Not exactly. I mean, just in general, are theaters haunted?" The tea tasted of smoke and oranges and green leaves, and she held it in her mouth, savoring the varying flavors, before she swallowed.

Giles was swirling the liquid in his mug, a large plain white cup meant for coffee rather than civilized English tea, watching it whirl round and round, and finally shook his head. "I can't imagine why they should be, unless someone's died in one. Hauntings generally require ghosts, and ghosts usually require deaths. Violent deaths, more often than not."

"Violent deaths? We have violent deaths?" Buffy, brushing cobwebs out of her hair, appeared in the door leading to the basement. "In the middle of the day?" She came over to the table and flopped down into a chair. "Giles, heavy boxes all moved."

"No, no," Willow said, smiling. "No deaths. I was just asking about haunted theaters."

"Good," Buffy said. "Wait, the theater is haunted?" Her brow wrinkled. "Are you sure?"

"Not that I can tell yet," Willow said. "I was just checking to see if haunted theaters were common."

Giles frowned. "As a general rule, applied to theaters as a whole, I would think not." He looked up. "*Has* anyone died violently in our local college theater?"

Willow smiled slightly, even through the inexplicable pang of disappointment. Giles would expect her to do her homework ahead of time, naturally. And naturally, she had. "I checked the newspaper files as far back as they went, and the police records. It's amazingly death-free."

Giles gave a *Well, there you are, then* kind of shrug.

Buffy grinned. "So, no ghosties in the theater," she

said, "Good. So, how's the class going? What really cool things am I missing because Giles is making me train?" She flicked a grin at Giles, who merely lifted an eyebrow and sipped his tea.

"My drama professor says that plays started out as rituals to propitiate the gods," Willow said. A thought struck her, and she turned to Giles. "Do you know anything about that?"

That got a flicker of interest from Giles, or maybe it was irritated pride. *One does know something more than just demonology, you know!* "Well, yes, of course originally, I'm sure it began that way," he said, "but it developed quite quickly into Sophocles and Aristophanes and all that lot. One doesn't think of *Lysistrata* as propitiating the gods, does one? Although there is some rather dreadful stuff in the Oedipus cycle and so on. The Furies. The king blinding himself. It all took place off stage. Where we get our term 'obscene' today, in fact."

Oops. Willow looked at Buffy, who was rolling her eyes toward heaven. She'd accidentally triggered Lecture Giles. Time to gently bring him back on track. "So you don't think there would be any connection to these superstitions today?"

He smiled. "I really don't see how there could be. As soon as scripts were developed, they became mass entertainment, and they lost any power as ritual they might have had. Unless you've got something specific you want to try to identify, Willow, I think you're just dealing with a colorful superstition. We've got to be particularly careful not to see demons behind every bush, considering the work we do—"

"Giles! We have several more shelves to check!" Anya apparently considered the short break long enough. She was standing across the shop, list in hand, literally tapping her foot in impatience, oblivious to the fact that a browsing customer was giving her a very wide, and wide-eyed, berth.

Buffy and Willow shared a grin, and Giles grimaced. "'Once more unto the breach . . . ,'" he muttered.

"Can I help?" Willow offered. "I'd love to list the books upstairs."

Giles hesitated, then set down his cup next to the now depleted plate of cookies. "Very well. But be careful, please, and if you can't read a title, don't open the volume. Just set it aside and I'll look at it later. And for heaven's sake, don't read anything out loud. Some of those books are really quite . . . quite . . ." He shook his head, unable to find words, and polished his glasses as a matter of reflex.

"Yeah, Will," Buffy said. "No demon-summoning. That way lies much badness. And dry-cleaning."

"Check," Willow said solemnly. "No reading aloud and no demon-summoning." She grabbed her backpack and dashed to the narrow staircase before Anya could think of a reason to keep her away, pleased at the chance to rummage through the shelves upstairs.

The upstairs balcony was wrought iron, and Willow could keep an eye on Buffy, sitting at the table and flipping through a glossy magazine, and Giles and Anya still cataloging the shelves below, distracted by the occasional customer coming in now and again looking for a tarot deck or a love charm. It was funny to see Anya trying her best to be charming and persuasive, two qualities not usually needed by the average vengeance demon, but Anya had learned fast that the easiest way to part a customer from his or her hard-earned cash was to be very, very nice to them. The problem was that Anya had the script for "very, very nice" down cold, but it still didn't sound entirely sincere. Willow had seen people shoving money into her hands in panic just to keep her from saying "Have a nice day" again. Somehow it was just . . . vaguely threatening, coming from Anya.

Willow had wondered more than once why Anya hadn't just become a bank robber. That would have been more in line with her direct approach to matters. Banks were where the money was, after all, and Anya loved money. And, Goddess knew, Anya was direct. But Anya was also extremely moral, Willow had decided. Even as a vengeance demon, she didn't go around simply inflicting dire punishments on random people; she only punished people who had earned punishment to begin with. So maybe bank robbery wasn't an option.

Still, watching her recite stilted lines like "Have a nice day! Come again soon!" just because Xander had patiently drilled her over and over, when she patently didn't mean a word of it and didn't understand why on earth she couldn't add "and please leave all your money here," did give her something to giggle over with Tara.

And come to think of it, Tara should be showing

up soon, so if she was going to find anything up here about dramatic ritual, Giles or no Giles, she'd better get to it. Moving to the far end of the upstairs bookcases, she began scanning the spines, looking for titles in languages she recognized and pulling them off the shelves to stack together. She and Tara could at least list those and leave the rest for Giles to worry about later.

Her eyes lit up as she began reading the titles under her breath, heedless of Giles's admonishment not to read aloud. *"The Malleus Maleficarum. A Study of African Herbs. The Greater and the Lesser Magicks of the Goths. Bacchantae. A Life of Aleister Crowley. The Six Thousand Demons of the Seventh Dimension. Vampyr. Studies in the Gemstone Rubric. Ritual, Chant, and Song. Demonology for Beginners. Journal of Demonology, Volume 16. Magik. Noisome Loathsome Fumes. The Art of Disguising. Lad: a Dog."*

She blinked. *"Lad: a Dog?"* Sure enough, someone had slipped in a copy of Albert Payson Terhune's late nineteen-teens classic about a collie. It had been one of her favorite books growing up. She slid it off the shelf and into her bag. Maybe Dawnie would like it. She reminded herself to pay Anya before she left. It wouldn't do to shoplift from a vengeance demon, former or not.

Sliding gracefully into a cross-legged position on the floor, she took out a notebook and began copying out the titles, authors, and publication information of the books. Some of them didn't have publication information; some of them looked as if they'd been printed by Gutenberg himself. The paper felt thick and waxy, and for one or two books she found herself handling them as little as possible and rubbing the feel of them away as soon as she put them down, scrubbing her hands against her corduroy skirt. The books seemed to sneer at her as she shoved them as far to the back of her "done" stack as she could.

Others she lingered over, as if they invited her, begged her to stop and read a while. She was flipping through the pages of *Elementary Irish Spellcasting* when the cheerful jangling of the bell announced yet another customer coming into the shop downstairs.

"Hello. Can we help you?" The sound of Giles's greeting barely registered; she was studying an Ogham inscription and its Latin translation, puzzling through the three-level Celtic invocation calling upon the three worlds to witness the intent of the spellcaster.

"I'm looking for a particular text," a man's voice said in response. "Do you have this?"

That accent was familiar. Willow blinked and looked down through the banister to the shop below and saw her professor from the drama class handing Anya a slip of paper. She read it, shook her head, frowning, and passed it to Giles, who was stepping off the ladder.

"I'm not certain," he said. "If we have it, it will be up here. Let me check."

Alarmed and not certain why, Willow scrambled back before Dr. Addams could see her sitting among the piles of books she'd pulled off the shelves. She couldn't hide from Giles, though, when he came upstairs.

"Good lord," he said mildly, looking around at the chaos she'd created, ignoring her frantic efforts to shush him. "I thought you were helping straighten things out."

"I am," she said, her voice just above a whisper. "That's my professor down there. I don't want him to know I'm here."

"Why not?" Since it was obvious he was talking to someone, he didn't lower his voice in turn, but he did look over the railing at Dr. Addams to add, "I'll be with you in just one moment, then, shall I?"

Willow shrugged, a little bewildered herself.

Giles took it in stride. "Very well. Here, do we have a copy of Liverakos's *Ritual, Chant, and Song*? I thought I saw a copy up here the other day."

Willow was sitting on it, in fact. Her hand closed on the cover of the volume, a worn red leather-bound folio edition engraved with an illustration of an early Greek amphitheater on the cover, and she automatically and emphatically shook her head in denial. "Nope. No copy here. Must have sold it. There were some carolers in here the other day; maybe one of them got it."

He looked at her steadily, his eyes bright blue through the steel-rimmed eyeglasses, and she knew that he knew she was lying through her teeth. It was months until Christmas, and the Feast of Mireille had been the week before.

Giles, one eyebrow lifted, said, "I see. That's all right then. Too bad." And he turned around and made his way down the steep stairs to the main shop floor, saying as he went, "I'm very sorry, sir, but my shop assistant says that we've sold our only copy. No, we don't have a record of the sale. Very sorry. You might try Powell's, perhaps, or The Tattered Cover. They're reputed to be quite good."

And Addams left, slamming the door behind him, cutting Anya off as she said, rotely, "Have a nice day! Come again soon!"

Late that evening, Willow sat on the stage of the theater at UC Sunnydale, her legs dangling over the edge of the stage into the orchestra pit. Tara had a night class. The theater was empty now. The last of the seniors had finished their work and packed up, expecting her to follow them out the door.

She might have, too, but she had turned out the lights and then stopped with her hand on the doorknob and turned back. Something had drawn her to the stage, and for just a moment she wanted to sit here by herself and listen to the quiet. She could hear her own breathing, the creaking of wood adjusting to the slowly changing temperature of the building as night cooled the Earth. Somewhere backstage something tiny rustled, a mouse probably.

The only light came from the glow of the exit signs over the doors, three of them, high up at the top of the stadium seating.

It wasn't uncomfortable in the dark, and she wasn't afraid. It was kind of nice, being the only one in the building. She sat and let her legs dangle, and she held the copy of *Ritual, Chant, and Song* close to her chest, and she listened to the quiet of the theater.

O there be players that I have seen play and heard others praise. . . . She thought about the drama students, their knack for quoting at the drop of a hat. Memorizing all those lines from all those plays, no doubt. Like Laurie, a lot of them had been at it since they were little kids. They'd never wanted to do anything else. *It must be nice to have known what you wanted to be,* she thought.

She knew what she wanted to be, finally, but it had taken her a long time to figure it out. Although to be fair, it wasn't like witches had role models on every street corner.

Suddenly she missed Jenny Calendar so much she could have cried. It wasn't fair. Giles tried to teach her, he tried his best, but he wasn't a witch. He wasn't a *woman.* He didn't understand what it was like. Not even Tara understood, sometimes, what it felt like. Sometimes she felt so, so *powerful.* . . . *I have thought some of nature's journeymen had made men and not made them well, they imitated humanity so abominably.*

It sounded—almost like a whisper. "What? Did somebody say something?" she called uncertainly, peering into the gloom of the darkened auditorium. "Lew? Laurie? Did you come back?"

Silence. Not quite the same silence as before. This silence pressed in upon her ears, more full somehow, more occupied than it had seemed a few moments before. The nails of her left hand pressed into the leather cover of the book, defining neat semicircles in the leather. Swallowing, she whispered into the darkness, *"Lux!"* and snapped the fingers of her other hand.

A tiny ball of yellow light popped into existence, sputtered, and died. "Darn it," she muttered. "*Lux,* I said!"

As if abashed, the ball of light popped back in, rising just above her head and casting a feeble glow that barely reached the backs of the first row of seats in front of her.

"Is somebody out there?"

More silence, as if the whole auditorium was full of . . . something . . . or someone . . . holding its breath and listening along with her, waiting for an answer.

Still clutching the book for dear life, Willow got to her feet, the little ball of light holding its position just above and in front of her. It began to dim at one point, and she glared at it. "Don't you dare," she snapped. "I'm not done with you."

As I foretold you . . . faded into air, into thin air . . .

"Who's out there?"

Feeling rather daring, since she wasn't absolutely sure there wasn't someone watching her doing unexplainably witchy things, she sent the little ball of light out into the theater as far as she could. Its golden glow illuminated the backs of two or three audience seats at once, hovering over them and then moving on until it left Willow alone in darkness on the stage and became not much more than a little wandering star in the shadows of the auditorium.

In the wake of the small light, the whispers came faster.

What's Hecuba to him, or he to Hecuba?

Attention must be paid!

The play, the play's the thing!

Sure would be a interestin' funeral. . . .

Heads. Heads. Heads.

For he today that sheds his blood with me. . . .

Sometimes they were so clear that they weren't whispers at all, and then sometimes she couldn't tell if she was really hearing the words or simply remembering them from hearing them so often from rehearsals, over and over and over again until the smell of the wood and the paint and the curtains triggered the memories of the words. Even two or three weeks of being around the theater crowd was enough to draw her in to what Lew called the "shared delusion of the stage." He had declaimed the phrase with cape and considerable grandeur and left Willow and the rest of the Intro class holding their sides with laughter as he marched back and forth producing wickedly accurate impressions of nearly every professor on campus, particularly Addams, whose affectations lent themselves to it with particular ease. "It's the shared delusion—we're all delusional about making a living at this, you see—"

"Okay, okay, I don't care if anybody's there or not," Willow called into the murmur. Her voice shook a little, and she tried again. "I'm going home, okay?"

Snapping her fingers in command, Willow stalked off, not looking behind her. The little globe of light zipped back to her and led the way backstage and out the stage door, and darkness floated back comfortably over auditorium and orchestra and stage.

The theater was finally, completely, empty.

The whispers did not go away.

It's the American Dream! The American Dream, dammit!

Daddy's all sticky wet. . . .

Chapter Six

London, England, 1880

He woke to maddening ravenous hunger, and darkness. He was lying on his back, his hands folded on his breast; when he tried to sit up, his head bashed against something hard covered by cloth. He howled and slammed his hands against the obstacle. It was tight and close and there wasn't much room to get leverage. He had to hit it again and again, kicking and twisting his body, clawing frantically, ripping the cloth away, pounding with all his strength to escape the confines of his containment.

There was a sharp crack as his hands broke through, sinking into something soft, and the rich, damp smell of new-turned earth came strongly to him. Fire burned along his forearms as his flesh scraped against the splintered wood. Some of the earth dribbled through the holes he had made, falling onto his chest and into his mouth. He spat to the side and heard the muddy spittle land on something very close by his head.

He pulled his hands free, sending more earth showering down onto him, and pushed against the wooden barrier above him. It creaked and cracked, and he pushed harder. The wood—cheap pine from the smell of it—gave way. Dirt poured in and he scrabbled at it, trying to keep it out of his mouth and nose. The smells of the earth and the splintered pine were over-powering, and he tore at the wood, unmindful of the sharp edges that gouged his flesh and the blood that ran down his hands and arms. He wanted *out,* away from the smells and the dark, and he pulled at the edges of the holes, widening and joining them. When there was room for his head and shoulders, he began scooping the dirt downward, reaching above him with both hands, frantic now to get free of the small space.

At length one hand broke through into open air, and he shoveled faster, pulling the dirt down in great armfuls, until finally his head broke through into the damp night air. Strangely, he could see perfectly well, even without his glasses. He spat out dirt, and contin-ued to spit until most of the dead, sterile taste left his mouth. If it hadn't been for that awful taste, he might have eaten the dirt, he was so hungry.

The hunger was astonishing. He'd never been this hungry before in his whole life; it gnawed in his belly like a ravening animal, clawed up the back of his throat, roared in his head. He was faint with it.

Everything seemed odd. The few stars that were strong enough to get through the foul London air winked at him, glinting red, and the tiny scrap of moon was red too. Every sound was magnified; he could hear the scrape of little squirrel feet in the trees, the squeak and scrabble of mice in the grass, the slow progress of worms in the earth.

He looked around him, confused. He was in a park or the ramble of some large house, in a small clearing. Beside him was a patch of new-dug dirt. Something white gleamed up at him from beneath the hole he'd made, and he was surprised to see that it was a coffin he'd been in. He was equally surprised that he could tell what it was in the faint light.

From somewhere close he heard footfalls, muffled by the damp grass but quite plain. A woman's voice, sharp with reproof, and another, higher voice, whimpering and begging to be let go, came to him through the trees.

They drew closer; now he could hear the rapid, stuttering beat of a heart and labored, ragged breathing. The woman's voice was very familiar. It pulled at something inside him, as though they were connected, somehow, and after a moment he relaxed. It was the woman from the alley, the one who'd offered him . . . what? And then she had done something to him. Something wonderful. He didn't know how he knew, and he couldn't remember precisely what it had been, but whatever it was, he was fiercely glad of it.

He looked off toward the voices. The woman glimmered in the starlight, her pale gown faintly red, her hair unbound and flowing over her shoulders in a black cloud. She was holding a skinny girl, about sixteen, one hand clamped over her mouth and the other arm around her chest. The girl's feet dangled about three inches off the ground, and she was struggling desperately, kicking and flailing, but the woman seemed not to notice as she moved through the trees. She seemed almost to float, her movement was so graceful. When she saw that he had noticed her, she gave him a dazzling smile.

"Ah, you're awake," she said. "I'm sorry to be so late, but Grandmother wouldn't help me hunt. I've brought you breakfast."

She carried the girl to him as though she were no more burden than a kitten and set her down in front of him. "Here," the dark woman said. "You must be ravenous." She stood watching him with an expectant air, but frowned when he shrank back from the girl.

Her clothes were filthy and torn, and she reeked of sweat and fear and urine and something else, something unhealthy, but underneath all that was another scent, something rich and hot that made his mouth water and sent the gnawing hunger spiraling up beyond bearing. He bit his lip, and was shocked to feel the two upper canines first. They were longer, and wickedly sharp; one of them punctured his lower lip, and without thinking he licked away the small bead of blood that welled up. And then he knew what that hot, rich smell was.

Suddenly everything, all sound, all sight, all scent, shrank to the girl, and he could hear her heart pounding, could feel the vibration of it on his skin, hear the sound of the blood as it pushed through the large vessels. The smell of it was like a promise of satisfaction, an end to the hunger that maddened him. A growl rose in his throat and he reached forward, snatching at the girl, pulling her toward him. The dark woman smiled and clapped her hands, giving a tiny bounce.

The girl struggled in his grip, but he held her easily, turning her so that her back pressed against his chest, lifting her jaw with one hand to expose the line of her neck. Somewhere in the back of his head a voice screamed, "No! Stop!" but he couldn't. He was starving, *starving*. . . .

With a feral snarl, he buried his fangs in her throat, and the voice went out as though it had never spoken. Hot, sweet blood gushed into his mouth and he swallowed. It was glorious and he wanted more. He began to suck greedily at the wound he'd made, gulping the girl's life as her heart slammed into a frantic rhythm and she screamed.

The scream did not last long, but turned into a low moan, then a sigh. She turned her head farther to the side and brought her hand up to clutch the back of his head, pressing his mouth harder against her throat. Her breath came short and she whimpered, her fingers threading through his hair. He pushed his hips forward as her fingers convulsed. She gave a sharp cry as he bit down harder, then shuddered and went slack, her arm falling to her side. Her heartbeat stuttered and slowed, slowed and stuttered, and then, finally . . . stopped.

For a moment he held her, his mouth still fastened

on her throat. The consuming hunger was gone, and so was the red haze that had seemed to cloud his vision when he woke, and warmth crept through him. He hadn't even realized he was cold. Then the woman came to him and gently pulled the dead girl from his grasp.

"There, now," she said. "You feel all better, don't you?" She lifted the limp body and tossed it aside. It landed in a sprawl at the base of a tree.

He sank to his knees in the short grass. He passed a trembling hand over his mouth, and when he looked down at it, it was covered with blood. His eyes went wide; he looked up at the dark woman.

"What . . . ," he began, and stopped at the feel of his lips moving over the long, sharp teeth. The woman bent down and laid a finger on his bloody mouth.

When her cold skin touched his, he remembered: coming outside in tears, her gentle voice promising him something glowing, her mouth on his throat, the pain of her sharp teeth piercing him, and then the most wonderful sensation he'd ever felt. . . .

He stared at her, awed. She was so beautiful, with her huge eyes and her glossy black hair and her red lips. He remembered touching her, putting his hand on her breast, remembered wanting her so badly that he'd have agreed to anything, as long as she kept touching him and talking to him. Kept *seeing* him.

"You . . . ," he began, but she pressed harder against his mouth, sliding her finger slowly down his bottom lip.

"Shh," she said. "All will be revealed in time." She

straightened, absently licking the blood off her finger and making a face at the taste. "Poor boy. Mummy should have gotten you a better one. This one was all spoiled and tastes of curdled milk." For a moment a darkness passed over her face, but, like a scudding cloud shadow, it was soon gone. "Oh, well," she said brightly, and shrugged. "There's always next time."

She held out her hand. Not knowing what else to do, he took it. She stepped close to him, pulling him to his feet as though he were a small child. She was stronger than she looked, and he landed against her chest, hard. It should have knocked the breath out of her, and he realized that she wasn't breathing except to talk. She wrapped one arm around him, holding him tight against her while she brushed her other hand through his hair. Earth from his grave, loosened by her fingers, drifted down inside his collar, but he scarcely noticed, distracted as he was by the feel of her body against his own.

He put his arms around her, let his head fall back into her hand, exposing his throat. She bent and licked the spot where she'd bitten him, and his arms tightened convulsively. He gave a small sigh, as he had done that night, and realized that it was one of the few breaths he'd actually drawn since he clawed his way out of the coffin.

The small sound excited her; he could smell the change in her scent. She began to breathe short, sharp pants, and when she lifted her head to look at him, her eyes were yellow and her face was . . . different, her teeth long and sharp and white. She was beautiful. He was overwhelmed with the urge to bite her; his own teeth ached with it.

"God," he breathed, "what did you do to me?"

"Hush," she said, pressing his head down onto her shoulder. Her white throat was against his lips, but he was afraid to do anything about it. "My brave knight," she crooned, still combing her fingers through his hair. "My lovely boy, my . . ." She stopped and let him go, frowning as her face changed back to what it had been before.

"What's your name?"

He was so disoriented by the suddenness of the question and the abrupt loss of contact, that he had to think about what she said for several seconds before he understood what she wanted to know, and it took him several more seconds to realize that he wasn't quite sure of the answer. His memories were there but . . . distant, fuzzy. Almost as though they belonged to someone else.

After a moment it came to him. "William."

"William," she said, rolling the name in her mouth, testing it. "William." She frowned again.

"That's wrong," she said, pouting a little. "It's not . . ." She seemed to be searching for a word, and after a second she found it. "It's not sharp enough for my handsome knight." She smiled at him and reached out to run her finger down the strong line of his cheek-bone. "But you'll have a new name, a fine name, soon." She took his hand and started off.

"Wait," he said sharply. He curled his fingers tightly around her wrist and jerked her back. "I want . . ."

But he had misjudged his strength, and she came to rest against him with a thump. He was still holding her wrist, his fingers digging hard into the tendons there, and she looked at his hand on her arm, then at him.

Her eyes were wide and a little glazed, her pupils dilated. "You're hurting me," she said, and her voice hummed with a dark joy. She laid the back of her other hand against his cheek, leaning toward him, taking tiny breaths, her eyes half-closed. "Do it again."

For a moment he stared at her, not sure he'd heard her properly. Then he caught the change in her scent, and knew she was completely serious. He gave her arm a slight twist, and she moaned, closing her eyes and letting her head fall back, her lips part. Her free hand snaked back, twining in the curls at the base of his skull, and her fingers tightened, pulling his head down until their mouths met.

She tasted of ripe plums, and when she ran her tongue over his sharp teeth, his knees buckled.

He let go of her wrist and wrapped his arms around her waist, carrying both of them to the ground. Her skirts spread on the ground, and she made a low, growling noise deep in her throat as the impact made him bite her tongue. Her blood in his mouth was bitter-sweet, like the chocolate that Mother sometimes shaved into hot milk, and . . .

The flash of memory brought him up short, and he pulled back. The dark woman—he realized that he did not even know her name—gave him a puzzled look from under her misshapen brows.

"What's wrong?" she said. "Didn't I taste good?"

She looked ready to pout if he gave the wrong answer.

He ignored the imminent pout. "Who are you?" he said, "*What* are you? What am I?"

The woman's face changed, the brow smoothing out, the eyes going back to chocolate brown. "I'm Drusilla," she said. "I'm sorry, it was quite rude of me not to introduce myself." She held out her hand to be kissed, just like the girls he met in society, and without thinking, he bent over it. When he looked up again, she was smiling. "You're my wise, brave knight. And I'm your lady. Just like in the stories." She looked like a lady from one of the courtly romances he used to read, with her black hair down around her shoulders and her skin glinting in the faint moonlight and her huge, haunted eyes. She was fey and beautiful, and she had changed him forever. He remembered now; she had offered him something . . . effulgent.

He could feel the new power in his body, and it made him fiercely happy. He smiled, and the pull of his lips over his long, sharp teeth gave him a feeling of strength that was completely foreign to the poncy poofter he'd been. It was a glorious feeling. "You . . . you made me . . . what you are."

Drusilla laughed and clapped her hands when she saw him smile. "Yes, my lovely boy," she said. "I made you for me, just for me." Her face changed, and she pulled him close, her hands strong on either side of his head, burrowing through his hair to rest against his skull. "All for me." She kissed him, pushed him down onto the damp grass, then sat up and started to remove her clothes. She looked like a goddess from some ancient legend, pale and gleaming in the moonlight, and he stared, awestruck. She was the most beautiful woman he'd ever seen, and she had given him a precious gift. Whatever she asked of him, he would do.

"Hurt me again," she said, holding out her hands to him. And he did.

They lay on the grass near his grave, clothed only in moonlight and each other. Drusilla was humming some tune he vaguely recalled from some other life as she lay, eyes closed, her head on his shoulder. The marks they had inflicted on each other were already beginning to heal, and he ran his fingers idly down her side. She was cold to the touch and very soft, and he had never even imagined the kinds of things they had done, but it had been glorious. His fingers stopped, hovering over her hip.

"This isn't a dream, is it?" he asked, and was a little alarmed at the trace of fear in his voice.

She broke off her humming. "No, silly. It's real, every bit, every bob, every syllable." Her voice took on a lilting, dreamy tone. "As real as tigers with their great green eyes." She sat up, opening her eyes. "Now, we'd better get dressed. The sun will be up in a few hours, and we have things to do."

She stood and looked about her for her shift. He watched her dress in silence, drinking in the sight of her, the way the moonlight silvered her dark hair, gleamed on her skin. She paused midway through buttoning up her basque. "Well?" she said, "What are you waiting for? Daddy and Grandmother will be along soon to get us, and Grandmother doesn't like being kept waiting." She motioned toward the heap of his clothes. "Go on, then."

Reluctantly he dressed, wondering who Daddy and Grandmother were. When he was done, Drusilla came over to him and stroked the ridges on his forehead.

"Here," she said, "can't go out looking like that. You'll scare away dinner. Better change back." She stood back, her eyebrows lifted, her head tilted, waiting for him to do as she'd said, but . . .

"Drusilla, dear," a voice said from behind them. He turned to find a tiny blond woman and a dark-haired smirking man standing several feet away.

"It's about time he woke up," the blonde woman went on. "Angelus . . ."

The dark man—Angelus—shrugged. "Don't be looking at me," he said in a lilting Irish accent. "Dru's the one made him."

The blonde woman heaved a great sigh and rolled her eyes heavenward, as if asking for patience.

"William," Drusilla said, giving a slight skip, "This is Angelus, my Angel, my sweet Daddy, and this is Darla. She's your great-grandmother." Darla sent a killing look toward Drusilla, but she seemed not to notice it. "And this is William. The bravest knight in all the land. The stars sang him to me."

"Not William," he interrupted. William was that soft ponce. What had Drusilla said? He needed a sharper name. And he knew just what it was. "My name is . . . Spike."

Drusilla spun around, eyes alight, hands clasped

together. "Spike! That's it! I knew it was something hard and sharp." She gave him a lascivious smile. "Just like you."

Angelus eyed Spike, clearly not impressed. "Drusilla, darlin', are you sure he's what you want? If not, you know we can always stake him and find you another playmate."

"Don't encourage her, Angelus," Darla said tiredly. "This one's fine, I'm sure. I for one don't have the patience to wait for another one to rise." She adjusted her hat—with its long green feather—and smoothed her hair. "Now, can we please go and find some dinner? I'm starving." She put her hand through Angelus's arm and gave a slight tug.

"Very well," Angelus said, smiling down at her. "Drusilla, bring young William—sorry, *Spike*—along." He lifted an eyebrow at him. "And see that he buttons his shirt up properly before we get to the street."

Drusilla giggled and her fingers flew over the buttons of his waistcoat; when it fell open she undid his shirt buttons, then hurriedly did them back up and rebuttoned the waistcoat. "There," she said, patting his shoulder. "Now you're all ready to go to the ball." She put her arm through his and started off after Angelus and Darla, but paused after a couple of steps. "Except for your face."

Spike concentrated for a moment and felt his bones changing, shifting, his teeth becoming smaller and very blunt, and he gave a delighted smile. "That was just . . ." He stopped, struggling for a word, but nothing even remotely appropriate suggested itself. He shook his head, laughing. Whatever she had done to him, he was glad of it. His new life promised to be quite a bit more interesting than his old one.

Chapter Seven

Sunnydale California, Fall semester, 2000

It does not surprise me, somehow, to find the auburn-haired girl from the Intro class in the Magic Box. Out of all the students in the class, her aura glowed brightest, as if it would only take a little more coaxing to flare into its full glory. If I were interested, at this late date, in taking on an apprentice, I might even consider courting her. (But I have no need of apprentices, and certainly not American teenagers!)

But she is a student, after all, and I suspect that the owner of the occulterie has a prior claim upon her. Certainly, when I returned to the place—the Magic Box . . . what an insipid name it is!—he had been aware that she was upstairs among the rarer books; there had been no surprise upon his face when he discovered her sitting cross-legged on the floor, surrounded as she was by stacks of volumes ranging from the common to the exquisitely precious.

"Willow," the shopkeeper had said, "I thought you were taking inventory?" It was clearly supposed to be a mild rebuke, but there was too much of a longstanding relationship between the two in the tone of the words. Much of a kind, these two: unable to go through books—touch books, handle books—without opening them, and once having opened them, they must skim, and once having begun to skim, they must read, drawn in by the fascination of the printed word. Not so much a rebuke as a shared joke.

She understood it as such, and answered it with a quick, rueful smile, raising her head to acknowledge him but keeping her place in the text with one finger lightly resting on the page—her hands were clean, too, not filthy with dirt and food recently eaten. She had respect for the age of the books she touched.

But then she saw me behind him, and the smile vanished and the light of welcome in her eyes was replaced with alarm, and the shopkeeper turned. Much more quickly than I would have expected, too. I cannot read his aura, I have just realized. I can see it. Of course I can see it—I am not completely inept! But it changes almost as a kaleidoscope changes, dark from one perspective, very bright from another, quite ordinary from yet another. If I had time . . . time! I laugh at myself; really, Albert, time is one of your greatest riches and now you lament its lack? I would investigate this further. I would write to the other Explorers *and see if they have heard of this Mr. Giles, perhaps under another name. So many of us have other names! He's not one of the Club, of that I am certain. But with that extraordinary aura, capable of disguising itself as nothing extraordinary at all, and owning that sort of business, he must be known somewhere, to someone. I am annoyed at myself that I did not see this on my previous visit.*

And he is knowledgeable, not one of those know-nothings who run New Age shops for—what is the phrase?— "pretend pagans and wannabe witches," yes. Abominable English but remarkably expressive American. At any rate, he recognized the Liverakos book, and when I asked about it on this second visit he went immediately upstairs. I knew it had not been sold; this time I followed him.

I had no idea the upstairs area of the shop was so large, and that there were so many books up there. If I were a lesser man, or not so close to my goal, I would postpone the entire ritual for the opportunity to plunder that treasury. Seeing it, considering what I have written here, I wonder if perhaps there may not be even more precious volumes elsewhere, hidden away from the eyes of mere students; this Giles is a merchant, perhaps, but a person of some taste and quality. An enigma.

But nothing to do with me. I must discipline myself. A tendency to follow the will-o'-the-wisp is characteristic of the learned; surely I have progressed past the merely fanciful pursuit of yet another intriguing line of inquiry to the single-minded passionate commitment to my ultimate goal?

Because I am close to it. I am so close to it I can taste it, I can touch it. I have stacks of books, scrolls, palimpsests of my own gathered over more than a century of research. I have read the words of the ancients in their own tongues, deciphered the secrets of the supplicants hidden in texts that were broken apart and scattered halfway across the earth. I have traced the development—no, not the development, say rather the degradation the deterioration!—of this magick from its original form thousands upon thousands of years ago to the pathetic remnants today, and I marvel. For all that it is a mere memory of a shadow of its original power, still it is so potent that someone who knows absolutely nothing of ritual can invoke it and create a separate living thing with a life apart from his own. And often will not even realize he has done so!

I am avoiding it still.

I must discipline myself. Discipline—that was always my weakness. Discipline, perhaps, and fear. Ages ago, I remember old Denbigh saying, "Never forget to fear the consequences." And we laughed at him. I will erase the memory of my second visit from the memory of this girl. There may be consequences to this pyramid of coincidence, and besides, I may well have use for her later.

I fear the consequences now. But I must do this. I have studied for a century for this. I made a mistake, but that was when I was young . . . and foolish. The ancients allowed themselves to be distracted in much the same way. Perhaps this is a mechanism the old gods and powers have created to protect themselves?

Perhaps—yes, yes, that is the key. Distraction. Multiplication of entities. The closer one comes to the solution, the more difficult it becomes to concentrate upon it. How elegant! How obvious! Yes! Yes!

I have it! I have it at last!

I conquered time for this, and now, damn you all, now I will conquer fate as well! We will deal with a single thread, Lachesis, and damn you, you will measure it again, and by my rule this time!

Chorus. Song. Ritual. Plays originally were supplications to the gods.

Then a single actor, usually supposed to be Thespis—thus today's actors were known as "thespians"—stepped out of the chorus, and dialog was created.

The second actor was not memorialized, nor the third.

Willow's notes were rewritten in black, for history. She compared them to the information in the Liverakos book, and found some interesting parallels. But where the notes from class seemed to work from Thespis forward, *Ritual, Chant, and Song* was more concerned with what came before a single man had the nerve to separate himself from the anonymity of the massed chorus speaking together to the gods on behalf of the polity.

The Greeks—or the villages that eventually became the Athenians, the Spartans, the Corinthians, and all the others, since before there was a nation there were city-states—used the chorus to appeal to the gods for good weather for their crops, for strength against their enemies, for justice for their citizens. Liverakos cited a case of a murder of a prominent citizen of the polis wherein the chorus was gathered "in a private place near unto the City, where verses were recited to supplicate to the Furies to pursue the murderer of him who had died, to hound him to uttermost madness, until he should rend the flesh from his very bones for the torment of them; and such was the power of their verses, and such was the power of their song, that the Furies did come out of the very Air and did sit in the temples of the Gods of that City, and they remained there until all the verses of their song were satisfied, and all the members of that Chorus were themselves dead for the horror of that Song which they had sung in the summoning of them."

"Wow," Willow said to herself. "Giles, you are so *wrong*."

Around her, the mutter of pre-class went quiet as Addams took center stage. He had a pipe in his hand, and he tapped the bowl against his palm and slipped it into his pocket. Willow hastily closed the book and slid it into her backpack, positioned a notebook on her lap, and assumed a look of complete innocence.

Addams surveyed the class, shoved his hands in his trouser pockets, and cleared his throat. "Well, now. We've discussed the classic Greek dramatists, Aristophanes, Sophocles, Euripedes, Aeschylos, the role of the masks, the construction of the theater, the dramatic contests or Dionysiads where the poets competed for honors and ivy crowns. From these humble roots came the theater"—he paused to look up and around himself— "of today. As you can see, in some respects not much has changed. Because of this, we can whip rather quickly through the Roman theater—yes? Miss, Rosenberg is it? You have a question?"

Willow took a deep breath. "I was wondering at what point you thought the break might have taken place between using drama for ritual purposes and using it mostly just for entertainment. Could it have been when the poets started separating individual characters out of the chorus? Would that have diluted the power of the ritual?"

Addams opened his mouth to respond and then closed it slowly again, pausing to stare at Willow for a long moment before answering her. "We really have no idea what the Greeks might have thought about what might have affected the power they were trying to invoke," he said at last. "Most of those plays were lost with the burning of the Great Library of Alexandria, and in any case whatever magick they were trying to do was just that: magick and mumbo-jumbo. But you make an interesting point, certainly, that with the creation of individual characters on the stage the potential for pure entertainment rather than pure religious ritual was certainly heightened. It's a pity we can never really know the answer to that question.

"Now, the Greeks did have some stage machines in the latter period. Not only did they use cranes to introduce what we have come to call the *deus ex machina*— you will note how the Romans stole the credit for that one, too—but they also used revolving pillars and wheeled platforms for simple scene changes. . . ."

Dear Reed,

I can hardly believe it. At long last I may have found, among these benighted—you will forgive me my little pun, I trust?—Americans, a student who actually made the connection between ritual and power which I have insisted all along is the path to recovering the rest of the spell for which we have searched for so very long. She is of course in one of the classes which I teach here, and today asked whether the power of the ritual might have been lost— with no prompting from me, I promise!—with the individuation of the chorus.

If there were time, I would very much like to see if this young lady could be brought into our Circles as we brought young men into the Explorers Club in the old days. Yes, I know we never considered women for membership then, but times have changed. Women are no longer relegated exclusively to the ranks of witches, slayers, housewives, and whores. Did you ever think to read such radical ideas coming from my pen, old friend? If I am to stay here much longer, I might even be tempted to discover whether the little chit actually has any talent.

The best news of all, however: I believe, too, that the book is here. All the scrying spells I have performed indicate that it is very near—frustratingly so. So near! I know it does not contain explicit instructions, but more and more I feel that I need it in order to bring together all I know and all I have done to see what I must see and do what I must do. I had it once

*and I will have it again, and this time I will know how
to use the wisdom it contains.*

*And I will do it, old friend. I will win my wager
with Moreham yet. Do you recall the night, so long
ago, when he attempted the spell upon the stage in
London? He was not prepared then, and let mere chaos
loose upon the audience. I do not intend to make the
same mistake!*

> *Yr. ob'dt sv't,*
> *Addams*

He sealed the envelope and addressed it, smiling
gently to himself. It was not a pleasant smile. He
would win his wager, yes.

And Cecily, dear Cecily, would smile upon him
again, if only in his dreams.

"Green makeup. Wow. Sallow people of the world,
beware." Buffy was not impressed with Willow's story
of the theater gremlins. She and Giles were working
out in the exercise room the Watcher had set up in the
back of the Magic Box. Giles, who was working up
rather more of a sweat than the Slayer, managed to say
between puffs, "I still . . . think . . . that . . . unless . . .
someone actually died—*oof*—in the theater"—he sat
down suddenly— "I really think you're probably . . .
dealing with a practical . . . joker. Quite a human being."

"Nobody's actually gotten hurt, have they?" Buffy
asked, offering her mentor a hand up.

"Well, no."

"Didn't you say that the swords had those tip

things taken off?" Tara asked. She had managed to stop in between her classes as well.

"But the property manager had checked and identified all the weapons that could have injured someone and what about the invisible oil on the floor?"

Giles frowned. "Now that, I admit, does sound a trifle odd."

"It could be a spell," Buffy said, shrugging. "Somebody playing a practical joke."

"But—" *But what about the whispers,* she started to protest, but looking around at the faces of her friends, she let a breath go and smiled. None of them was taking her seriously. Not even Tara. "Sure. No big. Just some practical joker."

"Besides, if there ever was anything demonic in the theater, it was probably Anouilh," Giles muttered darkly. "What that man did to *Antigone* . . ." He shook his head and turned to the counter, muttering under his breath. Willow looked at Tara and grinned.

"Are you going back over to the theater tonight?" Tara asked as they left the Magic Box, heading for a little Italian restaurant for dinner.

"I was thinking about it," Willow admitted.

"Aren't you pretty close to finishing up your fifteen hours already?"

"Um, well, I'm not sure. I've got to check." As it happened, that wasn't strictly true; Willow was as obsessive about keeping track of her theater hours as all the rest of her school work, and she only had an hour more to put in to meet the minimum requirement.

"But, you know, it doesn't mean I've got to stop, you know. It's kind of fun, Pollocking and stuff."

"Even with gremlins?" Tara was just as aware of the number of hours Willow was spending on theater work as Willow herself was, but she saw no harm in her partner pursuing a new interest.

"Well, as long as you've got night classes, it's either gremlins or Miss Kitty Fantastico, and she's got limited conversation."

Tara smiled. "As long as you don't go preferring gremlins to me."

"Hello? Jealous?"

Tara laughed, and the two of them twined their arms around each other as they went down the sidewalk.

"Would you like to come with me and see if you can hear them?" Willow suggested later over the tiramisu. "Giles doesn't believe me. He's busy with other stuff; I understand that. Demons trump green makeup and slippery floors every time."

"Giles never tried waxing a floor, I'll bet," Tara said wryly, scooping at a corner of the dessert and tapping excess nutmeg off the top. Willow shook her head. The dessert chef was absolutely prodigal with the superior spices, which was extreme yum, as far as Willow was concerned. "He has no idea just how demonic it can be."

"Humpf." *There has to be a spell for that,* Willow considered. *Why isn't there a book for basic household witchery in all those books Giles had upstairs?* Imagine how much time you could spend not doing dishes. And cleaning *bathrooms*—now *that* was practical magick. "Anyway. Want to come? Maybe you can figure it out."

Tara considered. They both knew Willow was far more powerful in the arcane arts than Tara, but working in the theater was eating into their together time. "Sure, why not?" Tara said, smiling. "When?"

"Well, I've got a Physics Lab from eight to ten tonight. I've been skipping it for most of the semester so far; I really ought to go. After that?"

Her partner blinked. "That's awfully late. There isn't going to be anybody there; it'll be locked up. How would we even get in?"

Willow gave her a look. "Hello, witches here," she said, waving her spoon like a wand.

Tara gave her a look right back and laid down her spoon. They were *good* witches, after all. Good witches did not go in for breaking and entering. "Maybe some other time."

Chapter Eight

London, England, 1880

Angelus led them along Piccadilly, toward the theaters surrounding the Circus, striding along with Darla on his arm as though he owned the pavement, and, indeed, from the way people stepped aside to let him pass, it was hard to believe that he didn't. Spike, his head pounding from the barrage of information his new sharp senses brought him, walked beside Drusilla, her hand tucked into the crook of his arm, letting her lead as he tried to deal with sounds and scents that he'd never been able to distinguish when he was human. He kept an eye on Angelus and Darla, several feet ahead; they seemed quite nonchalant about all the sudden noises around them, and as long as they were calm, Spike reasoned, there was no cause for him to panic. It was getting easier to sort out which were important and which he could safely ignore, but some things still made him start. When he did, Drusilla would pat his arm, and whisper soothing words, distracting him.

Angelus and Darla were arguing amiably about where they ought to hunt that night. Angelus favored Whitechapel, but Darla wasn't inclined to do that much walking, and eventually she wheedled Angelus into picking off one of the stage-door Johnnies who were waiting to catch a glimpse of one of the actresses coming out the stage door of the King's Theatre.

Dru giggled when they turned down the alley behind the theater. "This is going to be fun," she whispered in Spike's ear, her breath tickling his skin. "Watch." He turned his eyes reluctantly to Darla, who was moving in on their intended victim—a flower seller, waiting to make a sale to one of the young men.

The woman was not quite young, but not yet a matron, either. Darla sidled up next to her, pretending to try to see over the crowd, and bumped the woman. "Oh, I beg your pardon," she said, widening her eyes, and the woman gave her a pat on the arm.

"Quite all right," the woman said. She was a bit startled to see another woman there, but had the sense not to show it. "Are you waiting to see Mister Wingfield?"

Darla widened her eyes even more. "Oh, yes," she said, mostly breath and hardly any sound. "He's so . . ."

The woman laughed. "Yes, he is, isn't he?" She glanced at the crowd and then turned back to Darla, eyeing her with curiosity. "How many times have you seen the play?"

Darla went into a gushing recitation of the performances she'd seen, and fluttered the fingers of the hand she was holding behind her back. Angelus began to move, stepping to the woman's other side and gradually shifting toward them, just enough to make the woman unconsciously uncomfortable and take a step away from him.

As Angelus edged the woman closer to the mouth of the alley beside the building, Drusilla gave Spike a conspiratorial wink and a grin and drifted into the crowd waiting at the door, insinuating herself between the people as though she were fog. When she got to the middle of the crowd, she suddenly stiffened, gave a loud, whimpering moan, and clutched at the fellow in front of her.

The man turned around, saw Drusilla apparently in extreme distress, and caught her as she crumpled to the ground. The crowd parted with a collective cry, and the man eased Drusilla to the cobblestones, cradling her head in the crook of his arm. Several of the crowd knelt beside them, offering help.

Behind him, Spike heard a small gasp as Angelus and Darla snatched their victim into the side alley, the sound quickly muffled, as Drusilla gave a high-pitched cry and began to twitch and convulse. For a moment he wasn't sure she was feigning the attack, but in her thrashing, she caught his eye and gave him another wink. He waited until the faint sounds of struggle from the alley ceased, and then stepped forward.

"Here," he said, making his voice sound anxious and frightened, "Here, let me through." He shoved his way to Drusilla's side and knelt beside her. "Let me have her," he said to the man who had caught her. "I know what to do. This has happened before." The man relinquished his hold, settling Drusilla into Spike's arms carefully, and backed away.

"Is she going to be all right?" he said, wiping his brow with his handkerchief.

"She'll be fine," Spike said. "Won't you, sweet-heart?" He reached into his pocket and fumbled about, as though looking for something. "Confound it, I've left her medicine at home." He stood up, lifting Drusilla as though she weighed no more than a doll, and strode with her toward the alley where Darla and Angelus were waiting. "I've a cab waiting out front," he said over his shoulder. "Thank you for your help."

Drusilla began to shake in his arms, and he real-ized that she was trying not to giggle. When he was well into the darkness of the alley and was sure he wouldn't be seen, he set her down on her feet. She clapped both hands over her mouth, shaking with silent laughter.

"Well done, boy," Angelus said in a nearly sound-less whisper. He sounded a little surprised, as though he hadn't expected Spike to participate in their little game. Spike grinned at him.

"I thought it would be useful to get her out of there," he said.

Darla, holding on to the struggling woman, gave him an appraising look. "At least you're quicker about it than Angelus. He always takes an age to get back." She gave Angelus a catty smile, and he frowned.

"I do not," he said, shooting Darla a glare. "And now oughtn't we to have our dinner before she wears herself out and ruins the taste?"

Darla's smile widened. "You're right, darling." She tilted her chin at him, her hands being occupied with holding the woman. "Can you just get her sleeves, then?"

"Ooooh, Grandmother, let me!" Drusilla said, and, not waiting for a reply, took hold of the woman's dress sleeves and ripped them out at the seams. Darla rolled her eyes.

Lifting the woman's right arm, Drusilla held it out to Spike. "Here," she said. "Grandmother gets first bite, because she's the eldest, then Angelus, then me, and then you." She seemed quite cheerful.

Spike took the woman's arm, unsure of what he was supposed to do with it, but when first Darla and then Angelus struck swiftly at the woman's throat, and the scent of blood came to him, sweet and strong, he knew exactly what to do.

He waited for Drusilla to fasten her teeth into the bend of the woman's elbow, and as soon as she pierced the woman's flesh, he morphed into his other face and did the same.

Her blood was hot in his mouth, sweet and thick and quite different from the sickly child Drusilla had brought him when he crawled out of his coffin. He swallowed, growling a little at the glorious taste of her, and pulled harder as the woman thrashed about, trying vainly to shake the four of them off. Too soon, her struggles slowed then ceased, and no more blood flowed into his mouth. He lifted his head, wiped his mouth on the back of his hand and then licked the last of her rich life from his skin, savoring the final taste.

When he looked up, Darla was delicately wiping her lips. "Well," she said, "that was refreshing." She smiled up at Angelus, who was holding the limp corpse, and was about to speak when Drusilla began to make a high, keening sound.

Angelus thrust the body roughly at Spike and went to Drusilla, taking her by the shoulders.

"Dru, what is it?" he said, bending down to look into her eyes, which were wide and unfocused. "What do you see?"

The empty look on Dru's face frightened Spike. He pushed the body toward Darla, who gave him a contemptuous look and let the body fall to the ground. Spike went to Dru, his eyes blazing gold. "What's wrong?" he demanded, grabbing hold of Angelus's arm.

The older vampire shook him off with a twitch, never letting go of Drusilla. "It's a vision," he said tersely, and gave Dru a shake. "Drusilla! Darling, what do you see?"

All he got for reply was more keening. He gave her another, harder, shake, his brow creasing and his jaw muscles jumping. He drew back a hand, as though to strike her, but Spike caught his arm.

"No," he said, his voice low and deadly, and squeezed. He heard Angelus's bones creak. "That won't help."

Angelus looked down at him, amused. "And what would you know about it, boy?" he said, smirking.

"You've known her barely three hours." He jerked his arm; when that failed to loosen Spike's grip, he snarled, letting out the demon, and flung Spike back against the alley wall.

Spike was up in a second, snarling himself, and stepped between Angelus and Drusilla. "Leave her alone," he growled, baring his fangs.

Angelus showed his own teeth and drew back his fist. This time Darla caught his arm.

"Angelus, really, don't you know any better than to get between a fledgling and his sire?" Her voice was full of mocking amusement, and it seemed to deflate Angelus's anger. He took a step backward.

"Fine," he said sourly, flinging a hand into the air. "Go ahead, boy. See if you can do any better." He crossed his arms over his chest and leaned back against the brick wall, his face rippling back to human, his mouth set in a tight line.

Spike turned and set his hands gently on Drusilla's shoulders, holding her as Angelus had done. She was still keening, a sound that rose and fell and made the hairs on Spike's arms stand straight up. Her eyes were still unfocused, the pupils so large that her eyes were almost completely black, and she trembled underneath his hands.

"Drusilla," he said softly, "can you hear me?" She didn't reply, but the noise she was making stopped abruptly. He lifted a hand to her cheek, cupped it, and stroked his thumb over her cheekbone. "Drusilla, love," he said, and squeezed her shoulder with his other hand. "What is it? What's wrong?"

She nuzzled into his hand like a kitten. "Crows and weavers," she said, her voice far away. "Bright lights and stars and threads." She laid a hand over his and gently lifted it away from her face. "All the crows are coming, and we'll have a party. I must go and get the table set." She pushed past him, her eyes still unfocused, and walked up the alley toward the street.

Darla swore and started after her. "You had to drive her mad, didn't you?" she snapped over her shoulder. "You'll have to take care of the body. I'll go with her." She followed Drusilla, and when she caught up with her, grabbed her elbow and pulled her to a stop, then hailed a passing hansom and bundled Dru into it.

Angelus groaned and slumped against the wall. "Sure and she's going to make me pay for that," he said tiredly. "She hates having to deal with Dru when she's got one of her fits on her." He pushed himself away from the wall with a sigh. "Right, then. We'd better get this thing disposed of. Watch and learn, boy."

He bent and picked up the sleeves that Drusilla had torn from the woman's dress, handed one to Spike and proceeded to pull the other one up the dead woman's arm, tucking it into the dress at the top. Spike stood there, looking at the fabric.

"Why not just leave her here?"

"Because, you daft git, she's got the marks of four vampires on her. There are those in London who know what those marks mean. Too dangerous. Now put her sleeve on."

When Spike had complied, Angelus stood and

motioned to him. "All right, help me get her up." When they'd gotten the corpse to its feet, Angelus draped one dead arm around his neck and wrapped his arm around the woman's waist. "Lesson the first," he said, rolling the woman's dead weight forward with his inside hip. "The trick is to make it look like she's drunk or ill." He paused for a moment to tug the collar of the dress up a little, so that it hid the bite marks better. "And try to keep the head down. Now come on. We've got to get this to the river." He set off, dragging the dead woman, and Spike followed.

Angelus led Spike through a warren of alleys and back streets toward the river, carrying the dead woman slung over his shoulder. When they came to the water, they knotted stones into her petticoats and heaved her out into the middle of the Thames.

They returned to the house in Milbury Court by a different, more direct route. Angelus, glancing toward the east every few minutes, increased his pace until they were practically running. Spike was surprised to find that the pace did not tire him, nor was he the least bit winded.

They had just turned onto the street when Angelus swore and grabbed Spike by the coat sleeve. "Dawn's here," he said, giving a jerk. "Fly."

Spike stopped, amazed. "I can fly?" he said, a grin growing on his face, but Angelus only growled and gave a harder jerk on his sleeve.

"No, you great ponce. Now, *run*." He dropped Spike's sleeve and took off, seeming to vanish, he moved so fast. Spike, reasoning that if something was frightening Angelus enough to run, he ought to do the same, took off after him. The houses blurred as he passed them.

He might have passed his destination, but Angelus snatched at his collar and dragged him onto the walk. The first rays of sunlight were coming through the trees as they dashed up the pavement and onto the verandah, and Spike, not used to being awake at this hour, stopped to look. The light touched his face, warm.

Then it began to burn. The flesh began to sizzle and smoke, and Spike gave a strangled cry, leaping back into the shadows. He clapped a hand to his cheek.

"What . . . ," he said, and looked up to find Angelus giving him a ruthless grin.

"You're a vampire," he said. "Sunlight is deadly. Had that not occurred to you?"

"V-vampire?"

Angelus rolled his eyes. "Think, you prat. Surely you've heard the word before."

He had, of course, but the lurid stories he'd read bore little resemblance to his experience since he'd clawed his way out of a coffin. "But—," he began; Angelus cut him off.

"Drusilla will explain everything," he said, irritation plain in his voice. "Now we have to get inside. Unless you want another taste." He gestured to the plank flooring of the verandah, where the sunlight was creeping toward Spike's boot.

"Er, no," Spike said, stepping farther back. "Do

let's go in." Angelus gave a nasty laugh and opened the door.

Neither Darla nor Drusilla were to be seen. Spike looked around, a little curious to see how vampires lived, but he was disappointed to find an ordinary house, with unremarkable furniture and carpets that tended toward shabby. From somewhere upstairs he heard someone singing; it was the same familiar tune Dru had sung before. He followed the sound up a wide, carpeted staircase, down a hallway papered in an atrocious floral stripe, and into a smallish room at one corner of the house.

It might have belonged to a little girl, judging from the rose-printed wallpaper and the flounces and frills on the bedclothes, not to mention the row of china dolls lined up along the windowsill. The draperies were drawn against the sun, and the dolls sat propped against the heavy brocade, their skirts arranged prettily. But several of them wore blindfolds, and one or two had scraps of cloth tied around their mouths, as though they were gagged.

Drusilla sat in a small rocking chair, holding another doll in her lap, brushing its hair as she rocked and sang to it. She looked up when Spike stepped into the room.

"Hello," she said. "Have you met Miss Edith?" She held the doll up and lifted one of its porcelain arms, holding it out as though the doll wanted to shake hands.

"Er, no," Spike replied. There was an odd, faraway look in Dru's eyes, as though she couldn't quite remember who he was. She frowned when he did not move, and held the doll up a little higher, waggled its arm.

"Well, come and meet her, then," she said, her brows drawing further downward. "Miss Edith, this is . . ." Her face clouded. "This is . . ." She put her hand to her temple, a whine beginning in her throat. "I've forgotten your new name."

"Spike," he supplied, and her face brightened immediately.

"Spike," she told Miss Edith. "Spike, Miss Edith." She looked at Spike gravely, her eyes wide. Her lip began to tremble when he still made no move. "Come and shake hands like a gentleman," she said sharply, shaking the doll once again, "or Mummy shall be quite cross."

Spike stepped forward and took the doll's tiny hand. "How do you do, Miss Edith?" he said, watching Drusilla out of the corner of his eye. When she smiled, he went on. "It's an honor to meet you." He bent over the doll's hand, and Dru gave a delighted laugh that sounded like the chime of silver bells. She settled back in her chair and began to rock again. She didn't look at him, but resumed her song where she had left off.

"Drusilla?" he said, but she seemed not to hear him. He reached out and touched her cheek, and she looked up at him.

"Hullo," she said, as though she'd just noticed him. "Where have you been?"

He knelt at her feet and smiled up at her. "Looking for you, pet."

Chapter Nine

Sunnydale, California, Fall semester, 2000

Sometimes Willow thought she wasn't that much of a good witch after all. Good at *being* a witch, or getting good at it, maybe. But Tara was such a . . . wimp? Sometimes. She loved her, of course, but still. Sometimes.

It was nine o'clock, and the backstage door had just closed behind Laurie. The stage manager was carefully pulling the door closed and double-checking the lock. *Damn.* The stage crew usually stayed until eleven or even later most nights. She would have told Tara that, but every once in a while the moral high ground just got annoying. When she'd left Physics Lab, she'd stopped by the room, dropped off her books, and headed for the theater, intending to see who was there and what was going on. Now she really *was* going to have to break and enter.

And for all her big words, she didn't want to.

But there went Laurie, getting into her beat-up old Caravan and rolling out of the parking lot, and here was Willow.

She could either turn around with her tail between her legs, or she could break in and see the what.

Her teeth worried at her lower lip.

Okay, Liverakos aside, she was pretty sure the Furies were not waiting on the other side of that door.

What if a human prankster was doing all the stuff Laurie was worried about, and she ran into him? *Or her; equal time for female felons.* She began to wish she'd put more energy into talking Tara into coming with her. Or Xander.

Or Buffy. Buffy would be good here. Even though Buffy was probably on the other side of town patrolling, doing her Slayer job.

Or at least that she'd told Tara more about the voices.

Swallowing, Willow took a deep breath, let it out and marched over to the door. Mindful of fingerprints, she let her hand hover over the knob and whispered, "*Reserare.*"

Nothing happened.

Perhaps the door didn't speak Latin.

Willow frowned. "Okay," she muttered. "Door, not bilingual."

Wind shuddered through the trees and wafted the scent of rosemary to her, and she looked around quickly, making sure nobody and nothing was around, watching her. She nearly jumped out of her skin to find Buffy standing behind her, an amused look on her face.

"Buffy! I hate it when you sneak up on me like that!"

Buffy's amused look widened into a grin. "Hey," she said, "you know I patrol campus." She gestured at the door. "B and E, Will? And you didn't even ask me to help. Going after your theater ghosties?"

Willow sighed. "Yeah," she said. "But the stupid door won't open."

"Hey, I can help with that," Buffy said, and cocked her leg up to deliver a kick.

"No, no!" Willow said hastily, grabbing Buffy's arm. "I can get it. I'm just doing something wrong here. . . ." She broke off as the light bulb went on.

"Doofus," she muttered to herself, and tried again, this time directing the spell to the lock instead of to the door. *"Reserare!"*

The lock clicked open, loudly but obediently.

"Recludere!" The door, finally given a command it could obey, swung open. She turned to Buffy and grinned. "See?" she said. "Told you I could get it. Plus, no damaged door to explain."

Buffy laughed. "Yeah, that gets kind of tiresome. Want me to come with?"

Willow considered for a moment. "No," she said finally. "You guys are right and it's probably nothing. I'll check it out, no big. Besides," she pointed over Buffy's shoulder, "I think you might be needed over there." Buffy turned; on the other side of the quad, a well-muscled jock strutted down the sidewalk, puffing out his chest to impress the girl coming toward him.

He was too drunk to notice that the girl was a vampire.

Buffy rolled her eyes. "I ought to let her eat him and get him out of the gene pool," she said. She huffed out a sigh and started across the quad. "Yell if you run into any nasties," she called over her shoulder as she pulled a stake out of her pocket.

Willow watched for a second as Buffy pulled the vamp off the staggering jock and began to pummel her. Buffy seemed to be having a grand old time and didn't look as though she needed any help. Willow slipped inside the theater, pushing the door shut behind her.

It was *dark* in there. She'd had no idea how much ambient light there had been outside, from streetlights and office windows and car headlights. In here, there wasn't anything.

Well, that wasn't quite right either. There was the exit light over the door. As her eyes adjusted to the difference in illumination, she began to see shadows in the darkness and points of brightness on the floor showing where doorways were, so actors galloping for their cues wouldn't break their necks. And she could see the backstage fuse box, which had its own little independent battery-powered pinlight.

That helped a lot. Before she did anything about adding some light of her own, though, she was going to *listen*. Laurie was almost always the last one to leave— she wouldn't have locked up if there were anyone else in the building. But better safe than sorry, and she was here to listen, after all, wasn't she?

It was almost like a Zen meditation exercise. Or a Wicca one.

She slowed her breathing, became very quiet in herself.

Listened.

First, of course, she heard nothing.

Then herself—breath moving in and out of her nostrils, her lungs.

Her heart beating.

Blood shooshing in her ears.

Is this what vampires hear? a part of her wondered, and was hushed by the rest of her, listening.

Mice venturing out of the back rooms.

Wood beams contracting in cooling air.

The building settling for the night, resting.

Curtains sighing as dust fell from them to the floor.

Voices?

She raised one hand, opened her mouth, spoke without words a spell that would give her the ability to see in the darkness, that would keep others from seeing her. *I so hope this works. . . .*

The voices were coming from the front of the theater. She couldn't quite understand what they were saying. Creeping as softly as she could, she moved down the hallway toward the stage.

The closer she got, the more individual words and phrases she could make out, but nothing made sense. It sounded almost as if there was a whole crowd out there, but all she could hear were words, and nothing else. Something was missing, and she couldn't tell what.

Pausing by the back wing of the stage, she tried to see but couldn't. Her spell wasn't strong enough, and she was afraid to strengthen it. Frustrated, she reached for the edge of the curtain, wanting something to hold on to.

As she did so, someone passed her, coming out of absolutely nowhere, and she nearly screamed. But he simply walked past her, just onto the stage itself.

The man stopped and looked at her.

She knew him. Well, didn't know him exactly; she'd seen him last year, a senior in a production of *I'm Not Rappaport*. His name was Malcolm, and he'd played the role of Midge, the building superintendent, who sat on a bench in Central Park and gently debated life with Nat the equally aging radical. She was standing less than three feet away from him, and at this distance, practically close enough to hug him, she could really see how the stage makeup had been used to highlight and darken the lines and shadows on his face, to make a twenty-year-old black guy look like he was nearly seventy. His had been a terrific performance, one of the best she'd seen all year, and she'd told him so later when she saw him in the student union.

Now, even though he'd scared her out of her wits, she couldn't help but smile. Midge was such a sweet person, and Malcolm had made him so believable. But Malcom had graduated last year—what was he doing back here?

She opened her mouth to ask him, and as she did so, the figure before her stooped a little, and the lines of makeup blurred and faded. The powder in the hair softened. Malcolm's—Midge's—lips were wrinkled suddenly, and he looked tired, worn out.

He looked like an old man, nearly seventy years old, and he shook his head at her slowly. "You go on home now, girl," he whispered. "This is not a good place for you to be."

"Why not?" Willow asked. She was blinking, trying to figure out what she was seeing.

A sound from behind her, in the direction of the back door, distracted her. When she turned back, the stage was empty, Malcolm—Midge—was gone, and the voices were silent.

Malcolm Ismail had graduated in May 2000 and was now studying for a master's degree in chemical engineering at M.I.T. He had not, he assured Willow the next morning, been anywhere near UC Sunnydale in months. Not that he wasn't flattered that she remembered him from a play he'd done last year, but just why was she calling him out of the blue *now* to ask him about it?

Willow had absolutely no idea what to tell him. She did manage to ask if he remembered any stories about practical jokers in the theater while he'd been doing *Rappaport*.

"No more than usual," the amused and puzzled voice at the other end of the line said. "Look, I only got into doing the play because I was dating one of the lighting techs, and she talked me into trying out. It was fun while it lasted, but I'm more into earning a living, if you know what I mean. No, I don't remember any accidents or anything like that. No voices. Are you sure you're not just getting some bad drugs or something?"

"Oh, no, no drugs. Because, scary," Willow assured him. "Listen, thanks for your time. Really." She disconnected and stared at the phone in her hand.

It had been Ismail. It had absolutely been Ismail, no question. At least, it had been for at least a minute or so.

But then, when the man had actually spoken to her, it didn't sound at all like the grad student she'd just listened to. It had sounded like an old man, tired and uneducated, like Midge from the play.

But that was the whole point. Ismail was a really good actor.

But Ismail hadn't been *there.*

Shaking her head, Willow replaced the phone in its charger and started organizing her desk. Astrally projecting actors aside, she did have a full class load this semester, and Tara was right—she was nearly finished with her fifteen hours of work. She needed to choose a topic for a paper—well, she needed to make sure that Addams would accept a paper for extra credit, first. She didn't think she'd actually need the extra credit, but it never hurt, and it could be fun. She grinned wryly at herself. *Yeah, at the end of the day, still pretty much a study nerd.*

Faculty at UC Sunnydale posted office hours on the branch campus's Web site. The theater department only had four full-time professors and three associates, and some of them taught classes that were offered in coordination with other departments. Playwriting, for instance, was an English class as well as a theater class. The playwriting instructor wasn't really a member of the theater department at all—she was an English teacher in disguise.

Willow determined when she could find her professor in his office, at least theoretically. The next question was, what should she write a paper about? She snorted. *I'd like to do a paper about mysterious voices in the theater, Dr. Addams,* she could see herself saying. *Can you suggest some good references to start me off?*

So not likely.

Theater superstitions, maybe. There seemed to be a lot of those. She ran a quick search and sat back, only partly satisfied with the results. That many hits meant it was too . . . easy.

What about the stuff Addams had been talking about in that last lecture, stage machinery? She could ask Xander about it. She didn't get to see Xander nearly as much as she used to anymore—he had his job and Anya, and she had school and Tara, and sometimes she missed him so much. Stage machinery would be a perfect excuse to pick his brains, and then they could have popcorn and pizza, too.

There was all the other stuff she had to do this semester too, though. Maybe taking on another paper wasn't such a good idea. Physics. Greek. Chemistry. Botany.

Don't be silly, she chided herself. Intro to Drama was her fun class for the semester. This would be her fun paper. All she had to do was call and make sure Addams was in, and make an appointment to talk to him.

* * *

The young red-headed woman sitting across the desk from him folded her hands primly in her lap and crossed her ankles. She was wearing a bright blue skirt splashed with large yellow daisies—wobbly daisies that looked as if a young child had been given unfortunate access to crayons in the textile factory. It made her appear younger than she probably was. Younger and smaller, sitting in a large leather club chair in front of the floor-to-ceiling bookcases the faculty office came equipped with as a matter of course. And as a matter of course, the bookcases were stuffed with books. Delightfully stuffed. It was going to make moving on quite difficult, if he should have to do that; if he could not finally find what he was seeking here.

Surely he could find it here, if anywhere. The place had the reputation of being the Hellmouth, after all.

Albert Addams wondered for an instant if he had been wrong in his assessment of this student. She was obviously bright, but she seemed insecure. The stage manager's records showed that Willow Rosenberg had already completed the work option quite successfully, but here she was wanting to do a research paper as well. Perhaps she lacked the willfulness, the arrogance a really good magician required to manipulate powers beyond herself.

Still, there did appear to be some talent present. And if she was unable to put it to use herself, there were others who would be more than happy to make use of it. Talent should never go to waste. That was one of the first tenets of the Explorers Club. Real talent was too rare, too precious, to be allowed to dribble away unused, and if the owner could not or would not, well—

"I thought I'd like to do something on the stage machinery you mentioned the early Greeks used," she was saying. "Maybe trace how it developed into today's revolving stages."

He suppressed a smile. "Indeed. The sort of topic which one could cover adequately, I believe, in a master's thesis . . . or a sentence."

Round brown eyes blinked. *Yes, my dear, you were just insulted. Have you realized it yet? Good. It takes some of your peers a lifetime to notice.* "You made a remark in class recently about the shift in emphasis of the play from ritual to entertainment. Since you seem to have been listening during my lectures"—*unlike the rest of the clods*— "you will recall that the Dionysiads were actually contests for playwrights."

"Sort of early Sundance Festivals, only without the films," she said, nodding.

He winced. "Yes. Of course. Let me suggest to you, then, that you do a different sort of research paper. Since you seem to have an interest in the subject, I am going to provide you with a list of books. I wish you to create an annotated bibliography of early ritual in Greek plays. You do know what an annotated bibliography is?"

She looked dismayed and disappointed, but game. "It's a regular bibliography without the paper that goes with it. It's a list of reference books, with a description of each book and what it covers."

"An adequate description." He nodded and peered over the rims of his glasses at her. "In this case, however, I am providing you with the titles. You will prepare the bibliography after the style of the Modern Language Association style book. You will have to read the texts, of course, in order to prepare the annotations. No cheating, mind, by reviewing abstracts. Most of these titles, I fear, do not appear in the typical scholarly abstracts." He smiled, showing stained teeth. "After all, you are dealing with the Greek gods and myths." He paused. "Do you have any questions?"

Willow shook her head. This had been a really bad idea. She should have stuck to the work option and left it at that. Now she was going to be stuck doing scut work instead of fun research. She could see exactly where this was going: She was going to be looking up and reviewing obscure citations for his journal publications. She watched, depressed, as the professor opened a file drawer, fumbled through a folder, and finally chose a sheet of paper. He looked it over, then looked at her, still without handing it to her. At least it was only *one* sheet of paper.

Good. Now let us see if you can take a hint, a taste, a bait, my dear. . . . "I have one stipulation regarding the annotation for this bibliography, however. Each entry must note where the reference is to be found."

"Huh? I mean, I'm sorry? I'm not sure I understand."

He smiled, a superior, patient, world-weary smile. "I mean, Miss Rosenberg, that with each entry for your bibliography, I wish you to note whether the book, journal, article, or other entry can be actually

physically obtained in our fine university's library, or
in a bookstore in Timbuktoo, in an online journal, or
in the Magic Box occult store downtown. I want to be
able to assemble an actual library based upon your
bibliography, should I wish to do such a thing, no matter how fanciful the speculations in those references
might be."

"Oh . . . I see. I think." She looked doubtful, but
she clearly understood what he meant. And she had
caught the reference to the Magic Box as well; he had
seen the flicker in her eyes.

Now for the test, to see how much talent the child
really had.

"Here is the list." He handed her the page. She
began to scan it, but before she could more than glance
at it, he interrupted her. "Oh yes, one more thing." He
picked up, as if casually, a large purple crystal, an
amethyst geode paperweight that was sitting on top of
a stack of examination booklets, and touched the
glossy planes and facets, rubbing his fingers sensu-
ously across the sharp mineral tips of stone.

She looked up at once, her eyes a little unfocused.
An obedient child. *Very good.* "Yes?"

"Would you do me a favor, please, and bring me a
book from that shelf behind you?"

"Oh, sure." She got up at once, placed the list of
books he'd just handed her back on his desk without
looking at it, and stepped around the green leather
chair, going directly to the shelves.

She didn't ask, and he didn't tell her, which book
he required.

The mass of purple crystal in his hands pulsed gently, began to glow.

Willow scanned the leather bindings—no mere paper jackets here—and gold stamped titles, and smiled fondly as several of the books quivered and leaned out at her, as if begging, subtly, *Pick me, no, pick me! Me! I'm the one you want! No, I'm more interesting! Read me first! You'll like me!* Her eyes were still unfocused, and she didn't seem to find anything out of the ordinary with books moving by themselves.

As the books did so, the words on the list sitting on Addams's desk blurred and slid into a different configuration, held for a moment, and then scampered into yet another incarnation.

At the same time, Willow seemed to find a particular book for which she had been seeking, and stretched up on tiptoe to take it down. As she did, the rejected volumes slammed back into their upright positions on the shelf, the geode stopped glowing, and the gamboling print on the book list page slid back into its original, innocuous form. Willow turned, book in hand, and handed it to Addams. "Here you are." When he took the book from her, she blinked, a little puzzled to find herself holding it. "Thank you, Miss Rosenberg." He nodded at the list. "Your paper will be due the last Friday before the end of the semester. No extensions will be granted, but then I don't expect you're in the habit of requesting extensions, are you?"

She smiled, letting a little modest pride show. "Haven't had to get one yet." She looked at the paper again. This time nothing about it seemed to strike her as particularly unusual. "I don't think this will be any problem, Doctor Addams. Thanks for the assignment, anyway."

"If you have any problems, of course, please don't hesitate to call me. And please don't think you're not allowed to continue working in the theater if you're so inclined, Miss Rosenberg. An extra pair of hands never goes amiss, I'm sure." He smiled indulgently.

Willow stuffed the page into her backpack and walked out of the office. *Never goes amiss,* she thought. *Like he's ever done a day's work in his life.* Those hands were awfully soft and pudgy for a guy that tall. *Icky.*

She shivered. There was just something about that guy she just didn't like at all. Maybe it had been the way he'd fondled that geode.

She wished she hadn't signed up to do his paper, but she'd get it over with and never see him again. At least she really liked the stage crews. She was really glad he'd said she could keep working there.

And she *was* going to get to the bottom of the theater mystery, darn it. She wanted to know where those voices were coming from, and what that feeling of—whatever it was—was, every time she stayed late. Okay, so it wasn't an apocalypse like Buffy dealt with. And maybe the Furies thing was a long time ago, but this was *her* class, and she, Willow Rosenberg, was a real witch. And she was really going to pull out all the stops and find out what was what.

Albert Addams watched her go and smiled gently at the expression of resolution on the lovely face. Yes, quite a lot of talent there, even if unshaped. He could draw upon that very well. It would make a very nice supplement to his own power when the time came. Willow Rosenberg would do very nicely indeed.

After all, if someone had to be burned to a lifeless shell in propitiation for his centuries-old petition and the ultimate fulfillment of his quest, it was certainly not going to be Albert Addams, now was it?

Chapter Ten

London, England, 1880

They hunted in Whitechapel that night. Angelus gave him a cursory explanation of what to look for and what to avoid in a victim, how to size up a potential meal using his enhanced senses. Spike proved a quick study, and Angelus seemed delighted with his eagerness to learn about his new abilities, though he mocked Spike's attempts to chat up the whores.

"No, no, boy," he said, after one woman had laughed at Spike's advances and flounced away. "Don't be so damned prissy. You're the one with the money here, or at least that's what you want them to think. You needn't be polite. You just get them into a dark corner, then you drain 'em."

"But what about Drusilla?" Spike said, and then, as an afterthought, "and Darla?"

Angelus rolled his eyes. "We persuade a couple to come back to the house with us," he said, as though it were beyond obvious. "They'll not mind the notion of a shag in a comfortable bed instead of up against a wall for a change, and we offer to pay 'em extra."

And indeed, it worked out just that way. After they'd had their own dinners, and found a pair of girls for Darla and Drusilla, Angelus hired a cab to take the four of them back to Milbury Court, where they had a shabby-but-genteel townhouse.

For the next few days, this was their pattern. Angelus or Darla would stay with Drusilla, and the other would go out hunting with Spike. Spike by far preferred to hunt with Angelus; Darla was all contempt and lifted eyebrows, and he felt as though he were back in society, a barely-tolerated poor relation of someone important, and not the powerful creature he'd become. Darla never bothered to try teaching him anything, she merely gave him orders and he carried them out. Angelus had explained about stakes through the heart on their first excursion, and Spike never quite trusted Darla not to stake him if he disobeyed her. She never showed any interest in him either, except so far as he could keep her from having to do any actual work.

Angelus, on the other hand, seemed to be quite interested in Spike, and asked all sorts of probing questions about his background and his family and his friends. Spike declined to answer most of them. He remembered what Darla had said about Angelus driving Drusilla mad; Angelus's keen interest in someone was not always a good thing, he surmised. However, he saw no harm in answering Angelus's questions about how Drusilla had found him.

"She said you were beneath her?" Angelus said when he related his final conversation with Cecily. They were at one of the back tables in the Red Bear, nursing pints of stout and assessing the crowd. "The bitch."

Spike, who was actually drinking his beer instead of pretending to drink, nodded morosely. "She is," he agreed. "And all because her family had more money, more servants." He took another swig of the stout. "Didn't matter how much I loved her. I was just a . . . a thing of no consequence to her."

"The bitch," Angelus said again. "But at least she didn't laugh at you, like the rest of them, hey?"

Spike winced and took another drink. "No. At least she didn't laugh." That was, however, small comfort. The memory of the mocking laughter that had followed him as he fled the Addamses house made him seethe.

"Still," Angelus went on as he toyed with his drink, "beneath her. That had to hurt." He looked at Spike from underneath his lashes, a small smile playing at the corner of his mouth.

"It did." Spike finished his drink and was about to go up to the bar for another, but Angelus pushed his full glass across the table and moved Spike's empty one in front of him.

"Thanks," Spike said, staring into the dark beer. He frowned at what he saw. Or, rather, didn't see. He missed his reflection.

"You know," Angelus said, "you could make her sorry." He leaned back in his chair, a sly grin stretching his mouth. "I can think of all kinds of ways to make her pay. And several of them involving her being beneath *you*."

Spike nearly choked on his beer. "What?" he said, and Angelus's grin grew wider.

"Don't tell me you never thought about getting your own back."

"Oh, I have," Spike said grimly. "I have."

"And she's not the only one, either." Angelus leaned forward, propping his elbows on the table. "Those bastards, the ones who laughed at you, you should make *them* pay too."

"How?"

"I thought you'd never ask," Angelus said, his eyes flashing.

After the conversation with Angelus, Spike wasn't completely surprised when they met several of his erstwhile "friends" coming out of one of the less reputable gaming hells the next time they were out hunting.

It was nearly four A.M., and there were five of them, staggering out the door and leaning drunkenly on each other: Lasher and Gladham, Davey Roth, John Wigeon, and Alan Saunders. Lasher, in the lead as usual, stumbled to a halt and blinked puffy, bloodshot eyes at the two vampires.

"Well, bless my soul," Lasher said. His words were just starting to slur. "If it's not the bloody awful poet himself." He sniggered, and the rest of them followed suit.

Spike cringed at the hateful appellation. Angelus turned to look at him, smile growing wider by the second. Spike tried not to let that make him nervous.

"William," Angelus said, and his voice held mild reproof. All the while his eyes sparkled with wicked glee. "Aren't you going to introduce me to your friends?"

Gladham exchanged a glance with Wigeon, right eyebrow crawling toward his hairline. "Friends?" he said, obviously trying not to laugh, and Spike's jaw clenched. "This git is no friend of ours."

"Now, Charles," Lasher said, shaking a finger in Gladham's face, "you know how concerned we've been about William. We've not heard a word from him in weeks." He tried to assume a solicitous expression, but his lips kept twitching and ruining the effect.

"I thought we were celebrating that!" Saunders hooted.

"Where have you been, William?" Wigeon asked.

"He's been off somewhere writing more bloody awful poetry, that's where," Lasher said. "And he's come back to inflict it on Cecily."

"She'll be so delighted to hear it!"

It was Davey Roth who spoke. The other four found this so hilarious that they could barely stand up for laughing and had to hold one another upright.

Spike stepped toward them and seized Roth's

shirtfront. "Why don't you lot piss off?" he said. He locked his gaze with Roth's, his lip curled in a silent snarl, and lifted the other man several inches off the ground. Roth's scent was instantly infused with the sweet tang of fear, and Spike fought to keep his demon face hidden.

"Ooooh, look," Wigeon sniggered, completely oblivious to Roth's apparent levitation. "The bloody awful poet found a pair of bloody awful stones." Lasher and Gladham sniggered right along with him, and Saunders snorted.

Spike gave Roth a shake that snapped his head back and lifted him higher. Roth's face was beginning to turn purple, and the fear edged over into the heady scent of sheer terror. Spike's teeth ached from holding back the change, and he let go, let his demon out. Roth began to whimper and he kicked out, his feet flailing for contact, but Spike scarcely felt the blows. He gave Roth another, harder, shake, and the kicking stopped.

Lasher stopped laughing as Roth's whimpers turned into wheezing gasps for breath. "Here, what do you think you're doing?" he said, and laid his hand on Spike's arm. Spike turned, and for the first time Lasher saw the creature that William had become. He shrieked and leaped back, but Gladham was in the way and they both went sprawling on the sidewalk. Lasher thrashed about, hampering Gladham's attempts to help him up. Wigeon and Saunders began backing away, but found that Angelus was right behind them. He dropped his hands on their shoulders, holding them in place with what appeared to be bruising force, for they both cried out and tried to twist out of his grip.

"Now, now, boys," Angelus said, deliberately emphasizing his brogue. "Where do ye think ye're off to? I believe William here has a word or two for the lot of yez." He gave the two men a slight shake and grinned at Spike. "Only we don't call him William any more, do we, boyo?"

Roth batted at Spike's hand. "I know what you are," he wheezed, his eyes wide. "You're a vampire. You're . . . evil. Completely and utterly evil."

Spike gave a shrug. "Dunno about that, Davey-boy," he said, " but I expect you'd know, wouldn't you? Seeing as how you're the expert on so many things." He glanced at Lasher and Gladham, still tangled on the pavement. "Don't suppose they've ever told you how bloody annoying that gets, have they? Well, let me show you. . . ." He grasped Roth's chin in his free hand, jerked Roth's head to the side, and buried his fangs in Roth's neck.

Davey's blood was sweet with his terror, and Spike gulped it. It was so much better than the whores' blood he'd been drinking—there was no bitter undertaste of laudanum or gin, and because he knew—or William had known—Davey, there was the extra frisson of intimacy and a certain comfort, as though he were eating a favorite dish from childhood.

Too soon, Roth's heart slowed and stopped, and Spike dropped the body into the street. "Next?" he said, opening his mouth in a feral grin, blood dripping from his fangs.

"Oh, God," Gladham moaned, finally untangling himself from Lasher. "I knew things would turn out badly the minute I saw him. I knew it."

"Shut up, you fool," Lasher hissed, but Gladham didn't seem to hear. He covered his face with his hands and sat there trembling.

Spike reached down and hauled him to his feet, dangling him above the ground as he had Roth. "There, there, Charles," he said, affecting sympathy. "For once, you were right." He pulled Gladham close and struck in one movement, draining the man in seconds and tossing the body into the street beside Roth.

Lasher swore and scrambled to his feet, but Spike had him by the collar before he could run. "Tsk," Spike said. "Cyril, I'm not ready for you to leave yet." He backhanded Lasher across the face, knocking him into the brick wall behind them. Lasher crumpled to the ground, stunned.

Spike turned to Angelus. "Thank you for holding them for me," he said. He cocked his head to one side, considering. "I think Mister Saunders next, then," he said, and Angelus tossed Saunders to him.

Spike was just about to bite when he heard a change in the cadence of Lasher's heartbeat. He turned to look, holding Saunders still with one arm clamped around his chest, and saw that Lasher had gotten to his feet. Spike sighed. Turning back to his prisoner, he sighed. "Saunders, old man, nothing personal, but I don't have time to eat you." He took Saunders's head in his hands and twisted, hard. Saunders's spine gave with a gratifying wet crunch, and Spike flung the body away. Lasher, meanwhile, had fled, and was disappearing around the corner at the end of the block.

"Bloody hell," Spike said. He turned to Angelus.

"Take care of that one, would you?" Without waiting for a reply, he set off after Lasher, running at human speed.

Angelus grinned. "That's my boy," he said to Wigeon, who was nearly sobbing in his fright. "Make the chase last and torment the quarry. Now . . ."

Wigeon closed his eyes. "This isn't happening," he whimpered. "This is impossible. Everyone knows there's no such things as vampires, so this can't be happening."

Angelus shook his head. "You know," he said, his voice dripping scorn, "it always amazes me that some people can deny what's right in front of their eyes." Then he pulled Wigeon's head back and ripped out his throat.

Spike tracked Lasher over half of London, following the unique fear trail and the frantic rhythm of his quarry's heartbeat, sometimes hanging back for blocks, invisible, sometimes speeding up and letting Lasher catch sight of him. Sometimes he appeared nearly at Lasher's elbow, just out of reach, and Lasher would swear at him and jink. Spike let him think he was choosing the direction. The sudden stutter of Lasher's heartbeat at those moments made Spike's eyes burn gold.

It was nearing five A.M. when Spike finally tired of the cat-and-mouse game, sped up his pursuit, and drove Lasher toward the destination he'd had in mind the whole time—the railroad yard.

In the wee hours of the morning, the yard was

nearly deserted. The workshops were silent, and the cars on the sidings hunkered like huge crouching beasts. Spike could hear Lasher's heart laboring, his harsh breaths, and knew that his quarry was nearly ready to drop from exhaustion. When at last Lasher stumbled over a rail and sprawled headlong across the tracks, he found Spike waiting for him.

"Why, Cyril," Spike drawled, as though he'd just run into Lasher at their club. "I've been expecting you."

Lasher raised himself up on one elbow and swiped his sleeve across his cheek, which was smeared with soot and oil and dirt. "What do you want with me, you bastard?" he said, weak-voiced from exhaustion but still defiant.

"Tsk," Spike replied, smiling. "No need to insult Mother like that. She was quite respectably married when I was born, you know." Lasher just looked up at him, one eyebrow lifted. Spike shrugged.

"Very well, enough of the repartee." He squatted down beside Lasher, careful not to soil his clothes. "I have a proposal for you, mate." Reaching forward, he grabbed Lasher by the shirtfront and stood up.

"Angelus," he called, looking over toward where he knew his grandsire was standing. "Might you hold on to this fellow for me?"

Angelus stepped out of the shadows. "Glad to oblige," he said. He came over and took Lasher by the throat, lifting him up to eye level. Lasher's face began to turn a bright purple-red, and he made choking noises.

Spike cleared his throat. "Now then," he said

mildly, "I'd rather not have him dead, please."

Angelus grinned at Lasher, and gave him a slight shake. "What a shame," he quipped. "The other one was quite tasty, I thought." Lasher gurgled, his eyes going so wide that Spike thought his eyes might actually pop out of their sockets.

"No," Spike said, "it'll be his choice whether he dies tonight or not." Lasher gurgled again and somehow managed to make it sound like surprise.

"Why, Cyril, you don't think I'm completely uncivilized just because I've become a vampire, do you?" Spike shook his head in mock disappointment. "I'm crushed." He stepped between the tracks, scanning the rails and the crossties, until he found what he was looking for: a spike that hadn't quite been hammered all the way down. He bent down, worked his fingers underneath the edge of the head, and pulled, arms straining. It moved a little, and Spike gave it a couple of wiggles from side to side, then tried again. Lasher's eyes grew even wider, though that ought to have been impossible.

The spike finally came up on the third try. It was about six and a half inches long and a good half-inch thick, narrowing to a wedge-shaped point on one end and with a hooked head on the other. It showed quite a bit of rust, but the wedge end still looked wickedly sharp. Spike held it up before Lasher's face.

"Ah," he said, "I see you do remember what you said the last time we spoke. I don't believe you realized I'd heard you, but I did." He gestured to Angelus to let Lasher go, and Angelus set him roughly on the ground.

Lasher's legs buckled and there was the sudden sharp stench of urine as a dark stain spread on the front of his trousers.

Angelus wrinkled his nose at the smell. "Here, boy," he said. "Let me in on the joke, then. What is it about that thing that's made Mister High Society here piss himself?"

Spike smiled and reached down, taking hold of Lasher underneath one arm, and gently helped him to stand.

"My friend," he said, putting a bitter emphasis on the word, "heard a poem dear William had written and said that he'd rather have a railroad spike through his head than have to listen to any more." Lasher whimpered.

"There, man," Spike continued softly, giving Lasher a pat on the shoulder. "You were right. That poetry was appallingly bad. But here's my proposition." Without warning he seized Lasher's head and slammed the other man to the ground, his temple pressed onto one of the crossties. Lasher gave a cry of pain as a trickle of blood began to seep into the dirt beside his eye.

"I think my new situation may have improved my poetry," Spike went on. "I'll give you a choice, old man. And I warn you, there's only one right choice here. You can listen to the new poem I've written, or I can shove this railroad spike through your skull. Understand?"

Lasher moaned and Spike felt him try to nod. Angelus gave a bark of surprised laughter.

"Now that's a fine choice for the lad," he said. "I believe you may have potential, boy." He moved back to lean against one of the empty cars, making it shift a little, and waved a hand at Spike. "Go on then."

"Well?" Spike said, holding up the spike. "Which is it to be, Cyril?"

Lasher dragged himself up to a sitting position, looking from the spike to Spike's face. His heart was pounding, and the smell of the blood from the wound filled the air, making Spike's mouth water. Lasher licked his dry lips, opened his mouth, and tried to speak, but nothing came out. Spike lifted an eyebrow and cocked his head. "What was that, old man?" he said, giving Lasher a mocking grin.

"The . . . the poem," Lasher managed to whisper; looking down, he laced his hands together in his damp lap. His knuckles shone white in the faint moonlight.

"I'm sorry," Spike said. "I don't happen to have a new poem on me." As Lasher's head whipped up in realization, he rammed the railroad spike through Lasher's temple so hard that the point ripped out through Lasher's other ear.

Lasher's mouth opened as though in a scream, but he made no sound, and after a moment his muscles went slack and he sagged to the ground, his eyes open and staring.

Spike reached down to where the tip of the spike protruded from Lasher's ear and wiped a smear of blood from the metal. He looked at the dark stain on his fingertip for a second, then, almost absently, licked it off. Immediately he made a face and spat.

"Should have known," he said, disgusted. "All his taste was in his mouth."

Angelus pushed off from the railroad car, laughing. "Spike me lad," he said, "you *definitely* have potential." He put his arm around Spike's shoulder. "Now, let's be off and find some supper for our girls, shall we?"

As usual when they returned from hunting, Spike took Drusilla her supper, and as usual, Dru was almost too involved in her own world to notice. Though Angelus and Darla had both told him that she'd snap out of her fugue in a few days and that the best thing to do was let her alone until the fit passed, Spike was beginning to worry. Dru seemed very different from the woman who'd been waiting for him when he clawed his way out of the grave; she was fragile, almost frightened. She refused company, but being alone seemed to be making her madness worse.

Dru was sitting at the small vanity, brushing her hair, looking into the mirror as though she could see her reflection there. When he opened the door, she turned.

"Spike," she said, smiling. She laid the brush on the vanity and came to him, giving him a kiss on the cheek and completely ignoring the unconscious whore he had slung over his shoulder. When she drew back, her eyes were wide with delight and for the first time since her vision, the faraway look was gone from her eyes. "Why, what have you been doing tonight, you bad boy?" she said archly, tapping her nail against his mouth. She took a step backward, clapping her palms together. "I know. You've been wicked. You've got your own back." She clapped her hands again and took his hand, trying to dance, but the dead weight of the whore prevented her, and she finally noticed the woman.

"What's this?" Her voice announced an imminent pout, and Spike ducked his shoulder, letting the woman slide to the floor.

"Just your dinner, pet," he said. "Now, what did you want to know?"

Dru ducked her head, looking at him from underneath her lashes. She put a hand on his shoulder and began moving around behind him, her other hand making sinuous movements, her fingers waving. "My boy has been getting up to mischief," she said, all threat of pout gone. "Haven't you?"

Spike smiled at her. "Yes, love, I suppose I have," he said.

"I knew it," she said. "I could see it, hovering around you here." She reached over his shoulder, passed a hand over his brow, combing her fingers through his hair. "And here," she went on, laying her other hand on his chest and pressing up against his back. "And here." Her hands slid down, and Spike gasped as she pulled his hips back against her.

"Did you hurt them?" she said, her hands moving on him, and he could only manage a gulp and a nod. "Did you make them bleed and cry and call for their mummies?" Her voice was hypnotic, as were her hands, and he felt the nip of her sharp teeth on the back of his neck. "I can smell their pain and fear," she said, "all over you, and I want to taste it."

Suddenly she wasn't touching him at all, anywhere, and he gave a shuddering gasp at the abandonment.

"Here," she said, annoyed, "Where do you think *you're* going?" Spike, still groggy from the feel of her hands, took a moment to realize she wasn't talking to him, and he turned to find her holding the whore by the throat. He hadn't even heard the woman wake up.

Drusilla looked at Spike. "Should we let her watch, or eat her?" she said brightly, and then, without waiting for Spike to answer, "Eat her, I think. She doesn't deserve to watch." In an instant, her face changed and her teeth were in the woman's throat. After several deep swallows, she raised her head, mouth dripping. "Share?" she said, offering Spike the struggling woman. Dazed, he shook his head, and Dru shrugged and resumed feeding.

When the woman was dead, Dru dropped her to the floor and turned back to Spike, licking her lips. "Now," she said, "tell me all about your fun." She moved to the bed, sat down on it, and held out her hand to him, her eyes glowing. "I want to know everything."

Chapter Eleven

Later that evening Willow quietly pulled the theater door closed behind her and checked to make sure it was locked. It was just past midnight, but a full moon made the campus almost as bright as day. Shifting the strap of her backpack over one shoulder, she started down the concrete tree-lined walkway toward home.

She had gotten past the Chemical Engineering Building and the old English Building when she heard footsteps. She glanced back over her shoulder but saw only shadows silhouetted in the windows of the Chem E Building.

She hugged the strap a little more closely and walked faster.

The sound came again, along with the rustling of

leaves. She looked around again, noticing how moon-light washed the color out of everything around her.

Except the evil yellow glow in the eyes of the vam-pire standing in front of her. Skidding to an abrupt stop, Willow fumbled for a cross, trying desperately to remember a spell of protection, wishing desperately the Slayer was there, scrambling—

The vampire lunged.

Something else lunged as well. Willow managed to be in the intersection of the lunges and went sprawl-ing, knocked against a low concrete retaining wall, with the contents of her backpack scattered over the sidewalk, with black and pink and purple pens rolling and sliding under the feet of two snarling vampires. She pressed back against the wall, making herself as small as she possibly could, as one of the monsters in front of her battered and ripped at the other and was smashed at in return, and finally one exploded into a ball of black dust. The remaining demon spun around, hissing, fangs dripping, eyes glaring, ready to leap upon her and rip out her throat.

"*Spike?*" she said, not quite sure whether to scream or just sigh in exasperation.

The vampire paused.

A moment later his features smoothed into a human visage, the fangs shrank and disappeared into merely human teeth, and the expression changed from savage threat to disappointment and disgust.

"Didn't even bother you a bit, did it, then?" he said, his voice thick with disgust, and picked up some of the scattered books and handed them to her. "I should just give it up entirely, shouldn't I? Can't even put a decent scare into you. So much for the Big Bad."

"Were you *following* me?" she asked, getting to her feet and brushing at a raw spot on her knee. "Why?"

"Well, sure I was. You're a tasty bait, aren't you? Stands to reason somebody's going to jump you sooner or later. Gives me *somebody* to pound on." He stepped back to give her room to sort herself out. "Since I bloody well can't eat humans anymore now this bloody chip in my brain makes my head feel like it's going to explode if I so much as look at one of you sideways."

A little pile of dust, the remains of the loser in the fight, marred the sidewalk, and he sneered at it. "Took them long enough to figure out you stayed late most every night, the twits. Thought they'd never cop to it."

Tasty bait? Willow blushed. Spike saw it and grinned wickedly, making her blush even more. He was very good-looking, in a punk rock kind of way, and even if, well, gay now, she could still appreciate a hottie with probably zero percent body fat—well, maybe two; how many calories did blood have, anyway? *I just called Spike a hottie,* Willow thought. *Tara wouldn't like that, I'll bet.*

Tara would also definitely not like the idea that Spike was following Willow around at night hoping that some demon would attack her, just so the neutralized vamp would have somebody to take his violent frustrations out on either. Definitely too weird.

A gust of wind ruffled the mound of dust, caught it up, and whipped it away.

Time to change the subject.

"Hey, you wouldn't know anything about theater gremlins, would you?" she asked desperately.

"What?" the vampire asked, baffled as well as deeply cranky that Willow was obviously not in the least terrified of him.

"Theater gremlins. I mean, you're English, right? And you're really old, so I thought maybe you might know about . . ." Her voice trailed off lamely.

"That's logical, that is. I suppose you've asked your Watcher pal then? He's English too, and *he's* really old," Spike mocked.

"You're older than he is," she said gamely. "Even if you don't look it."

"Well thank you for *that* much, anyway." He studied her for a moment, looked longingly at the oozing raw spot on her knee and away again. "So he didn't know anything about it?"

"He said the theater couldn't be haunted unless somebody had been killed in it, and I couldn't find any records of anybody dying in it or anything. I went back as far as I could, back to the day the theater was built, even before in case it was built on some old Indian campground or something like that. And it isn't. This could be the only building lot in California that nobody ever died on.

"But then why are all those things happening? I don't believe it's a practical joker. And how come my professor's looking for magick books?"

"Whoa, there, Red. Take a breath. What kind of things are happening?" He hopped up on the retaining

wall and got out his cigarettes, balancing on one foot
and then the other, swinging the open coat around like
massive black wings.

He's doing his Big Bad persona, Willow realized.
Keeping in practice.

"Well, you know," she went on, ignoring his pos-
ing. "Funny things with the costumes, and now there
are holes in the flats—those are the pieces of scenery,
not apartments—"

"I know what flats are." He looked down at her,
indignant. What she'd just said penetrated, and she had
the grace to look abashed.

"Uh, that was pretty dumb, wasn't it?"

"Worthy of your Mister Build-It," Spike agreed.
"So somebody's putting their foot through the walls.
Sounds like clumsiness to me. So what?"

"There's whispers," she admitted at last.

"O-ho, now that sounds interesting. Whispers.
Somebody's cooing sweet somethings in your shell-
like ears? Tell me about whispers." He grinned
wickedly at her, and waggled his eyebrows. Making
fun of her. She didn't have to put up with that.

"Well." Willow sorted out the contents of her backpack, counted the colored pens, discovered the purple
one missing, and chased it down in the gutter. One of
the books wouldn't line up right, and she had to pull
them all out again and pack them back properly.

The vampire sat on the retaining wall, smoking a
cigarette and watching her patiently. He was a hunter.
He was very good at patience. His skin glowed pale in
the moonlight, very pale against the black of his jeans

and T-shirt, the leather of his duster. His peroxided hair shone almost white.

With everything back together precisely the way she wanted it, Willow slung the strap over her shoulder as if to go on her way again, shooting him a withering glare. Spike chuckled.

"All right, all right. I'll be good. Whispers," he said, and crushed out his cigarette on the stone. He cocked his head and assumed a serious expression, as though he were really interested. Willow tried not to be mollified.

"Oh. Yeah." She sighed, and leaned back against the wall herself, a wary distance away. Yes, he was perfectly safe to be around. But . . . he was still Spike, and if there was any possible way for him to get around that chip, he'd find it, and he wouldn't necessarily advertise the fact ahead of time either. Better safe than sorry.

"Okay," she said defiantly. "Sometimes when I'm by myself at night in the theater, I can hear whispers."

"Little voices, then?" He looked at her steadily. "I take it you don't think you've gone round the twist?"

"No," she snapped. "I have not."

He smiled slyly. "Just checking. You told Daddy Giles about this? What does he say?"

"No. Giles doesn't think there's anything to it. I mean, I told him about the incidents and things, and he doesn't take it seriously."

He shrugged, lit another cigarette, and sent a long stream of smoke out into the night air. Willow looked at it and wondered why he bothered. Vampires didn't have to breathe. They were dead, after all. So why smoke?

Of course, he doesn't have to worry about carcinogens, she thought, *and he wouldn't care about the effects of second-hand smoke on people he was planning to eat anyway, so I suppose in a warped sort of way it makes sense. Or at least it isn't strictly non-logical.*

"Maybe he's right. Your incidents aren't much more than little pranks. Haven't even got any decent injuries, have you? Sure you're not just looking for something to be important about, little witch?"

"I am *not,*" she snapped, and stood up and started to walk off, her shoulders square and offended.

She hadn't gone more than six feet before she found the vampire standing in front of her. She gave a little yip of surprise, then glared at him. He grinned at her. *Right, vampire speed. I hate it when he does that.*

"So what do the whispers say?" All right, it wasn't a supernatural apology. It was Spike, not ready to end the conversation yet.

Neither was she, she supposed. She let the tension ease out of her spine and she sighed.

"Sometimes I can't even tell. Sometimes it just sounds like lines from plays, all kinds of different plays. I can recognize some lines from plays, I mean. Other times it sounds like conversation. You can't really tell, you know. It's just that tonight they sounded scared. Frantic, almost." She paused and looked inquiringly at him. "So is that any kind of demon you know about?"

He gave it serious thought. It was one of the things

that made Spike one of the more unusual monsters Willow had ever heard of—he was not only capable of carrying on an intelligent conversation with a human being, he was willing to pay lip service to someone else's point of view. Of course, if he hadn't been carrying the Initiative's disabling chip in his brain, he'd probably be doing it while simultaneously eating them, but still, it was kind of neat.

"Don't think I have," he said. "I'd like to hear these whispers. Sounds like an interesting way to kill an evening. Since I don't seem to be killing much else these days."

Willow brushed dust off her bag and refrained from making an obvious rejoinder. "I can put some hours in tomorrow evening," she said. "It's Wednesday. Tara's got a class, so she won't be back until late anyway. I usually show up to watch the directing class rehearsals and then do whatever work they need done. You could come around eight or so and stick around with me. I don't know if you'll hear anything, though. Nobody ever hears them but me."

"That's because you're a crazy witch, hearing voices that aren't there."

"That's not funny!"

"Not meant to be." But he grinned anyway. "So," he said, and Willow had the odd feeling that he was trying very hard to be casual, "what does Buffy think about all this whispering business?"

"I, uh, I haven't told her about the whispers." Spike grinned at that. "Hey," Willow said, trying to sound righteous, "I told her about the other stuff." Her eyes narrowed. "And why do you care what Buffy thinks, anyway?"

"No reason. Why would there be a reason for me to ask about Buffy? Just making conversation." He tossed his cigarette down and ground it out with his boot. Did he sound . . . defensive? She lifted an eyebrow at him, and he rolled his eyes.

"So I guess you're not in the mood for conversation, then," he said. "Right. I'll just be off." He gave her a mocking salute and faded into the darkness.

Willow resumed her walk home, but no more sounds of footfalls interrupted her journey. She was fairly certain she knew why. It was reassuring, in a way; but it was even more reassuring to know that the chip that kept Spike harmless was still fully operational. Because if it ever failed . . . well, never mind.

Early the next afternoon, before class, Willow stopped by the Magic Box, a copy of the bibliography list in her backpack. She wasn't sure why, but she had a confused memory of seeing most of the books on the list upstairs at the Box.

There were fifteen books on the list. No, eighteen. She stopped just inside the door, oblivious to the clanging of the bell, and looked at it again, counting carefully.

Sixteen.

She could have sworn that the last time she counted there were fifteen. Where did that extra book come from?

The print on the list swam before her eyes, rearranging itself.

"Willow? Is something wrong?"

She looked up to see Giles coming toward her, looking concerned. Rapidly folding the paper up and sticking it into her backpack, she smiled and shook her head. "Nope. No wrong here. Just getting the blurry-eyes from studying too hard, I think."

"Good heavens," Giles said, grinning at Willow as she headed for the teapot and the cookies he kept specifically for the Scooby Gang. "Willow Rosenberg, admitting to studying too hard? The world has come to an end before, granted, but never quite like this."

Rolling her eyes at him, the young witch poured herself a cup of tea, snagged a couple of oatmeal cookies, and slung her backpack strap over the back of a handy chair. She sat down and nibbled and sipped, alternately, staring into space.

Buffy came out of the exercise room, a towel around her neck. She'd worked up a decent glow beating the stuffing out of the heavy bag and was quite cheerful about it. "Hey, Will. What's up?"

Willow looked up, startled, as if the words had taken a long moment to penetrate. "Oh. Hi, Buffy. Giles. What's happening?"

Watcher and Slayer exchanged glances.

"We were kinda on the asking-*you*-that page," Buffy informed her.

"Oh. Sorry. I was sort of elsewhere thoughtwise."

"And that would be where?"

Willow smiled. "I was thinking about homework."

Buffy rolled her eyes. "That's the Willow I know and love but do not understand," she proclaimed.

"Giles, this is for you to deal with. I myself am doing Dawnish stuff, and then demons beware." She flexed a bicep, looked at it with mock pride. "The Slayer's back in town."

"The Slayer hasn't left recently," Willow pointed out.

"It's the spirit of the thing," Buffy informed her.

"I see."

Giles had refrained from trying to participate in this exchange, instead taking the opportunity to polish his glasses.

"I have to look up a bunch of books and review them for a paper," Willow said. "I thought I would check upstairs, see if any of them are here."

Giles slowly tapped his glasses on the table. "This is for a class?"

"Uh-huh." Willow nodded vigorously.

"I cannot imagine what sort of class would require you to review the sort of books we have here in the shop," he said, puzzled. "One would think that you would go to the university library for this assignment. May I see your list of books, Willow?"

"Sure. I have it right here. . . ." Reaching around into the backpack hanging on the chair, she rummaged.

And rummaged again.

"It was right here," she said, and pulled the backpack into her lap. Yanking the opening wide, she pulled each book, notebook, and piece of paper out individually, examining it. "It's gone. I don't get it. I just *had* it." Her voice was rising with panic.

"Willow, Willow, it's okay. Chill. It's all right. I'm

sure the prof will give you another copy." Buffy was moving the books into stacks for her friend, concerned, until Willow snatched them back again. "Or you just left it in your room. It's no big. Will, come on. Come back to us."

"No, you don't get it. I had it just now. I know I did. I put it right here. How could I lose it?"

"Willow, please don't panic." Giles sounded a trifle panicky himself. "Buffy is right. It's only a list; I'm quite sure the professor will give you another copy.

"And you've been working extremely hard recently. It's no wonder that you might misplace something. It's perfectly normal, for heaven's sake. You've always set high standards for yourself, carried heavy class loads, and you've been simply invaluable to me. To us.

"Look, why don't you go home and rest. Give your classes a miss for the rest of the day—"

He stopped, realizing that both women were looking at him as if he had just grown a second head.

"Who are you and what have you done with the real Rupert Giles?" Buffy demanded. It wasn't entirely clear that she was joking.

"I'm serious," he insisted. "Willow is overreacting to a perfectly normal situation. It's a sign of stress. I'm simply suggesting . . ."

"*I'm* overreacting?" she asked. "Giles, *you're* suggesting that I *cut class*."

"I'm suggesting that you take a few well-deserved hours off. You simply misplaced a piece of paper, nothing more. It doesn't merit the kind of reaction you've just demonstrated."

Willow looked at the piles of books, papers, note-books and pens scattered on the table in front of her. Tea had slopped out of one of the teacups and was soaking into the cardboard cover of one of the note-books and dripping onto the piece of paper that stuck out from the bottom.

"I don't believe this," she said, plucking the sheet of typing paper out from between the pages of the notebook. "Sheesh. It must have shoved in there when . . . before." She paused briefly, scanning the list, counting. "Fifteen. That's what I thought." She folded it carefully in half and placed it back between the pages of the notebook. "Wow. I'd better get going. I'm going to be late for class." She gave Buffy and Giles a See-I'm-just-fine fake smile and began to gather her things.

She repacked her bag, swung it into place, and got to her feet. "I guess I'll have to check that stuff out later. See you, guys. Good hunting, Buffy. And Giles—" She gave him a smile of incredible sweetness. "I know you're just worried about me, but it's okay, really." She snickered. "Cutting class? And you think *I'm* stressed?"

Shaking her head, she grabbed one last cookie and made for the door, leaving the other two staring after her.

"And what, exactly, do you make of that?" Giles said, replacing his glasses and pinching the bridge of his nose.

Buffy let go a deep breath. "I make that I'm really glad I'm the muscles of the outfit," she said. "Has Anya been working you too hard doing inventory?"

"I say," Giles retorted, stung. "I'm not the one becoming nearly hysterical over a lost piece of paper. And she was the one who originally suggested she was studying too hard, I'll have you know. She seems to be obsessing about that drama class she's taking. I wish she'd drop it. It would simplify matters considerably."

"Now that *would* be the end of the world," Buffy said. "Willow give up on a class? Never happen. She's stubborn about things like that. Only she calls it 'resolute.'"

Giles sighed. "Perhaps you'd better look into this problem at the theater, Buffy." He sat down at the table, brushing the crumbs from Willow's cookie into a small heap. "I'm not so sure Willow's thinking clearly about this, judging by her reactions just now."

"I tried," Buffy said. "Made it a point to be patrolling on campus the other night. But she didn't seem to want my help." She shrugged when Giles lifted an eyebrow at her. "I'll keep an eye on her. If things get out of hand, I'll step in. Honestly, it doesn't sound too serious." She stood. "I'd better get going. Dawn should be home from school in a few, and I want to be there when she comes in." She headed for the door. "Don't worry about Willow. She can take care of herself."

"I hope you're right," Giles muttered as the bell jangled behind Buffy.

Chapter Twelve

London, England, 1880

Angelus found Spike in Drusilla's room the next evening and shoved him unceremoniously out of the bed. Drusilla, putting her hair up at the vanity, shot Angelus a reproving look.

"He's mine to play with, you know," she said frostily, and Angelus snorted.

"I am right here," Spike said from the floor, where he was trying to extricate himself from the bedcovers.

"I see you're feeling better, Dru," Angelus said, ignoring Spike's protest.

"Oh, yes," she said, her eyes shining. "My Spike brought me a lovely present, all that pain and fear. It was quite tasty."

Angelus made a sound that might have indicated

understanding or slight disapproval. "Well," he said, "I'm glad to see you're up to going out again. I believe Spike needs some new clothes."

Drusilla gave a small hop in her chair. "Ooooh, shopping!" she said, clapping her hands.

"Shopping?" Spike, finally out from under the bedclothes and getting dressed, stopped with his pants half-buttoned. "All the shops will be closed."

"Oh, I know a few places," Angelus said, his eyes twinkling. "Don't worry. We'll have you into something fashionable in no time."

"Something fashionable!" Spike looked down at his tweed suit, which, he had to admit, was rather showing the need for a good brush-up. "What's wrong with this suit?"

"Well, it's hardly going to do to wear to a ball or to the theater, now is it?" Angelus said. He flashed Spike a saucy grin.

"Ball?" Spike shook his head. "I think not. They barely tolerated me at balls when I was alive. Don't really feature getting into one now I'm dead."

"But Spike," Angelus said, his grin getting wider. "I believe you have some unfinished business with society."

"Yes," Dru said, putting the last pin into her hair and patting the curls into place. "That nasty girl with the big eyes, you're not done with her." She came to where Spike was trying to tie his cravat and took the cloth out of his hands, and in a matter of seconds the thing was knotted properly.

"What, you mean Cecily?" Spike's eyes narrowed at the thought, and he smiled.

"Yes," Dru said. "Horrid girl. She hurt my knight, and she must be punished." She gave the cravat a last tug. "There. My Angel is right, though. You do need new clothes. These are beginning to smell." She picked up her hat and began to pin it on.

"They were beginning to smell when you buried him, dear." Darla, standing in the door, wrinkled her nose and managed to look down it at Spike, though he was taller than she by several inches. "Are we going shopping?" She looked up at Angelus.

He rolled his eyes. "Yes, we are," he said with a resigned sigh. He offered her his arm. "I was only planning to go to the tailor's, but I suppose we can stop by Madame Verdi's afterward."

Darla took his arm and gave him a radiant smile. "Darling, you do know how to pamper a girl," she said, and led him out of the room.

Drusilla took Spike's arm and snuggled close to his side. "The last time we went to Madame Verdi's," she said in a conspiratorial whisper, "Darla bought five new gowns, and Angelus had to eat an earl to pay for them. He was old and fat, and Angelus said he tasted of snuff." She giggled. "And he told Darla that if she wanted any more new gowns, she'd just have to eat a countess and steal hers."

"I heard that," Darla called from the stairs.

Dru gave another giggle and leaned to whisper in Spike's ear. "She was quite put out."

"I heard that, too!" Darla's tone was bordering on peevish, and Drusilla winked at Spike and rolled her eyes.

"We'd better go," she said. "It's liable to be crowded at the tailor's if we don't hurry."

As they strolled through the London streets, still full of people even at eight, Spike wondered what kind of tailor kept his shop open to customers so late at night. When they arrived at the shop, tucked away in a narrow side street, after having left Darla and Drusilla off at Mme. Verdi's, he found his answer.

The tailor, whom Angelus introduced as Bensen, was a vampire.

Spike looked at Angelus, brows lifted in a silent question, and Angelus laughed.

"He's the only tailor in London who caters to vampires," Angelus explained. "He was turned more than a hundred years ago. His sire was tired of having to find a new tailor whenever the fashions changed, and set him up here. Bensen never minded. Sewing was his passion when he was alive, and he saw no reason not to go on doing what he knew best." Angelus leaned close to Spike. "Whatever you do," he whispered, "don't annoy him. You'll end up with some awful suit that doesn't fit properly and makes you look like a fool."

"Yes, young man, you will." Bensen looked up from where he was measuring the sleeve for a vampire with flowing black hair and peered at Spike. "So stay on my good side."

Spike, bemused, nodded. As they waited for

Bensen to finish with the long-haired vampire, Spike turned to Angelus.

"What's this all about?" he said. "Why do you care about Cecily?"

Angelus shrugged. "I don't. She's just another bitch from the English snobs to me. But you do, don't you, boy? She made you look like a fool. Me, I'd shame her before her friends. I'd cut her wrists and leave her drained body in her bathtub for her family to find."

"As long as I get to kill her," Spike said with a grim smile, "I'll be happy."

"Tsk," Angelus said. "Did you hear that, Bensen?" he called to the tailor, who was carefully removing the long-haired vampire's coat. Bensen looked up, smiling around a mouthful of pins.

"The boy has no sense of style, Angelus. Not like you."

Angelus turned back to Spike. "And after you showed such promise last night, too." He gave a great sigh and shook his head.

"What are we to do with him, Bensen?"

"I suppose you'll just have to take him in hand," Bensen said, and the dark-haired vampire snorted, as did Angelus.

"All in good time," Angelus said.

Spike, aware that he had somehow missed the joke, glared at Angelus. "So, then, how would you handle Cecily?" he said. "Shame her how, exactly?"

Angelus smiled a terrible smile. "Ah, now," he said, settling himself as Spike stepped up onto the fitting dais, "there are so many ways, boy, so many ways. . . ."

The next night, Spike and Angelus began looking for Cecily. They prowled the city in the early evening, strolling along the fashionable streets in hopes of finding a party or a ball, but society was strangely quiet. The public places where the moneyed classes gathered were little better, and it was only when Angelus bought an evening newspaper that they found out that a great many of that week's social events had been cancelled because of the latest spate of murders. Angelus took great delight in reading to Spike the lurid descriptions of his victims, along with the wildly speculative theories on how Cyril Lasher had ended up with a railroad spike through his brain.

"Well," Angelus said as he tossed the newspaper aside, "it seems we'll have a bit of a wait before we can take care of your little friend. Perhaps you ought to try to look up some of your set and see if they have any idea when the parties are going to start back up again. None of them seem to know you died. Should be easy enough."

It turned out to be easier than Spike expected. He ran into Sally Trumble early the next evening, coming out of the chemist's and looking drawn and wan. She didn't see him until he reached out to keep her from running him over. She began to apologize, but broke off when she recognized him.

"William?" she said, her eyes wide with shock. "You're all right?"

"Good day, Sally," he said, letting go of her arms.

"Of course I'm all right. Why shouldn't I be?"

"My dear, we thought you dead," she said with a shudder. "Your poor mother has been frantic."

Spike affected surprise. "Didn't she find my letter?" he said. "I left it in plain sight on the mantelpiece." As he'd expected, Sally shook her head. "Oh, dear," Spike said, "I've been staying with friends in the country. I thought she knew." He bit his lip, drew his brows down in a worried frown. "I must see her at once and reassure her," he said. "But come, you don't look well, Sally. What's wrong?"

"Oh, it's been just awful," she said, pressing one hand to her chest. Spike smiled to himself. He could well imagine how awful it had been for her; he'd long thought that she and Alan Saunders had been engaged in a secret romantic entanglement.

He slipped his hand underneath her elbow. "Here," he said, concern in his voice, "there's a sweet shop just round the corner that's open. Let's go and have some tea, and you can tell me what's happened." To his considerable surprise, she agreed.

When they'd gotten their tea, he led her to a small table toward the back of the shop, and she poured out the whole story of his disappearance. She said that all his friends had been worried about him and that his mother had even approached the police, afraid he'd been one of the victims of the murderer that had been haunting London for the last several weeks. He was quite sure she was telling the truth about his mother, but suspected that she was exaggerating how concerned his "friends" had been, out of politeness. Then she came to the police finding Cyril Lasher with a railroad spike through his head at the railroad yard. Spike made appropriately horrified sounds, but he was secretly thrilled at her gory description.

"And as if that weren't enough," she said, her voice starting to show strain, "four of Cyril's friends were found murdered in the street. John Wigeon and Davey Roth, Charles Gladham and Al—Alan S—Saunders." She stopped and took a gulp of her tea, blinking hard.

"Good God!" Spike exclaimed, and reached across the table to take her hand. "Sally, I had no idea!"

She looked up at him, nearly goggling. "Haven't you been reading the papers?" she said, clearly unable to believe he hadn't heard.

"Oh, no," he said, very earnestly. "My . . . friends and I have hardly been out of the house. We've been having a sort of retreat, you see." He gave her his most solemn face. "A writers' retreat."

She gave a little start and pulled her hand away, and Spike took a sip of his tea to hide a smile at her discomfiture. "Have the police found the murderer?"

Sally shook her head. "They're still investigating," she said. "It's been awful. They've been round to everyone, asking the most dreadful questions. Poor Cecily Addams. . . ." She broke off, giving Spike a queer look. "Do you know, William, you haven't mentioned Cecily once the whole time we've been here?"

He swore to himself. He'd been so busy trying to be sympathetic that he'd forgotten to be William.

"Well," he said, twisting his face into a pained expression and looking down into his teacup, "after . . .

after . . ." He stopped, swallowed, went on. "After what she said to me . . ." He sneaked a look at Sally from underneath his lashes; she looked horribly embarrassed, and Spike knew that he'd guessed correctly and Cecily had wasted no time in sharing their last conversation with her friends. No doubt with much hand-wringing and pauses for sympathy.

"Oh," Sally said. "Oh. Yes. Er, quite, I can quite see why you wouldn't . . . er, hrm." She gulped the dregs of her tea and brought her napkin up to cover her red face.

"How . . . ," Spike said, looking up her with hopeful eyes, then back down into his teacup. "Well. Perhaps I ought not to ask." He gave a long sigh, and waited, watching her surreptitiously.

For a moment she seemed torn between what she wanted to say and what she'd been taught to do in these kinds of situations. Her training won out, and she reached across the table and gave his hand a quick, light pat. "She's as well as can be expected," she said, trying for a comforting tone. "When your mother came round asking about you, she was dreadfully afraid you'd . . . you'd done yourself harm because of her."

And didn't the bitch just love the idea that I'd gone and killed myself over her, Spike thought. *Probably thought it was hugely romantic.* He looked up at Sally, his eyes as huge as he could make them. "I suppose that would have been the proper thing for a rejected lover to do," he said, "but I find that I'm just too much of a coward to do it." He gave her a sad smile. "I'm afraid I'm as much of a failure at being a romantic as I am at being a poet."

She opened her mouth, then shut it. Clearly she had never expected him to admit to his lack of talent, and she gave him a long look.

"My," she said, surprised into forthrightness. "That's not something you'd have said two weeks ago. Whoever your friends are, whatever you're doing on this retreat, it's done you good."

"Yes, it has," he said blandly. "I'm a changed man."

"You certainly are." She tilted her head, staring at him with a speculative expression. "You know," she said, her eyes suddenly narrowing, "I think it might do Cecily good to see that you're quite all right, and that she hasn't driven you to some desperate act." Spike was surprised at the steel in her voice; he'd always thought that she and Cecily were good friends, but there was something in Sally's face that made him think that perhaps she disapproved of Cecily's treatment of him, and he found himself almost liking the girl.

"There haven't been any parties since . . . since the murders," she said, her expression clouding for a second, "but Naismith's is opening its doors again next week. Perhaps you ought to come. If you're free."

He struggled to contain his triumph, and put on a thoughtful expression. "Perhaps I shall," he said, "if you don't think it would be too . . . awkward?"

Sally smiled. "I daresay it will," she said. "Give us something to talk about besides this dismal murder business." She gave him a wan smile and stood.

"Thank you, William," she said, holding out her hand. He took it and bowed over it, his fingers resting on her wrist where the pulse beat. The feel of her heartbeat underneath his hand, the rich red scent of her blood, so close under the skin, made his mouth water, and when he looked up at her, she started back, her eyes widening, pupils dilating, caught in the hunger he couldn't keep out of his face. He let her go, and she blinked. She rubbed at her temple, looking slightly lost.

"Er," she said, obviously trying to collect herself. "You've been most kind to listen to me all this time," she said, frowning a little. "I'm glad to see you well, and do please think about Naismith's. I would . . . I hope you will come." She stared at him for a moment longer, as though she didn't quite know what to make of him, then gave him a hesitant nod and went on her way.

Spike sat down again, smiling broadly. Angelus was going to be pleased that it had all gone so well.

Chapter Thirteen

Sunnydale, California, Fall semester, 2000

You know, Willow thought, as she squirmed in her seat in the auditorium the next night, *some occult scholar somewhere could have given some thought to the possibility that people could just possibly die of embarrassment.* Spike, sprawled in the seat next to her, seemed to be fully prepared to explore the possibility of murder and mayhem by pure silken rhetoric, and apparently it delighted him at least as much as the bloody kind.

"Gawd, will you listen to that cow," he was saying, his voice pitched just low enough that the words weren't—she so hoped—distinguishable to the girl up on the stage. His tone certainly was, judging by the hate-filled glances she shot toward the audience in between consultations with the student director. "They'd do better to get one of those talking chickens at the drive-up for all the guts she's putting into it. "'Ere, yes, you do seem a bit orf, m'lud, runnin' a bit of fever are you?'" The Scenes from Shakespeare class was rehearsing the first "mad" scene from *Hamlet*. "The nunnery wouldn't have her."

"Spike, *shut up*!" Willow whispered desperately. "They're gonna throw us out of here!"

"What, baby actors can't take a little distracting from the pit?" He grinned. "In my time, sweets, we'd be throwin' rotten oranges and dead squirrels at 'em. See if they can remember all their fancy words and such *then*."

Willow got up and moved several seats down, pointedly separating herself from the troublemaker.

The troublemaker stuck out his lower lip, pouted, and got up and followed her. Willow rolled her eyes and held up her hands in helpless apology to the student director, who marched up the aisle to them.

"Look," he said, "we're trying to do some serious work here, and we'd appreciate it if you'd respect that."

"Oh," Spike said. "Serious work. Had no idea." He looked at the stage, where Hamlet and Ophelia were commiserating with each other and sneaking peeks at the book. "So sorry about that. Thought you were just, you know, acting."

Willow cringed.

The student director pushed his glasses up on his nose in a gesture oddly reminiscent of Rupert Giles.

"They're *trying*," he said, and then lowered his voice. "Doing their best. But it's hard to put your soul up there when somebody's making fun of you, you know? So if you could give them a break, okay?"

Willow fully expected Spike to laugh out loud in the other man's face, and for an instant he looked as if he was going to. But an odd look flickered over his face, the instant passed, and instead he sprawled back in the seat, propped his Doc Martens up on the back of the seat in front of him, and waved one languid hand in permission. "Oh, all right then. Go on. I'll keep my opinions to myself. But for God's sake, teach that woman to emote, would you? It's actually painful to watch her."

The director smiled. "Thanks. We'll try to make it a little less agonizing."

And it was, though Willow found herself watching the changing expressions on Spike's face out of the corner of her eye as much as she did the scenes on stage. After the *Hamlet* (sigh of relief through barely parted lips as exeunt stage left), the seduction scene from Richard III (barely restrained smile and glittering eyes, and Willow with the uncomfortable feeling that Spike was a breath away from game face as the stage Richard made his plea to the Lady Anne over the dead body of her murdered father-in-law: "Vouchsafe, divine perfection of a woman, of these supposed evils, to give me leave By circumstance, but to acquit myself . . ."), and a really disastrous recitation of *A Lover's Complaint* (eyes tightly closed and eyebrows knotted), the Scenes class called it quits for the night.

The Intro class, hewers of wood and drawers of water all, were put to work sorting costumes for the performances. When Willow looked up to the audience, Spike had vanished. She tried not to think where he might have gotten himself. At least the chip would prevent him from being too magisterial a drama critic . . . she hoped.

"Okay, that's enough," Laurie said two hours later, stretching mightily. "Will, you're not going to close up again, are you? Seems like you're always the last one out."

"Oh, that's okay." Willow was sitting cross-legged on the concrete floor of the women's dressing room, partially buried under piles of satins and silks and half-pinned tippet sleeves and caps with fake pearls, talking around pins in her mouth. Removing them carefully, she lifted a brown velveteen skirt and tucked up a hem. "I should bring Tara down here and show her this. She loves this kind of stuff."

"Tara's your roommate?"

"Uh, yeah." She got to her feet and shook out the skirt. "She's my girlfriend." She was finally used to saying the words out loud, but she was never sure how the other person would take it. Sometimes she thought she was just stating a fact, but from the reaction she got, she was making a militant statement.

Apparently this was a "just the facts" occasion. Laurie said, "Well, if she can handle a sewing machine, we can use the help. Bring her on down."

They could hear voices backstage and doors slamming. "I'll hang these things up." Willow indicated the pile still on the floor and tables. "You go ahead."

"Are you sure?"

"Yep, no problem. Really. Offering. So go ahead, okay?"

"Well, if you say so." Laurie gave her a tired grin. "I have to say, we haven't had as many little incidents since you've been the last one out. Maybe you're just more careful about locking up."

"Yeah, I'll bet that's it." Willow waved good-bye and stood listening to Laurie's footsteps as she checked the other rooms and crossed the backstage. The door crashed closed again. It was suddenly quiet.

She busied herself picking up and sorting out, wincing when she pricked herself with a stray pin. If anybody was still in the theater, they had plenty of time to go.

Still quiet.

Everything was tidy. Even the fake pearls were all picked up and put away in a little plastic box to be sewn back onto Lady Anne's cap the next day.

Willow took a deep breath and left the dressing room. The lights backstage were always dim, not meant to be seen from out front. She walked down the short hall to the wings of the stage. The house lights were down; a dim light illuminated the stage. She stepped out onto it and peered into the auditorium, at a disadvantage because of the lighting. "Spike?" she called softly. "Are you out there?"

As if in response, the house lights rose, until stage and auditorium were equally well lit. And except for herself, they were both empty. Shielding her eyes from the spotlights, she looked to the lighting booth, and a figure there raised a hand in acknowledgment. Just in case she didn't get the message, the lights around her blinked a couple of times.

She took a deep breath. "Okay," she said, and held out one hand, palm down, and lowered it slowly.

The lights dimmed.

"Okay," she repeated. "Whoever you are. Whatever you are. I'm listening."

At first, there was nothing, and she wondered, fleetingly, if she had to be in the audience, or sitting down, or something, to hear—

Once upon a time

Oh, it's a wonderful house, Momma!

I feel like a cat on a hot

The kindness of strangers

A husband for Antigone

Eeny meeny miney moe

The whispers.

Where are they?

Gone. Gone missing. More of us gone missing, taken. Lost. Lost!

They came from all directions, beside her, behind her, above her, echoed off the stage curtains, scurried in the orchestra pit. So many voices, so many whispers.

She realized suddenly that she'd stopped breathing, and she drew in a huge breath as quietly as she could, and began to say the words of the spell she'd prepared, calling, as softly as she could, on magick, to allow her to see the unseen, to see the whisperers—

And there before her, seated in the audience, the

misty shapes of characters appeared. She recognized Hamlet—not this evening's, but another, stronger image—and Hedda Gabbler and Mother Goose and Big Daddy and Blanche and Lysistrata and Huck Finn, images she recognized from plays she had read and seen and from the posters in the lobby.

Some of them were thin; others were stronger and more vivid, more real. They were talking together and laughing and comparing notes and shaking out their costumes, as if they were the customers, not constrained anymore by the lines she heard in whispers, or the blocking of the play, but given a life of their own.

There was Malcolm Ismail again—no. No, it wasn't Malcolm at all. It was Midge, the old man, clear as she had seen him one week earlier, and standing next to him was Nat, the other character from the play—only Nat was pale and indistinct by comparison. The actor who played Nat had been so totally bad that she had repressed his name.

They were, she understood suddenly, all the characters that had ever been created on this stage and brought to life there, stepped down to claim a place in the audience and watch and stand judgment on each of the creations that were added to their number, hundreds of them, maybe thousands for all of the plays that all of the students in all of the classes had performed from the time this theater had been built, forty years ago. The vivid ones were the product of the good actors, and the weak and crippled ones the product of the bad actors, but all of them had some kind of life and some kind of substance. And they interacted with one another as if the universe of created characters had a perfectly normal existence next to her own, ignoring her standing on the stage because she wasn't a part of them—neither a character nor a creator.

Awed, Willow was almost afraid to breathe, but Spike had no such compunctions (or requirements). Slouching out of the lighting booth and into the auditorium, lighting a cigarette as he came, he lifted an eyebrow at the assembly. Willow opened her mouth to tell him he couldn't smoke in the theater, but before she could do so, he said, "All right then, you lot. What in hell's goin' on in this theater?"

There's a lot to be said for the direct approach, Willow thought.

"That's right, I'm talking to you, prince of bloody Denmark. Pay attention then."

Abruptly, the characters realized that Spike was actually addressing one of their own— that he and the woman standing at the edge of the stage could actually see them. There were screams of terror, and the characters fled from Spike. He smiled, rather pleased at the reaction, but didn't pursue them.

"How can you do that?" asked a tired, graying Willy Loman, shivering, when it was clear that nothing more was going to happen. A woman standing next to him patted him on the shoulder. *Attention must be paid* . . . "You're not supposed to see us."

"It's, uh, magick," Willow explained, with embarrassed pride. "I kept hearing these whispers, and I thought they might have something to do with all the things going on in the theater—"

"Aaahhhhhh . . ." A huge sigh swept over the characters, and they nodded to one another.

"You heard us?" Hedda Gabbler asked.

"Just said so, didn't she?"

"Spike, please. Yes. So I was just wondering. Are *you* what haunts the theater? Do you haunt *every* theater?"

"I wouldn't say haunt," Thoreau, complete with book in hand, said. "We have a few ghosts among us," he nodded to Banquo dead, who took a bow along with Banquo living and Hamlet's father, "but *we* aren't ghosts. *We* are *characters* . . . with lives of our own."

"And of course we like to welcome newcomers to our ranks," Creon added. "Why shouldn't we? We're perfectly hospitable. Even the serial killers among us." The Greek king, dressed in a 1940s business suit as Anouilh's play would have him, shoved his hands into his pockets and then took them out again and crossed his arms and uncrossed them again.

Willow blinked, recognizing the murderer from *Night Must Fall* raising a hand in acknowledgment at the reference, along with a couple of giggling grandmothers in lace mantillas.

Midge caught her eye and smiled at her, sharing the secret of their earlier meeting.

"Well, isn't that just comfy cozy," Spike said. "Guess that solves your mystery, then. There you have it, green makeup and oily floors and all."

Dead silence. Then Creon shook his head. "That wasn't us. That was the other."

"What other?" Willow was still trying to identify characters in the milling crowd before her. Some of the wispier individuals looked as if they might not last very long, tagging along the periphery and fading even as she looked at them. "Who are they?" she asked a woman standing near her, in a lower voice, indicating the mistier characters.

The woman looked over and sniffed in haughty fashion. "Poorly drawn, unmemorable, without soul, barely brought to life at all. Better they were never born than to live so." She herself could never be mistaken for any of that. Her dark hair was piled high on her head, held in place with a fillet of gold, and her wide dark eyes were outlined in dramatic khol. She wore a simple Greek dress, with wide bands of gold around her otherwise bare upper arms, and two small children clung to her skirts. "Still, they were stronger before this thing that feeds upon us came to our stage."

"Something feeds on you?"

Several of the characters nodded assent. The woman went on. "Some nights when all of you are gone—even you—there is a thing that moves among us, a terrible thing. It rises from the incantations made upon this stage, but it is not yet born. Not yet. Its creator has not yet found the proper text for it. But it is from these rehearsals that come the troubles that disturb the creators, and it sucks at us, their creations. It drains the weak ones dry, sending them to madness."

"Well, isn't *that* a shocker," Spike said ironically. "A monster's growing here. Who'd have thought it? Come on, m'lady. We *are* sitting on the Hellmouth, after all. What's a little more madness among friends? And wouldn't you be the one to know it?"

The Greek woman stepped forward, holding her children by the hand, and looked him in the eye. From the new angle, Willow saw with shock that each of the children had a thick line of red across the throat, and she recognized who the woman had to be: mad Medea, who killed her children.

Apparently makeup served for murder, because the murdered children, sliced throats or not, were having a wonderful time playing peekaboo behind their mother's dress. Meanwhile their royal mother was facing down a vampire without apparent effort. "You are a demon, a monster," the Greek said, "but even you have limits. There are things you cannot do, too terrible for you to do. This thing has no limits that we know."

"Hey!" he protested. "That's not *my* fault. I didn't ask for the bloody chip to be put in. You take out the damn chip and you'll see how limitless I can be."

A very flimsy Cortez that Willow remembered from last year's production of *Royal Hunt of the Sun* burst forth with execrable Spanish, to the effect that there were monsters and there were powers, and the powers that could come forth from the incantations made on this stage could destroy them all.

"What does he mean, 'destroy us all'?" Willow wanted to know. "Does he mean all the characters, or, like, *us* us? And what happened to the actor that created you, by the way? Wasn't he a junior last year? He's not with the seniors, I don't think—" She broke off. This was the Hellmouth, after all; you got used to classmates disappearing from the face of the earth at no notice.

The characters fell silent again, as if the question was a terrible faux pas, and the Cortez screamed and faded away into thin air before her eyes.

"We don't usually refer to the creators, you know," a very pompous Watson informed her. "Once we're created, we're not *them* anymore. Very annoying to be confused with some lout of an actor. It's as Creon said: We have separate lives of our own. The creators are . . . the actors. You know. Well, they're not us. They give us shape and voice, but once we're created, set free, well, often we outlive them. We're more alive, more brilliant, more interesting, most of the time. Besides," he said, lowering his voice and fiddling nervously with a pipe, "the poor boy was replaced after only three performances. Eaten by a vampire, you know. So not perhaps a terribly *memorable* performance." Willow nodded, not at all astonished at the news.

"Hold on though," Spike said. He was sitting now on the edge of the stage, still watching the nervous crowd of characters. "What's this about incantations? Something that isn't quite with you yet? What's this all about?"

Creon was not only a modernized Greek king, but a leader among the characters, Willow decided. There was quite a debate among the crowd before he stepped back out to face the two of them. Medea stood with him, her murdered children still playing hide-and-seek with the folds of her dress, while the rest of the characters pressed back, as if disassociating themselves from the information being passed along.

"Late at night—not every night, or we would all be gone by now—a man comes, speaking lines from the ancient plays. He is seeking the words that will invoke the Fates themselves," the king said. Spike was lighting another cigarette as he spoke, and he flinched, as if he had burned himself on the match. But he said nothing, and lit another, as Creon continued. "He is seeking the old plays—older than mine, older even than Medea's." The queen nodded agreement. "He has not found them yet, but he is stirring great powers, the same great magicks that give us characters life itself, and it is twisting the fabric of the magick in this theater. What the creators see now is the very tip of the turmoil we characters have experienced—we are being destroyed by what this man is attempting. But if he succeeds, what we experience will be as nothing to what he will unleash upon your world.

"We believe that if he seeks a ritual play as ancient as the very first of the plays, he must be invoking the Fates themselves, because there must be a Fate that he wishes to change. But if he does that, he will undo all the Fates of all the world—they will all come unraveled."

"Does he realize that?" Willow wanted to know. She had a sinking feeling she knew exactly who the characters were talking about.

"We believe," the queen said gravely, "that he does not care. He is not a creator, this man, but a destroyer, for all that he touches is destroyed."

Chapter Fourteen

London, England, 1880

Darla was pouting. "Drusilla, *dear*," she said in an acidly sweet voice, "do please stop that dreadful humming. People are staring." She smiled at an elderly man who was passing them, his copious eyebrows drawn down over his nose and his mouth pursed in disapproval.

They were walking in the low-rent end of the theater district, waiting for the shows to let out. There were always stage-door Johnnies who lingered too long, and they were easy pickings.

"I'm calling to the dark star," Drusilla said, making a face at the old man. He harrumphed at her, dark eyes snapping with temper, and, mustaches bristling, made a point of ignoring them as he passed.

"Well, dear, I don't think your star is listening." Darla was beginning to sound snappish, but she didn't care. Drusilla had been humming the same monotonous tune ever since they'd left the house, and Darla was finding it increasingly harder to quash the urge to snatch one of the passersby and commit mayhem.

"Oh, he's listening, Grandmummy," Dru said. She stopped dead in the middle of the sidewalk, causing the people behind her to exclaim and dodge around her. They jostled her, but she didn't seem to notice.

Darla winced. No matter how many times she protested, Angelus's little chit insisted on calling her by that ridiculous name, and Angelus, the beast, only laughed at her when she suggested that he try to talk Dru out of the habit. Darla tucked her hand under Drusilla's elbow and pulled her along. Dru, of course, resumed her humming. Darla ground her teeth.

"Well, I wish the bugger would hurry up and answer you," she muttered, and rolled her eyes.

Drusilla stopped again, and her hum changed from a tune to a slowly rising minor-key warble. "Ooooh," she said, turning to face the theater they were passing. "He's here, Grandmummy. I can feel him." She curved her hands into claws, waving them toward the building as though she were a kitten batting at a string. "He's calling the ravens." She stepped up to the door and laid her hand on it, her eyes closed, humming at the building.

"Oh, for heaven's sake," Darla said. "Drusilla. Stop that at once. Come away from there." She took hold of Dru's arm, but Dru turned to her with a fey, forbidding expression on her face.

"No," she said her voice thrumming with a dark joy, "the dark star is calling me. We must go in." And she pulled the door off the hinges, set it carefully to one side, and walked into the theater.

"Wonderful," Darla said, flinging up her hands, and followed her in.

Drusilla walked straight to the doors into the theater proper and pulled them open. Several of the audience turned to look at them, brows beetling in disapproval at the noise.

On the opposite side of the auditorium, near the stage, a small, brownish man who reminded Darla of a weasel was chanting something in an ancient language. When he finished, he clapped his hands three times, then reached into a pocket and flung something onto the stage. There was a bright flash of light and the audience gasped.

Phantoms appeared on the stage. The audience made an appreciative *ahhhh* sound, and there was a smattering of applause. Drusilla, bouncing on the balls of her feet like a little girl, made little chirpy laughing sounds. "Look, Grandmummy, look!" she said. "It's all about to come undone!"

Though the audience thought the phantoms were part of the show, it was clear that the actors knew better. Even from the back of the theater, Darla could see how wide their eyes were as they tried to ignore the specters and continue the play. Unfortunately the distraction proved too much for one fellow's memory, and he stood staring at a phantom dressed just as he was, his mouth hanging open, the revolver he had been using to threaten another character dangling unnoticed from his slack hand.

The phantom, shrieking obscenities, flew toward the man and snatched the gun from his hand. Setting the weapon flush against the actor's chest, the ghost pulled the trigger, and the gun went off with a muffled roar. At that point-blank range, even the dummy round in the gun was deadly; the man screamed and fell, and the gun clattered to the boards. Blood fountained out of his chest in a crimson flood that soon covered half the stage.

The audience screamed. Many of them sprang from their seats, hands clutched to their mouths in horror as the other apparitions swooped down from the stage and began to attack the people in the first few rows.

Drusilla, still bouncing, clapped her hands.

Meanwhile, one of the phantoms ran back up onto the stage and, seizing the drapery from a false window, set it directly on the working gas jet that provided part of the lighting. The fabric, dry and dusty, blazed up at once, and soon the walls of the set were burning. The flames licked at the heavy velvet curtains and the black legs at the sides of the set, and crept along the hardwood planking of the floor, and soon the stage was an inferno. The actors fled the stage, and the audience, now in a panic, began to move for the doors, pushing and stumbling and screaming.

"Oh, dear," Darla said, realizing what was about to happen, and grabbed Drusilla's arm. Drusilla turned to her, eyes grown enormous.

"This is wrong," she said plaintively as Darla grabbed the last two men out of the back row of seats with one hand and hurled them into the midst of the raging crowd.

"Really," Darla said, and jerked Dru into the empty row. "I'd never have guessed." The crowd surged up the aisle, and Darla snagged a fleeing woman as she passed. "Well," she said, vamping out, "we might as well make the most of this." She drained the woman quickly, then tossed her corpse into the crowd, where it was soon trampled. "Help yourself, dear," she shouted to Dru over the roar of the flames and the crowd, and delicately wiped her mouth before she grabbed a large man. "Plenty for us both."

But Drusilla mumbled, "Wrong, wrong," and stepped into the crowded aisle. Using her vampire strength, she began to push her way toward the stage.

By the time the mob had shoved its way past her, Darla had drained the large man, three matrons, and a spotty, downy-cheeked youth, and was feeling quite full. She took her handkerchief out of her reticule and dabbed at the corners of her mouth, then checked the front of her new outfit for spots. Finding none, she smoothed her skirts and looked around her.

Drusilla was nowhere to be seen. The fire was starting to creep out into the hall; Darla could smell the stench of the horsehair stuffing of the seats as it burned, the singed-wool smell of the carpets. Smoke rolled up the aisle, making her squint. At least she didn't need to breathe.

The aisles were three deep in bodies, most of them

trampled beyond recognition, but there was the occasional moan from someone who was not quite dead yet.

Darla turned, taking in as much of the auditorium as she could in one sweep, but still didn't see Drusilla. "Where *can* she have gotten to?" she said, pursing her red lips and stamping her foot. "Drusilla! Where are you? We've got to get out of here before the place comes down around our ears!" The smoke she'd taken in to call for Dru made her cough, but she shouted again. Angelus would be furious if she let Drusilla burn.

"Here, Grandmummy!" A pale arm lifted above one of the seats. Blood dripped down it, and Darla realized that the sleeve of Drusilla's gown had been ripped away.

She shook her head. "And it was brand new, too," she said sadly as she picked her way toward Drusilla.

Naismith's was already crowded by the time Spike and Angelus arrived, quite late, and carriages were still drawing up at the doors to let off passengers. Spike caught glimpses of colorful gowns and glittering lights and snatches of music every time the footmen opened the doors to admit another arrival.

As they crossed the crowded street, another carriage pulled up. The footman stepped up to open the door, handing out first Albert Addams and then Cecily, who was dressed in a gown of deep rose with a daring décolletage. Spike growled low in his throat.

Cecily smiled her thanks to the footman and stepped down from the carriage, looking around for her friends. Her eyes flew wide and she gasped when she saw Spike, and she turned quickly away. He could hear her heart start to pound.

Spike's growl deepened to a snarl, his lips skinning back over his suddenly long teeth and a red haze blurring his vision; he wanted more than anything to spring forward and rip her pretty white throat out, feel her hot blood spurt into his mouth, hear her scream bubble and die in her throat as he drained the life from her. He felt his face start to change, and his muscles tensed in preparation for the leap.

Without warning, Angelus was between him and the carriage, his hands on Spike's shoulders, fingers biting into flesh as he held the younger vampire there with his full strength. "Stop it, you fool," he hissed. "You'll ruin everything."

For a moment, Spike continued to struggle against Angelus's greater strength, unable to make any sense of his words. Angelus gave him a rough shake, then another. "People are starting to stare, man. Put your face away," he said. Spike, not quite comprehending anything but his grandsire's anger, complied.

"What the hell was that?" Angelus said, his voice like the crack of a whip. "You never do that in a crowd of humans, you damned fool!"

"Nobody saw," Spike said, a bit sullenly. He thought he'd been prepared to see her, but the look on Cecily's face, her dismay at the very sight of him, was far worse than anything he had imagined.

"Thanks to me," Angelus said. "Have you got yourself under control enough to go in there and do this my way?" He pinned Spike in place with a glare, and Spike gave a grudging nod.

"Good," Angelus said. "Now come along." He stepped aside and motioned Spike to go ahead of him. "Don't embarrass me again, boy," he said as Spike passed him, and the threat in Angelus's voice raised the hair on the back of Spike's neck.

The main room was packed. Spike followed Angelus as he pushed through the crowd, listening to the whispers that followed in their wake. By the time they got to the other side of the room, Spike had learned that not only had Cecily rejected him, but he had variously flung himself off London Bridge, shot himself in the head, and gone out and gotten into a brawl with a stevedore who beat him to death. He found it all quite amusing, until Angelus stopped and he nearly bloodied his nose on the other man's back. "What the . . . ," he began, and Angelus stepped aside.

Spike found himself face to face with Cecily. Her nostrils flared, and for a moment he held her gaze, then, quite deliberately, turned his head and walked in the other direction, giving her the cut direct. The buzz of shocked whispers behind him was as sweet as the taste of blood.

"Don't get cocky, now," Angelus murmured in his ear. "You've got the hook in her mouth, it isn't set yet." He stopped beside the refreshment table, took a cup of punch from the liveried servant, and passed it to Spike, darting a quick, appraising glance around the room as he did so. "That one," he said, nodding toward a girl in a dreadful shade of green, sitting between two frowning matrons. She looked slightly familiar. "Remember what I told you, now," Angelus said, taking another cup of punch from the servant. "Here, give her this." He thrust the cup into Spike's other hand.

Spike set his jaw and started toward the girl, trying not to slosh the punch and cudgeling his brain for her name. Thankfully, it came to him just as he stepped into her line of vision.

"Good evening, Miss Danbury," he said, bowing to her. She looked startled to hear her name, and even more startled to be hearing it from him. She flicked a quick look at the woman on her left, who squinted at Spike and then gave a slight nod, before acknowledging him.

"Good evening, sir," she said, a pretty blush coloring her cheeks. "It's good to see you well." She fiddled with her closed fan, her fingers tapping on the silk.

Spike smiled at her. "Yes," he said, "I hear that I ought to be quite dead of unrequited love." He winked at her, and her color deepened. "Don't look dead, do I?"

Miss Danbury dimpled and shook her head. Her mother's lips twitched, then settled back into a frown.

Spike held out a cup of punch. "May I offer you some refreshment?" he asked. "You looked quite thirsty."

Miss Danbury checked silently with her mother again, and at her nod, took the cup Spike was offering. "Thank you," she said. "I was beginning to feel positively parched." When she had drunk the punch, Spike took the cup from her and set it on a nearby table with several other empty cups.

Just then the musicians struck up a new tune, and he held out his hand. "Miss Danbury, if your card is not full, will you honor me with a dance?" Miss Danbury let out a squeak and nearly dropped her fan, from which dangled her quite empty dance card. This time she didn't bother to check with her mother; she stood and set her hand in his.

"I would be delighted, sir," she said, and stepped into his arms.

She turned out to be quite an accomplished dancer, and Spike found that she was also very amusing, when not under her mother's withering glare. By the end of their dance, he was almost sorry that he mightn't ask her for another, but when he brought her back to her mother, he found Angelus standing there, chatting up a very dazed Mrs. Danbury as though they had known each other for years. Which might not have been so far off the mark, Spike realized as Angelus aimed him at another shy, neglected wallflower, for as they walked away he heard Mrs. Danbury and her companion exchanging a whispered conversation about a young man they'd known when they were girls and how like him Angelus was.

Spike was quite gratified to find that he was the main topic of conversation that evening. The girls put their heads together and whispered about how different he seemed, and the gentlemen frowned and shot disapproving glares his way whenever he chose a new dance partner. He smiled blandly back at them, showing his teeth, and the knowledge that he could snap their puny necks whenever he chose gave him an aura of danger that made the men blink and look away, and the ladies flutter and blush and look up at him with wide-eyed fascination. He found he rather enjoyed being thought of as dangerous.

As he danced with one young lady after another, he made it a point to cross Cecily's path as often as possible, though he never once looked her way or acknowledged her. At some point, he knew, she would tire of the crowd and the noise, and seek out a quiet place to be alone for a few minutes, and he fully intended to follow her and have his vengeance.

Finally, at a lull in the music, she whispered something to her friends and headed off by herself, toward one of the many curtained alcoves on the second floor. Spike broke away from his current partner with a murmured excuse and, catching Angelus's eye across the room, indicated that he was going after her. Angelus nodded and started threading his way through the crowd.

Spike had barely gotten three steps when Albert Addams stepped in front of him. His face was set in stern lines, and he laid a hand on Spike's arm.

"Well, well," Addams said, "I certainly didn't expect to see you here." Spike looked pointedly at Addams's hand on his arm, then at Addams, and let his eyes flash amber. Addams jerked back, staring, his mouth slack. "Good God," he said, darting a glance toward the stairs where Cecily stood on the landing. When he looked back, his eyes grew even bigger; Angelus was standing beside Spike.

"Good evening, sir," he said, holding out his hand. "William, do introduce us."

"I believe we've already met," Addams said, obviously trying to keep his voice from shaking. Angelus gave him a predatory smile.

"Yes, now that you mention it, I believe we have," he said. "At Madame Dover's, was it?"

Addams blanched, and Spike heard his heart start to pound triple time. "Yes, well," he stammered, "it's . . . I . . . If you'll excuse me, I believe I need to find my daughter. It's time we were going." He turned and fled toward the stairs.

Spike looked at Angelus, who was laughing silently. "What the blazes was that all about?" he demanded. "You've met him?"

"Not exactly," Angelus said, stepping aside with a bow to let a matron and her daughter pass. "Peggy Dover runs a house that he frequents, and I'm often in that neighborhood. He's seen me there."

Spike's brows drew together. "House?" he said. "What house?"

Angelus sighed and shook his head, casting a glance heavenward. "A brothel, Spike, a brothel," he said patiently. Then he grinned, his eyes sparkling with malice. "And not just any brothel, either, boyo. Not all of Peggy's girls are human, and I'd be willing to wager large sums that our Mister Addams there likes the vampire girls." He rubbed his hands together. "Well, now, this night is just opening up all kinds of possibilities." He tapped Spike on the chest. "Come along. He'll be dragging the girl home, now that he knows there are vampires here. We'll have to catch them as they come down the stairs."

They made their way through the crowd to the staircase in the foyer. Sure enough, after a few minutes Addams came hurrying down with a very put-out Cecily in tow.

"Papa," she said, her mouth drawn into what might have been a pout, "it's quite early. What on earth is wrong?" But her father didn't answer. He only took her arm and hurried her along.

Angelus maneuvered the two of them into a spot at the foot of the stairs that would be directly in Addams's path and, as Addams and Cecily neared their position, stumbled between the girl and her father, separating them and knocking Cecily into Spike's waiting arms.

She gave a small cry and clutched at his shoulders as he steadied her, his hands on her waist, and for a moment, as he looked into her eyes, he remembered how much he had worshipped her . . . before. His face softened, and he reached up to brush a curl away from her cheek.

She flinched from him. There was strange mixture of disgust and fear in her eyes, and the last words he'd heard her speak echoed in Spike's brain: *You're beneath me.* He jerked his hand back, let go of her, and tried to smother the snarl that rose in his throat like bile.

Alarm flared in her face, and she put a hand up to her throat, where Spike could see her pulse drumming. "William," she said, her voice a trifle unsteady, "how . . . how are you?" She moved her other hand, as though to touch him, perhaps, and he stepped back.

Beside him, Angelus gave a hiss of pain and sprang back from his position between Spike and Addams, clutching his left hand. Spike caught the scent of charred flesh and saw steam rising from a cross-shaped burn in Angelus's palm.

Addams, holding a small gold crucifix so that it dangled between his fingers and rested on his palm, stepped between Spike and Cecily. Spike hissed in a breath at the sight of the cross and a sudden deep sense of revulsion made him step back from it. He shot a glare at Angelus.

"I think you forgot to mention something, mate," he said dryly.

Addams reached behind him and took Cecily by the hand, then came down the last few steps. Spike and Angelus retreated as he advanced, hands in their pockets, trying to seem as though he weren't forcing them back.

"Cecily," Addams said when they reached the foyer, "we are going home now, and I want you to promise me that should these . . . gentlemen come round to visit at any time in future, you will not invite them into our house." His tone brooked no disagreement, and he never took his eyes off the two vampires.

Cecily, however, seemed not to notice her father's determination. "But Papa," she began. "William—"

"Is no longer welcome in my house," Addams said through his teeth. "He can be nothing but danger to you, Cecily, and neither he nor any of his associates will step one foot inside my doors."

Had he been watching his daughter instead of the vampires, Addams might have regretted his choice of words. Spike, who was watching Cecily, noted the slight flare of her nostrils at the word "danger," and the speculative look she gave him. *And the hook is set,* he thought with an inward smile.

"Oh, don't worry, Addams, old man," he said. Addams's face turned a mottled purple at the presumptuousness of the address. "I've had quite a few invitations to call on some very charming girls this evening. I shan't get round to Cecily for quite some time, I expect." His tone was perfect nonchalance, and it had the desired effect on Cecily, whose hands clenched in her skirts, crushing the silk. Spike totted up a mental mark to himself.

Cecily came forward and laid a hand on Spike's arm. "Papa," she said, forcing a smile, "I've known William for ages, and he's no more dangerous than a mouse."

Spike laid his hand over hers. "Oh," he said, pitching his voice low and intimate, stroking his thumb across the backs of her fingers. Her eyes went wide, and she drew in a quick breath at the caress. "I think you'll find our last conversation has caused quite a change in me," he went on. "Perhaps your father's right. Perhaps I am . . . dangerous." He stared into her eyes and concentrated on the sound of her heart and her scent, and let himself feel the blood-hunger. She made a small, whimpery sound deep in her throat. Spike, satisfied at the effect, stepped back. She staggered a little and began to pluck at her skirts without seeming to realize she was doing it.

For a moment, none of them moved. Then Cecily blinked rapidly and gave her skirts a twitch to smooth them. "Oh, I don't believe that for a minute," she said, and rapped his arm with her fan.

Addams slipped his arm about her waist, his mouth set in a grim line, his eyes flashing anger. His grip must have been painful, even through her corsets, because she winced.

"Come along, girl," Addams commanded, and, holding the crucifix in front of him, gestured for the vampires to let him pass. After a moment of impasse, Spike looked at Angelus, who nodded; Spike glared at him, but Angelus simply stepped aside, and Spike, clearly unhappy, followed suit. Addams hurried a protesting Cecily out the door, calling to the footman to have his carriage brought round as quickly as possible.

Spike stood watching them, his expression stony as the carriage pulled up and they got in and drove off. Rage seethed behind his eyes; he'd been so close, and the scent of her blood had filled him with a raging hunger that boiled up in his chest, pounding there like a heartbeat. He turned to Angelus.

"We could have stopped them, you know," he said.

Angelus shook his head. "No, we couldn't," he replied, gesturing at the Ton, now queuing up at the doors for their wraps and calling for their carriages. "Too much of a scene if he'd tried to stop us, and he would have." He took Spike's arm and joined the line of people at the coat-check stand. "I've seen enough worried fathers to be sure of that." He patted Spike on the arm. "Don't worry, boy, you'll have another chance at her. But we may need to exercise a bit of patience."

"I don't want to be patient. I want to kill the bitch!" Spike snarled. Heads turned toward them, showing shocked expressions, and Angelus's hand tightened on Spike's arm hard enough to leave bruises.

"Mind your tongue!" Angelus hissed, and then, smiling, he raised his voice. "Oh, dear, no," he said, laughing, "That line won't do at all. It's so hard to rhyme." When a titter rippled through the immediate crowd, he relaxed his grip and pushed to the front of the queue, ignoring the protests of the rest of the line, to collect their things. Then he shoved Spike ahead of him out the door.

They stalked along in silence for several blocks, until they were well away from Naismith's, and then Spike stopped dead in the street, turning his fully vamped face on Angelus, who rolled his eyes and leaned against the nearest lamppost. The gaslight cast his face in a saturnine shadow.

"If you'd kept him away, I could have been upstairs with her before he realized!" Spike snarled, his eyes blazing gold. He could smell Cecily on his hands, on his clothes where she had touched him, and the scent was pushing his hunger past bearing.

"Bollocks," Angelus replied, buffing his nails on his waistcoat. "How many unwilling females have you ever made off with, boy? It's not as easy as you think."

"She wasn't unwilling, was she?"

Angelus looked up. "Ah, now," he said, "beginning to feel a bit of our power, are we?" He gave Spike a cold, mocking smile. "Let me tell you something, you bloody young fool. In the middle of a party crowded with humans is just about the worst place you'll come across to make a kill, unless you're devilish clever. Better vampires than you have ended up dust trying it." He lifted one shoulder, affecting a modest shrug. "Me, now, I've made an art of it, you might say, but then I've had a long time to practice my skills. You'd best leave that sort of thing to your betters and figure out another way to get this girl alone." He pushed off the lamppost.

"Come along," he said over his shoulder as he walked past Spike. "Smelling all that warm blood flowing has made me hungry."

"I can go to her house now. She'll let me in." Spike smiled, lips pulling back over sharp teeth, as he remembered the cloudy, bemused expression on Cecily's face when he'd said he might be dangerous. She was fascinated by that danger; he had seen it. He could use that fascination to get into the house.

Angelus gave a hoot of laughter and shook his head. "Boy, if you live a month without getting dusted, I'll be bleeding well amazed," he said. "Do you really think her father won't stay there with her, hoping you'll try something that stupid? Or that the servants won't remember you, once they've found her dead body in the morning? Face it, we've lost this opportunity, and we'll just have to find another way."

"No!" Spike slammed his fist into the lamppost.

Angelus stopped, turned slowly around. "What do you mean, 'no,' boy?"

Spike put his hand to his mouth and sucked at the thick blood that welled up between his fingers. "I'm not waiting," he said as he shook the numbness from his already-healing fist. "I'm going to kill her *now*."

He turned on his heel, but before he could take a step, he found himself lying on the ground. He tried to sit up, shaking his head, and Angelus, yellow eyes blazing, hauled him up by his hair and pinned him against the lamppost with bone-jarring force, holding him there with a forearm across his throat.

"You listen to me, boy, because I'm only going to tell you this once." Each word was like the flick of a very sharp knife. "I'm the master here. If I say we wait, then we wait. Are we clear on that?" Angelus gave a shove on his throat to emphasize the question, and Spike nodded as well as he was able, under the circumstances. Angelus held him there for a moment longer, then let go. Spike slid to the ground, one hand at his aching throat, the other pressed to his side, where he was fairly sure a rib was broken.

"Get up from there," Angelus said contemptuously, dusting his hands off on his trousers. "I'll not have you ruining those clothes. They cost me a pretty penny." He stalked off down the street, not waiting to see whether Spike obeyed him or not.

After a moment Spike pushed himself to his feet. He leaned against the lamppost for support, resting his head on the cold metal. "Bloody bastard," he croaked, sending a killing look after Angelus.

"And don't you forget it, boy." Angelus's voice came floating back to him, and he grimaced, then limped off after the older vampire, hissing as his steps jarred the broken rib.

Chapter Fifteen

Sunnydale, California, Fall semester, 2000

"**W**ell, *now* maybe Giles will listen to me," Willow said with a sense of considerable satisfaction as she and Spike left the university theater. "Let's wait and see if this guy shows up tonight. We can find out who he is and what kind of spell it is, and tell Giles. Then he'll believe me."

"Unless he shows up and succeeds, in which case Giles won't have to believe you. Of course, that's only if you think you have to go running to your fusty Watcher with every little thing. You couldn't possibly do anything all by yourself, anyway."

"I could so," Willow said indignantly. "I heard those characters, when not even Giles could. He was all listening to choral music, and he didn't even hear them worrying. And they were loud."

"All right," Spike said agreeably. "We'll wait. It'll be different for you, won't it? No running to Giles and no studying ahead of time either. I thought you lot were true believers in swotting the books before you tackled monsters. Not this time, eh? Just wait around and leap on him. Sounds more my line. Only since they think he's one of you, I'll just sit back and watch, maybe give you a few pointers on style. Be interesting to see what you're going to do with him once you've got him."

Willow stopped and wheeled to face him. "Just what do you think you're doing, anyway? Are you being encouragy or not?"

"Me?" Spike said, in his most unconvincing manner. "Didn't think the Slayer's friends needed any encouragement from the likes of me."

"Well, first you say one thing and then you say another. Only I'm not sure what you're saying. Whether I should—we should—stay and watch or not, I mean."

"Isn't up to me, now is it? Besides, don't you have somebody waiting for you at home? And they said whoever it is doesn't show up every night anyway. You'd probably be quite safe if you just left it."

In any event, a fuming Willow waited outside the theater exactly two and a half hours by her watch, trying her best to ignore the tangled arguments the vampire advanced for, variously: staying; leaving; consulting Giles; rousing Giles and bringing the

Watcher, the Slayer, and the entire Scooby Gang to the theater at once; pretending the whole business was a figment of her imagination; and going back into the theater to demand the characters talk to her again. Every argument made sense until the next sentence came out of his mouth. At the end of the time she'd arbitrarily chosen, Willow was ready to stake the vampire herself. And other than a slowly rolling campus patrol car, absolutely nothing had moved.

By the time she got home, she was too tired to try to explain to Tara why she was so late. All she wanted to do was go to bed and sleep without dreams.

She had no luck there, either. Images of Buffy as a flapper doing a fast Charleston kept popping up out of nowhere, and every time she tried to tell the Slayer that there was a problem, her friend glared at her and shouted, "Can't you see I'm busy? You're going to make me miss a step! I can't afford to miss a step!"

The next day, before her morning physics class, Willow stopped off at the university library and looked for the books on Addams's list.

Not one of the books listed was in the university library, not even on interlibrary loan. But one of them was the Liverakos book that she'd "borrowed" from the Magic Box.

Since she happened to be looking things up, she did a search through the online catalog for the Fates.

The problem, she quickly discovered, was that there was way too much information available on Greek mythology. She could identify the Fates easily enough: Clotho the spinner, Lachesis the one who measures, and

Atropos who cuts the thread of life. Nobody, apparently, messed with the Fates, not even the gods of Olympus. But they weren't the same as the Furies, Alecto, Tisiphone, and Megaera. Although, Lachesis apparently could call in the Furies by deciding what kind of life you were going to have, and Atropos could save you from them by killing you, although that was sort of drastic, Willow thought, and not really saving much.

There were lots of plays about Furies pursuing people; poor Oedipus really had it rough. After all, he didn't *know* it was his father he'd killed or his mother he'd married. It wasn't like he'd done it on purpose. But she couldn't find anything about summoning or controlling the Fates. It was as if the Fates were left strictly alone, even by playwrights who had no problem making fun of the gods. Some things were just better not messed with, apparently.

The Greek gods really were all through the plays, she realized, reading on. Addams had alluded to the Dionysiads, but they were up to Restoration drama in class now. He hadn't said that the original drama festivals were all religious festivals for the god Dionysus, who was also the god of wine. The myth said he'd been ripped to pieces by the Titans and restored to life, and his followers, the Maenads, had the reputation for going crazy and behaving violently. So naturally, during his festivals writers competed for public attention with choruses that eventually evolved into the modern play.

Maybe that's where the image of the hard-drinking writer got started? she wondered.

And while it was all fascinating, absolutely none

of it helped her figure out what was going on with the characters in the UC Sunnydale theater.

"Back to the Magic Box for me," she said with a sigh, and then, looking at a wall clock, squeaked with alarm and scrambled for her botany class. She'd completely missed physics.

Willow had just put her backpack on the floor between her feet when someone pushed down the seat beside her and flopped into it. She wrinkled her nose at an oddly familiar scent of singed steak, and looked up into wickedly glittering blue eyes and an equally glittering dark smile. He swept his black leather duster over the place next to him, ensuring that no one would try to cozy up. *Not that anyone in his right mind would,* she thought.

"Spike, what are you doing here? This is my class!" she yelped. Two rows of students turned around to see what was going on. She made an apologetic face. Spike propped his feet up on the back of the next row.

The student occupying the seat in front of the vampire turned around to protest. Spike arched an eyebrow. The boy drew in a single breath and changed his mind, then picked up his books and moved away.

"You can't be here," Willow went on, much more quietly. The class was just past the settling-in stage and beginning to enter the where's-the-teacher stage. "This is a class. You're not enrolled."

"What's the matter?" he asked. At least, she was slightly relieved to find, he was keeping his voice down. "You think you're the only one who can broaden your horizons? Educate your mind? People audit classes all the time." His accent, some species of lower-class British, was even broader and deeper than usual. Willow had no idea whether it was Cockney or South London or something else entirely; all she knew was that Spike seemed to be able to turn it off and on at will. Sometimes it almost disappeared; she'd heard him mimic Giles's university tones flawlessly. Now he was rooting around the opposite end of the linguistic spectrum.

"Well be quiet," she said helplessly. He had her on that auditing thing. It was just . . . creepy to think Spike was going to watch her take notes.

The characteristic hush that marked the entrance of a professor fell across the class as Dr. Addams walked across the stage and into the center stage light. Willow looked up, preparing her notebook with the appropriate pen color of the day.

And suddenly her skin crawled as she heard the all-too-familiar hissing snarl of the vampire next to her.

Jerking around in her seat, she saw Spike, not the human, with smooth skin, high cheekbones, and smooth forehead, but the demon, the monster, the predator, with knotted skull, mouth gaping, and fangs ready to rend soft human flesh. His feet weren't up on the seat back anymore. He was sitting forward, his hands digging into the rim of the chair in front of him, every muscle tensed to launch death over the dozen rows that separated it from the stage. *Chip,* Willow reminded herself, but knowing that he couldn't actually hurt anyone didn't keep her heart from slamming into

high gear. She'd been on too many patrols, come a
hair's breadth to fangy death too many times, to see a
vampire in game face and not react to it.

An instant later, the face was gone, and sitting next
to her, to all appearances, was simply a human male,
easing himself back against the cushion.

"Heart's beating ninety to the dozen, lamb chop,"
he observed, not looking at her. "Careful you don't
have yourself a stroke."

She simply stared at him, mouth open in shock,
and then frantically glanced around their immediate
neighbors. Amazingly, no one else seemed to have
noticed anything.

He has the chip, she reminded herself. *He can't
harm a human being without excruciating pain.* She'd
seen it herself. She'd been the very first beneficiary of
it, in fact, and it had been proven over and over and
over again, and she knew for an absolute fact that
Spike was absolutely, completely, totally harmless. He
could not harm a human being, no matter how frustrated that made him.

It still took her a good two minutes for her heart
rate to get back to normal. She could tell by the way he
kept smirking at her. He was better than a blood pressure monitor.

Meanwhile, Addams was beginning a dry and
uninteresting lecture about Restoration and eighteenth-
century drama, with side commentary about the
restoration of the monarchy to the British throne. Spike
added a few comments of his own about Nell Gwyn
and orange sellers.

"Shut up," Willow said between gritted teeth. "You weren't alive then."

"Know people who were," he responded.

She blinked. "You do?" It was possible, she realized. It was actually possible. *And wow, the research paper I could write if I could interview—*

"She was a tasty bit too," he informed her. "Met the guy who ate her."

"A, eeeuw. And B, shut up." Addams was peering up toward them, she noticed, probably trying to see who was talking during his lecture. He was fumbling with his notes, reading from them much more than he usually did; even the side remarks sounded as if they had been prepared ahead of time. He dashed through the re-opening of the theaters in record time, barely mentioning the impact of Cromwell's Puritans, skimmed the contributions of the major playwrights, and summed up the tenor of the most popular plays in what Willow considered a highly perfunctory fashion. Indeed, he had completed his hour and a half's lecture in less than forty minutes.

"Any questions?" he said, with a clear air of, *There had better not be; I'm a busy man and I have better things to do.* "Class dismissed."

"Wow," Willow said, and capped her pen.

"I think we ought to keep an eye on this bloke," Spike said meditatively. "I do."

"You do? What happened to all that let's-talk-to-Giles-and-get-Buffy—" She was talking over her shoulder as they edged out of the row of seats.

"No." It was short and harsh and definite. "This

isn't Slayer and Watcher stuff. I can handle this myself." Instead of heading up to the main doors leading to the audience, Willow found herself being guided down toward the stage, where an obviously irritated Addams was entangled in a throng of freshmen and sophomores asking questions about the final.

The two of them were standing on the periphery of the little group. Willow would have walked off, but Spike's hand was still painfully tight on her elbow, and she was absolutely certain he wasn't trying to hurt her, because otherwise he would have been doubled over in pain. Instead he was watching Addams, studying him as if he were going to draw his portrait from memory.

"Doctor Addams," he said at last.

The professor was exasperated. "Yes, what is it?" He recognized Willow, looked again at Spike, his brow wrinkling. Almost as though he thought he ought to recognize Spike, but couldn't, quite. "Are you in my class?"

"I'd say you were in a class by yourself," Spike said gently.

Willow bit her lip, started to rebuke him and then remembered that momentary shift into game face at the beginning of the class. He'd let go of her arm and chip, but still—

"I was just wondering," the vampire went on, "how long do you have to study to get to be an expert on this stuff? Years and years? I mean, how long do you think it would take a bloke like me to get to know the kind of things a smart man like you knows, about acting and poetry and all?"

The words were respectful, almost subservient. The tone was almost humble. Willow did not believe it for a second, and she wanted very very much to be far far away from whatever game Spike was playing now.

From the look on his face, Addams could tell he was being mocked, but couldn't decide what to do about it. He hesitated half a beat, and then said brusquely, "More than your lifetime, I'm afraid. Now if you don't mind, I have some things to take care of. Excuse me, ladies and gentlemen." With that, he brushed his way past the few remaining students and out through the wings of the stage.

"More than *my* lifetime?" Spike murmured, staring after him. "Oh my, Doctor Addams. *Wrong answer.*"

Disappointed, the abandoned students began to wander up the aisles. Willow grabbed Spike's arm as he, too, started to leave.

"Hold on just one minute, buster," she said in her bossiest voice. "Just what the heck was that all about?"

Spike looked down at her small hand, pale against the black leather of his duster. His eyes gleamed dangerously, and she hastily removed her hand.

"That was about unfinished business," Spike said grimly, and stalked up the aisle, not looking to see if she followed.

Chapter Sixteen

London, England, 1880

The Addamses carriage drew up at the front door and the footman swung down to let the passengers out. Cecily was out first, barely taking the fellow's hand as she leaped to the ground and stalked up the steps. Addams followed, nodding to the footman and sighing as he went into the house.

She was waiting for him in the foyer, two hectic spots of color in her cheeks, fists clenched in her skirts, bosom heaving hard enough to threaten indecency.

"How could you, Papa?" she demanded as soon as he had shut the door. Addams heard the squeak of a hinge as Clermont backed through the door into the kitchen and discreetly closed it again.

"How could you humiliate me that way, in front of

my friends?" The hair was standing up on her arms, and her eyes snapped. He hadn't seen her this furious since she was three years old.

"That is quite enough, young lady," he barked, drawing himself up to his full height and glowering down at her. "There will be no further discussion of this subject. Is that perfectly clear?" He glared at her, not blinking, until she lowered her head.

"Yes, Papa," she said, her voice breaking, but he caught the determined set of her mouth afterward and the stubborn gleam in her eye, and sighed.

"Cecily," he said, gentling his voice, "I'm sorry about the scene, but that young man . . ." He paused, considering. He'd already told her that William was dangerous, and that had only piqued her interest. How to squelch that interest?

"I'm afraid your friend William has fallen in with a very bad crowd. Worse even than that pack of young rakehells who cat about after Lovell." The mention of one of London's most profligate libertines gave Cecily pause, and Addams was encouraged. He stepped closer to her, ran a hand over her hair as he used to do when she was a child. "My darling," he said, "I couldn't bear the thought of anything harming you, and those associates of William's, well, they have . . . appetites that would horrify you." She shuddered at that, and he smiled.

"I only want to protect you, child," he said. "Now come and kiss me and say you forgive me?" He held his arms open for her, and after a moment she came into them.

"I do beg your pardon, Papa," she said humbly, sniffling a little into his waistcoat. "You're right to be worried, I think. William seemed very different. He was so . . ." She seemed to be searching for a word. "So . . . confident. And he didn't used to be that way at all."

Addams patted his daughter's back. "Appetites," he said, dropping a kiss on the top of her head. "Now you be off to bed, darling. This has been a terrible evening for you, I'm sure. Let Cook pamper you."

He fully intended to sit up all night in the foyer with a cross and stake, in case young William was as stupid as most new vampires and tried to storm the house, but shortly after Cecily went up to bed, there was an urgent knock at the front door. He opened it himself, before Clermont even got the kitchen door open, and found Denholm Reed standing on the stoop, his eyes wild, chewing at his mustache. A cab was drawn up in front of the door, the driver looking expectantly toward them as though waiting.

"Bertie, thank God," Reed said, grabbing him by the sleeve and attempting to haul him out the door. "You've got to come to the Explorers' Club straight away. Something awful has happened. Moreham tried to raise the Furies and it all went wrong and—"

Addams caught hold of the doorframe, jerking Reed to a stop both physically and verbally.

"Slow down, man!" he snapped. "I scarcely got a word of that." He'd gotten the relevant words, though, "Moreham" and "Furies," and a black feeling of dread began to rise up in his throat.

Reed grasped his sleeve again, took several deep breaths, and began again. "Moreham. He found the spell. Tried to use it tonight. Something went wrong." He looked up at Addams, his eyes huge. "You've got to come to the Club, Bertie. Moreham is furious because he thinks the spell's destroyed, but several of the others don't think so." He tugged on Addams's arm again.

"That damned arrogant fool!" Addams gnawed on his lower lip. Clearly he needed to go to the Explorers' Club, but what about Cecily? Did he dare leave her here alone?

Reed's white, desperately excited face decided him. This was too good an opportunity to pass up, and as long as no one invited the vampire in, Cecily would be quite safe.

"Wait here," he said, disengaging Reed's hand from his sleeve. "I'll get my hat and coat."

Leaving Reed on the step, he hurried back inside, calling for Clermont. He gave strict orders, on pain of immediate dismissal without a character, that until he returned, no one was to be let into the house, no matter how desperate the reason, and that Miss Cecily was under no circumstances whatsoever to be allowed out of it, even if it meant they had to tie her to the bed to keep her there.

Clermont, never turning a hair, gave his word that he would see to it, and, jamming his hat on his head and putting on his coat as he went out the door, Addams got into Reed's waiting cab and they drove off for the Explorers' Club.

* * *

When Spike arrived at the rented house, he found Darla in the parlor, working her way through a second decanter of sherry, apparently to drown out Dru's crooning, a rising and falling pitch that came in monotonous waves from upstairs. She was quite drunk and grinned blearily at him when he asked what had happened.

"Damn vision," Darla said, stumbling over the vowels. "And then the ghosts." She took another swig of the sherry. "Oh, and the fire. Mustn't forget the fire. . . ." She giggled and tried to pour more wine into her glass. She didn't seem to realize she was missing the glass entirely. She let her head fall back onto the arm of the sofa, still giggling.

Spike went up the stairs two at a time, at vampire speed, afraid of what he'd find in Dru's room, but she was only bruised, not burned. "My Spike," she said, coming to him and pulling him into the room. "He's here, my dark star, my stoat-man. He's here." She took his hand and laid it along her cheek, looking up at him with her tongue creeping playfully out of the corner of her mouth.

"What, here in the house?" Spike looked around, a trifle alarmed.

"No, silly, in the theater. I saw him tonight, and he did such wonderful things!"

"What wonderful things, pet?" He stroked her hair and she closed her eyes, enjoying the touch.

"Mmmm," she said, the sound almost a purr. "Ravens and fire and fear and screaming. Beautiful chaos." She opened her eyes and stood up, her lower lip stuck out in a pout. "But something went wrong.

The stoat-man didn't finish his song, and the crows all flew away. And then the nasty rude people wouldn't let me up. I got quite stepped on." She put a hand to her side, and Spike heard the grinding of broken bones. He winced, and pressed his palm against his own broken rib in sympathy.

Dru stepped closer and laid her head on his shoulder. "Find him for me, Spike," she said. "He'll turn the world inside out for me if you find him."

"And that would be good because ... ?" Spike said.

"Because then we'll always be happy together," she said. "Always and always, you and me and Grandmummy and Angelus."

"Just one big happy family, then?"

"That's right," she said. "One big happy family, and no nasty shocks."

Downstairs, he heard the front door open. Angelus called out for Darla, and Drusilla stopped stock still, her nostrils flaring.

"My Angel," she said, her voice breathy, almost reverent, and Spike wondered if she would ever sound like that when she spoke of him.

"Why is Darla passed out drunk in the parlor?" Angelus stamped into the room, glowering at the both of them.

Spike indicated Drusilla. "They seem to have run into a problem while they were out."

"Problem?" Angelus was instantly alert. "What kind of problem?"

"Dru had a vision," Spike said, but before he could go on, Drusilla spoke.

"The little brown stoat-man," she said, coming to Angelus and trailing her fingers along his arm. "He wants to bring the dark star out of hiding, the dark star that will pull everything inside out." She giggled. "Like a stocking when you take it off." Her fingers tightened on his arm, nails digging through his coat, and he winced. "He must peel us off like stockings," she said, her eyes burning with a knowledge that she wasn't quite able to communicate, "or there'll be no more happy family, ever again." She put her hands to her temples and moaned, rocking back and forth, working her fingers into her hair and pulling as though to tear the troubling thoughts out of her head.

Spike took her hands in his and tried to still her fingers. "Shh, now," he said. "Easy, love. We'll find this fellow for you and make everything right. Can you tell me any more about this stoat-man?"

Her expression grew sly. "He thinks he's found the incantation," she said, her voice low and conspiratorial, "but he's left out an important bit. He forgot the old words in the play, you see." She pulled Spike down to whisper to him. "The phantoms know."

"Find him for me, Spike," Dru breathed into his ear. "Find him and keep our family safe." Her hand crept underneath the collar of his waistcoat and she laid her head on his shoulder, looking up at him with pleading eyes, and Spike quite lost his train of thought.

"I will, I promise," he said, caught in her huge dark eyes, willing to give her anything she asked.

Dru gave herself a slight shake and drew away from Spike. "But I'm forgetting," she said. "Tell me all about that nasty bad girl and what you did to her."

Spike sighed. "Not much to tell, I'm afraid," he said, "She got away."

Dru gave him a pat on the arm. "Don't worry," she said matter-of-factly. "I'm sure you'll get her next time."

The next evening Spike and Angelus went back to Naismith's. They saw neither Addams nor Cecily, but when Spike suggested they leave, Angelus clapped him on the back, grinning.

"No, we're staying," he said. "You're going to charm every one of those girls, the pretty ones and the plain ones and even the ugly ones, and you're going to charm their mothers even more. Meanwhile I will be dishing the dirt on you. And giving you an inheritance, I'm thinking. That'll certainly attract their attention."

"But—"

"Don't argue with me, boy. I've been seducing young ladies out from under their fathers' noses longer than you've even existed, and I know what I'm about. Get her friends on your side, make her feel she's missing something, and she'll want to see what it is. We'll get that little bitch right where we want her before the season's out, if you play your cards right." The prospect of the chase seemed to delight him. "Now put all those dancing lessons I'm sure your mummy gave you to good use." He nodded to Miss Abercorn, who had caught Spike's eye and was fluttering her fan at him.

Spike sat out more dances that evening than he had the night before, fetching punch and biscuits for the young ladies and flattering their mothers shamelessly. By the end of the night, he'd received informal invitations to several musicales, two dinner parties, and a ball, all of which he agreed enthusiastically to attend.

Angelus had also done his work well; about midway through the evening, Spike began to hear his name mentioned in the whispered conversations that sprang up behind his back. The young ladies were aflutter about a mysterious heartbreak in his past, and the mothers were buzzing about the rumor that he'd recently come into quite a sum of money. The fathers gave him speculative looks and the single men began to shoot dark looks his way.

By the time they collected their coats and hats, Spike's face ached from smiling, and he felt that if he never saw another cup of punch again, it would be too soon.

"Do let's go and kill something," he muttered to Angelus as they left. "I need to get the taste of this place out of my mouth." Angelus laughed, and led him on a savage hunt.

Predictably, Cecily was absent from the next few events they attended, but Spike made the most of the occasions. He made veiled allusions to Cecily, and strong hints that she was the one who had broken his heart. It amused him to no end. Even though most of the young ladies he spoke with knew exactly that, to have it couched in mysterious hints and snatches, with a few distant looks and a self-deprecating joke thrown in here and there, brought their sympathies firmly

around to his side. The whispers that inevitably followed him began to take on a different tone toward
Cecily.

"It's dreadful." Sally Trumble said to him as they
went in to dinner at Chloe Danvers's one evening.
"Clermont is like a dragon guarding the door, and her
father's in a terrible temper over something that happened at his club. He's hardly ever home, she says, and
when he is, he's in his study, poring over old books. He
has promised to take her to Lady Arnett's ball,
though." She gave him a sly look out of the corner of
her eye as he pulled out her chair for her. "You will be
attending that, won't you?"

He gave her a stern glance as he sat down. "And if
I am?"

She smiled smugly and nodded. "Good," she said.
"I shall look forward to seeing you there. Shall I tell
Cecily you're going, or let it be a surprise?"

"Oh," Spike said, a wicked glint in his eyes as he
picked up his napkin, "do let it be a surprise."

The ballroom was upstairs; Spike and Angelus
climbed the wide marble stairs and stood for a moment
looking in. The huge room was glittering; the gas jets
were lit, and the chandeliers, still unfitted for the new-
fangled lighting, glowed with hundreds of candles, the
light winking off the crystal bobbles and prisms and
gleaming on the highly polished parquet floor.

The musicians were in the middle of a waltz, and
gentlemen in black-and-white evening dress spun
around the floor with their partners, their silk skirts in

a panoply of colors making the room look like a spring flower garden. Liveried servants moved about the room, fetching trays of drinks and removing empty glasses.

Angelus began to scan the room, looking for their quarry, and after a moment's search pointed her out to Spike with a grin.

"Well, well," he said, indicating the dance floor.

Cecily was dancing with a short, slightly rumpled brown-haired man with a ferret-like face, whom Spike had never seen before.

"That fellow," Angelus said, "has no deep love for Albert Addams. I've seen them both at Peggy Dover's, and they came to blows over some damned thing or other. I've a feeling he's going to be an asset to us tonight. I wonder what's brought him here."

"As long as he can distract Addams until I can get to Cecily, I don't care a bloody hang why he's here." Spike looked back at the dancers. Cecily was trying to be politely attentive, but it was obvious that something was making her nervous; she kept darting glances over her partner's shoulder and turning her head to look over her own shoulder. Her lapses seemed not to annoy the fellow in the least, until Cecily, in the middle of a turn, caught sight of Spike and trod on her partner's toe. He stumbled, and she apologized, blushing, as he steered them toward the chairs along the edges of the room. Cecily's eyes grew quite wide when she realized that he was moving directly toward Spike.

"Is this the fellow you were looking for, Miss Addams?" the fellow said when they stopped. Cecily's face grew even redder, and she put her fan up to hide it.

"Oh, n-no, I wasn't . . ." She stammered, looking from her dance partner to Spike. "That is, I . . ."

The man held out his hand to Spike. "Miss Addams doesn't seem inclined to introduce us," he said, smiling at her to take any reproof from the words. "I'm Jack Moreham." He was giving Spike a rather odd look, as though he could sense the undercurrents between him and Cecily, and Spike's eyes narrowed.

Spike took his hand. Moreham's eyes flickered a little at the coolness of Spike's skin, and he tensed, but shook hands without further comment. "William . . . ," Spike began.

"Oh, dear me," Cecily exclaimed, interrupting the introduction. "I do believe Papa is trying to catch my attention," she said. "Please excuse me." She caught up her skirt and hurried away from them as fast as was decently possible.

Moreham lifted a quizzical eyebrow. "Interesting girl," he said dryly, looking after her swaying skirt. He turned to Spike. "Then again, you seem to be an interesting fellow yourself. Does she deserve you?"

Spike's lips twisted in an ironic smile. "Oh, yes," he said, "I believe she does."

"I'd look out for her father, then," Moreham said, inclining his head toward Addams, who was heading straight toward them, his face thunderously purple.

"Believe I will," Spike said. "Thanks." He turned and insinuated himself into a knot of chattering young ladies, who all exclaimed in delight and began to simper at him.

"Addams!" Moreham said behind him, and stepped straight into the older man's path. "It's been an age! Lucky I ran into you, old man. I have a question about one of those rare books you're always coming across. . . ."

Spike could hear Addams's teeth grinding even over the girls' chatter, and he grinned as he let them sweep him up into their conversation and away from Cecily's father.

Spike spent the evening flirting outrageously with the young ladies, making them laugh and blush. He was equally flirtatious with the girls' mothers, and he made sure that Cecily caught him doing it at every opportunity; he watched with much satisfaction as she grew more and more puzzled at her friends' attitudes toward him.

Angelus caught up with him during the orchestra's interval. "You've almost got her," he said, his voiced pitched for vampire hearing, and clapped Spike on the back. "If you don't mind a piece of advice, I'd give her one of those soulful looks, let her know there are still feelings for her under all that hurt." He winked and laid a finger beside his nose. "Lie, in other words."

Spike grinned back at him and answered in the same low tone. "What, you mean make her feel sorry for me? If I could have done that, I wouldn't be a vampire right now, would I?" He cocked his head thoughtfully. "I must remember to thank the bitch for that."

He followed Angelus's advice, and gave it a twist of his own, letting his smile slip occasionally as his gaze rested on Cecily, then seeming to realize what he was doing and resuming his conversations with a forced cheerfulness. As the evening wore on, he let the episodes lengthen, eventually excusing himself in the middle of a conversation to "get some air." He stood in the shadows on the balcony outside the ballroom, listening to the murmurs of sympathy, smiling to himself.

When he went back into the ballroom, his posture slightly drooping, and settled himself wearily into a chair, waving off all company, Cecily was watching him surreptitiously. He caught her gaze for a second, then turned abruptly away, biting his lower lip, and put his hand over his eyes.

Between his fingers, he could see her stricken look, and when she started to walk over to him, he struggled to hide his fierce smile.

"William?" Her voice was hesitant, and he stiffened in the chair as though he hadn't seen her coming.

Angelus, who had apparently been staying near to him, keeping tabs on his progress, began to drift closer. Spike stood, positioning himself so that Cecily was between him and Angelus.

"I beg your pardon, Miss Addams," he said coldly. "I believe Lady Barrett is trying to attract my attention. If you'll excuse me . . ." He made as if to leave.

"Wait!" she said, and laid her hand on his arm. He tensed the muscles under her hand, making them tremble a little. "William, please, I need to speak to you," she said earnestly, looking up at him with a pleading expression that he knew all too well.

"I can't," he said, roughening his voice and turning away so she wouldn't see the triumphant flash of gold in his eyes. "I . . . It's too . . . too painful." Over her shoulder, he saw Angelus's approving glance. "Please, Cecily." He looked directly into her eyes and bit the inside of his cheek hard enough to make tears well up. "I need to go." He took her hand, as though to lift it off his arm, but instead of letting it go, he ran the ball of his thumb along the underside of her palm. She sucked in a sudden breath and laid her other hand over his.

"William, I beg of you," she said, squeezing his fingers. "Please, you must hear me out." Her hand was trembling, and so was her voice.

Angelus was nodding at him, making tiny go-ahead motions with his hand, and Spike pretended to let her pleas soften him.

"Very well," he said, biting his lip again, and turned his hand so that her palm lay in his. "If you insist." He gave a tiny sigh. "Shall we go down into the garden, then? Separately. There'll be talk if we go together, and I'd rather not expose you to that."

She nodded. "I'll meet you by the fountain," she said, and slid her hand away, unconsciously brushing her fingers along his to prolong the contact. Then, without another word, she turned and left him.

As soon as she was gone, Angelus came over to him. "You'd better hurry," he said. "Her father saw her talking to you, and I believe he's about to go looking for her. I'll delay him if I can." He gave Spike a shove toward the doors and set off determinedly across the ballroom.

Spike made his way downstairs and out into the garden, which was decorated with strings of tiny paper lanterns that cast enough light to see one's footing, but not enough to banish the shadows entirely. Spike, of course, could see perfectly well without the lanterns and moved through the deepest of the shadows, and Cecily did not see him coming. He watched her for a moment as she stood beside the rim of the small pool where a very prosaic dolphin spouted a stream of water into a series of seashells.

She was beautiful in the soft lantern light. Her hair was piled on top of her head, with one lone curl dangling down the side of her neck, and her eyes shone huge and dark in the reflection of the lanterns. Her gown was cut low, exposing her white throat. Spike's lips pulled back over his teeth in a hungry grin. Poor little girl—she had no idea what ugly death was waiting for her. Just as he'd had no idea, that last night of his life.

He stepped out of the shadows, and she started, her hand going to her chest as her heart skipped a beat.

"William," she said, "I . . ." She didn't seem to know how to go on, so he did it for her.

"'Oh, William,'" he said bitterly, mocking her, "'I didn't want you because you were so boring, and now all my friends think I'm horrible and mean.' Is that it?"

"No!" But she put her hand to her cheek as though his words had been a blow.

"You punished me for loving you," he went on. "I was awkward and callow and naïve, and I embarrassed you. Is that nearer to the mark?"

"I . . ." She looked down, smoothing at an imaginary wrinkle in her skirt. "They all tell me how different you are," she said, "and I can see that they're right. You've changed since . . . since that night."

His laugh was jarring in the quiet of the garden. "Yes, by God, I have," he said, bitter humor in his tone. "More than you can possibly imagine."

"Perhaps I . . . Perhaps . . . ."

"Perhaps you were wrong about me?" She nodded, still not looking at him.

"God, what a little sheep you are!" She looked up at him then, her mouth parted in an O of surprise. "Yes, I said sheep," he told her with a cruel laugh. "When all your friends laughed at me, I wasn't good enough for you, but now that they all seem to like me, you're willing to give me another chance."

"That's not true!" She seemed genuinely stung. Then she put a shaking hand up to her mouth. "Oh, God," she said, "it is." She sank down on the edge of the pool, careless of her skirts, and put her head in her hands. Her shoulders began to shake.

"Oh, please," Spike said. "Spare me your tears."

She looked up at him, her throat working. "I know that I don't deserve to be forgiven," she said thickly. "But is there nothing I can say to make amends? Nothing I can do?"

"Oh, yes," he said, and for a moment hope shone in her eyes. He reached out, brushed the lone curl away from her neck. His cold finger pebbled the skin and she trembled, waiting for his next words.

"You can die," he said softly giving her a terrible, cold smile, and as his face changed, he caught her by the back of the head, dragged her upward, and sank his fangs into her throat exactly where his finger had rested. *Just there,* he thought as her blood gushed into his mouth.

She cried out at the sudden, tearing pain, and her hands came up to clutch at his shoulders. "Oh, God!" she choked out. "No, please . . ." Her hands scrabbled at the fabric of his coat and she breathed out a last, soft gasp. "S-stop. . . ."

And, for reasons he was never able to fathom afterward, he did. He tore his mouth from her neck, and she sagged to the ground, pressing her hand to her bleeding throat, sobbing quietly. Spike looked down at her, still alive, and shook his head, stunned by what he'd just done. Just failed to do.

"Finish her, you fool!" Angelus, as if from thin air, appeared at his side and shook him by the shoulder.

Spike pushed Cecily behind him. "I'm going to kill her, damn you, but not until I've made her suffer," he snarled. "Keep your bleeding hands off. She's mine."

To his immense surprise, Angelus stepped back, grinning. "You're learning, boy. You're learning." He looked at Cecily, still holding her hand to her throat. The bleeding was starting to slow, but her dress was smeared with gore. "Tsk," Angelus said. "There's no way we'll get her out of here looking like that." He took off his cape and wrapped it around her, pulling the collar up to hide the bite that stood out like a beacon against her white skin. She stood like a biddable child and let him do it, her eyes staring at nothing and her breathing coming in short, shallow pants.

"Now then, girl," said Angelus, taking her chin in his fingers and forcing her to look up at him, "if you want to live a little longer, you'll do exactly as I say. We're going to leave now, and you're going to come with us. If anyone sees us leaving, you're going to assure them that you're going with us freely and of your own will. If you can't do that, well, William here will kill you, and then . . ." He brought his demon out with astonishing speed. "Well, then I'll come back and find your dear Papa, rip his head right off his shoulders, and play at ninepins with it. Understand me, girl?"

Cecily's eyes nearly started from their sockets, and she nodded, wincing as the motion pulled at the congealing edges of her wound.

"Good." Angelus looked at Spike. "Ready, then?" Spike nodded and put his arm around Cecily's shoulder, tucking her into his body so that the bite was hidden against him. Then the three of them walked to the garden gate and out onto the street.

They were almost to the corner when Lady Arnett's footman stopped them.

"'Hoy, there," he said, his boots ringing on the sidewalk as he dashed after them. "Is that Miss Addams?"

Spike turned, his arm still around Cecily. "Yes, it is," he said, taking hold of Cecily's hand in a grip that ground her bones together. To her credit, or perhaps because she was in shock, she did not even flinch. "Why?"

"Begging your pardon, sir. Her father has just

called for their carriage, and said she must wait here for him. Some sort of emergency." The footman tugged at his forelock and flicked a glance at Cecily, who leaned against Spike.

"There's been a change of plans," Angelus interjected smoothly. "I just spoke to Mister Addams on my way out, and he's asked that *we* take the lass home instead. She's a bit under the weather, as you can see, and he needs to attend to his emergency."

The footman looked from Angelus to Cecily. "Miss?" he said, stepping forward. "Is that right?"

"Y . . . yes," Cecily said weakly, her eyes fixed on Spike's face. He smiled down at her.

"Poor lamb," he said, kissing her gently on the forehead. "Let's get you home and into bed where I can take care of you properly." She shuddered against him, and he pulled Angelus's cloak more tightly around her, then turned back to the footman. "Don't suppose you've seen a cab about, then?" The footman shook his head, and Spike sighed. "Well, perhaps we'll turn one up in a bit." He aimed a dismissive nod at the footman. "Come along, darling. We'll be home before you know it." Angelus, at a look from Spike, came and put his arm around Cecily's waist from the other side, and together they half-carried her down the street, leaving the footman staring silently after them.

They locked Cecily in one of the upstairs bedrooms. She was logy from loss of blood, and they didn't bother to tie her up, but left her sitting on the bed.

She looked up as Spike followed Angelus out of

the room. "William?" she said, and there was something so deliciously lost in her voice that Spike turned around.

"You bit me." She seemed vaguely puzzled.

"Yes, I did," he replied.

"Why did you bite me?"

"Because I'm a vampire, pet. It's what I do."

"Oh." She seemed to accept that explanation as a matter of course, and Spike wondered if it was because her father had explained such things to her or if she was in such a state of shock that she couldn't grasp the wrongness of it.

Her hands twisted in the fabric of her skirt, knotting it into clumps between her fingers. "Papa is going to be dreadfully worried about me," she said, a faint frown drawing her brows together.

"Yes, I expect he is."

"I need to go home soon." Her voice was becoming petulant, and he hid a smile.

"You can't go yet. I'm not done with you." A flicker of alarm crossed her face; it was beginning to sink in.

"But . . ." She put a hand to her neck. "But I can't stay here with you all night," she said, as though she were explaining to a child. "I'll be ruined."

He let his demon face out. "Yes, I know." He opened his mouth, showing her his sharp teeth, and gave a low chuckle. "That's the point, love."

Chapter Seventeen

Sunnydale, California, Fall semester, 2000

Several days later, with Tara gone and Miss Kitty safely if indignantly shut up in her carrier, Willow set up a spell circle with wards and candles, and got out the book list that Addams had given her. It hadn't vanished on her again, but every time she looked at it, she could swear it was different. There was definitely something wrong there, and despite what both Spike and Giles might suggest, she did *not* need her head examined, thank you very much. The problem wasn't her; it was the list, she was sure. She placed the paper in the middle of the circle and murmured the words of a spell, at the same time sprinkling sea salt and distilled water over it for purification. "Reveal," she said when the incantation was finished.

Interesting, she thought, as an image arose from the paper, almost as a hologram might. She sort of expected one of the figures to lean forward and say in an impassioned voice, "Help me, Obi-Wan Kenobi," but none of them wore a white robe or cinnamon-bun hair.

Instead they wore very old-fashioned three-piece suits and ribbon ties, high stiff collars, and leather shoes. Five or six men—it was hard to tell because they were constantly moving, and the images weren't very big to begin with—were gathered around a small table covered with green felt. A card table, perhaps? They were talking, but she couldn't hear what they were saying.

One of them looked exactly like Dr. Addams, only dressed in that strange period costume. He was leaning forward, with one hand upon the green felt surface supporting him. In the other hand he held a red book.

Almost all the men were holding at least one book apiece, she noticed. Some of them were showing passages to others. One man, a small weasely-looking fellow dressed all in brown, was hiding his book, clearly refusing to share. Willow frowned. She didn't like it when people refused to play nice.

She could make out a few details of the room, as well: the marble fireplace behind them, the coat of arms mounted over the mantel showing a ship, ocean waves, a tree.

One by one, the men in the image placed their books on the table in front of Dr. Addams. The very last to do so was the small brown man, and he did so with great reluctance, and at the last moment he tried to snatch his book back, and the red volume belonging to Addams as well. He did not succeed. The rest of the men, witnessing his effort, escorted him out of the scope of the image.

She was busy watching what happened to the little figure of the man, and thus failed to see what had happened to the books on the table. When she looked again, they were all gone.

Milliseconds later, so was the image.

She heaved a deep sigh and began to blow out the candles, breaking the spell circle. She had just leaned forward to quench the last one when the command came through, clear and distinct and undeniable, in Dr. Addams's voice: *Bring them to me, and forget.*

Unwillingly, she got to her feet and went to the bookshelf, pulled out the books she had rummaged from the shelves of her own library, of Tara's, of Giles's, and of the Magic Box over the past three days. The battered, red leather bound volume on top was *Ritual, Chant, and Song.*

If she hurried, she could drop them off before lunch. That would give her plenty of time to forget she had ever had them in her possession before anyone discovered a particular book missing and started raising any questions.

Meanwhile, she was needed tonight, she could tell. She should take a nap that afternoon before class, build up her strength. So she could be ready.

It took the Rosenberg girl longer than he'd expected to figure out the spell he'd put on the book list. It was a trifle disappointing.

Professor Addams was in his office preparing for the next day's lecture when the tampering spell he'd also put on the paper set off a tiny shower of fireworks in the air over his desk. With a muttered curse, he smothered the fallen sparks that threatened to ignite the blotter, then sat back in his chair.

She'd be here soon. Good. He wondered if she'd been successful at finding all the books. From the looks of the magick shop, and the stuffiness of the proprietor, he'd be willing to wager large sums of money that several of them had been up in the loft there.

He reached into the desk drawer and took out the geode he'd used to fog her mind before. It never hurt to be prepared, even though it wasn't likely that she'd be so quick getting here.

She arrived about twenty minutes later, looking a little foggy and carrying an armful of books. One of them was a battered folio bound in red leather, and Addams sat forward in his chair, his eyes widening.

"Miss Rosenberg," he said, keeping his voice calm, "do please sit down." He passed his hand over the geode; it rippled, and Willow sat obediently in the chair before the desk.

"I brought the books you wanted," she said.

"How very kind of you. You may put them on the desk now." She did, and slowly, almost afraid that the red book would not be the one he hoped, he slid it from the bottom of the stack.

It was Liverakos's *Ritual, Chant, and Song.* Addams took a deep, quavering breath. "By God," he whispered, "at last. At last!" Reverently, he opened the book, smoothing the title page with a palm, relishing the texture of the paper.

The book was old, dating back to Elizabethan times, early in the history of the printing press. The printing was not nearly as clean as modern books; there were gaps in some of the letters and not all of them were the same font or size, and the spelling was eccentric. "Rituall, Chant, and Songe," the first line read, and underneath that, "A true Coppie of the originall compendium of Anton Liverakos in the reigne of Ricardus II."

In the chair, the Rosenberg girl stirred, frowning. Addams looked up, his hand still on the book. "Yes, Miss Rosenberg?" he said.

"I haven't done the bibliography yet," she said. "You're not going to keep those books, are you?"

Damn, but the chit had a strong will. Addams stroked the geode once more. "But my dear," he said, his voice low and hypnotic, "you turned your bibliography in days ago. Don't you remember? And an excellent job you did, too. I should think you've earned an *A*."

Willow beamed at him, but her eyes were still unfocused. "Oh, good," she said. "*A*'s are good. I get lots of *A*'s."

"I daresay you do," Addams said, smothering a laugh. "All right now, off with you." He took the geode in both hands, stroking his thumbs across the spikes of crystals along the edges. The air between them rippled, glowed purple. "When you get back to your room, you'll forget all about the books, save that you used them for your paper and have returned them to their rightful places."

Willow stood. "I've finished the paper, returned the books, and got an *A*," she said, nodding. "Go, me. Good afternoon, Professor." She walked to the door, her eyes fixed on a spot that seemed to move with her.

"Willow." She stopped, her hand on the doorknob. "Yes?"

"One last thing. You must be in the theater tonight. Be there at eight."

She nodded slowly. "Eight." Then she turned the knob and walked out of the office.

When the door closed behind her, Addams returned his attention to the large book. "Soon," he murmured as he turned the pages. "Soon . . ."

Spike slipped into the theater building through the open loading-dock door and beat the flames out on his blanket. It was foolishness, going out in the daylight when it wasn't strictly necessary, and he could easily have waited until dark, but the memory of Addams's face, his supercilious expression, made Spike's dead blood rage. He didn't know how the bastard had survived the last hundred and twenty-some years, but he was bloody well about to find out. And this time Addams would recognize him. He'd make sure of that.

He made his way onto the stage, Doc Martens clocking on the plywood covering, making no attempt to be quiet. Sometimes acting like you belonged where you were was the best disguise. The stage was empty, but a student stuck her head out of the passageway to the dressing rooms, and Spike lifted a casual hand at her. When she saw his face, she gave a disgusted snort and ducked back. He grinned.

"Guess I showed her," he said, and, walking to the edge of the stage, he leaped across the orchestra pit, landing gracefully in front of the first row of seats. He pulled out a cigarette and lit it as he sauntered over to the stairwell door that flanked the stage and pulled it open.

The theater department offices were on the basement level; he'd called the secretary to find out, and she'd helpfully given him directions to Addams's office. He clattered down the stairs, his mouth twisted in a fearful smile around his cigarette.

He was just about to open the door at the bottom of the stairwell when it opened of its own accord, and the witch came through.

"Well, well, fancy meetin' you here, Red," Spike said, but Willow didn't seem to hear him. She walked straight past him, her eyes focused on a spot about three feet in front of her nose.

"Oi!" Something was very wrong, here. Willow never ignored him. "Witch!"

She still didn't seem to hear him, and he vaulted over the railing to land on the stairs in front of her. That seemed to get her attention; she gasped, her eyes focused on him, and she flailed her arms as her foot slipped. He reached forward and caught her, lifting her onto the step beside him.

"Spike?" she said, her brow furrowing. "What the . . . ?"

"You tell me, pet," he said, shrugging. "You were walking around like a zombie." She seemed to have regained her balance, and he let go of her. She sat down on the landing.

"Uh, what am I doing in a stairwell? And which stairwell is it?" Her voice was small, and she cut her eyes, which were very wide, up at him.

"Theater," he said. "The basement level, where the offices are. As for why you're here, I have no idea." He shrugged again, threw down the butt of his smoke, and ground it out with his boot. "Don't you remember?"

She shook her head.

"What's the last thing you do remember?"

She thought about that for a minute. "Um, I was in my room, doing a revelation spell on the book list Doctor Addams gave me. There was something funny about it."

"What did you find?"

Willow tilted her head, squinting at the far wall. "I . . . I don't remember." She looked up at Spike. "I know he put some kind of spell on that paper. I'm sure of it. And the spell I cast to find it should have worked. So why didn't it?"

Spike's eyes narrowed. "Maybe it did work, love."

"But . . ." Then her eyebrows flew up into her bangs. "There must have been a secondary spell piggy-backed onto the main one. A forgetting spell."

"Or a warning that you were tampering."

Willow looked at Spike, her mouth open in surprise.

"What?" he snapped, annoyed. *They all think I'm too stupid to understand anything.* "I do know a couple of things about magick, you know."

"You do?" Willow, seeming to sense his annoyance, swallowed. "I mean, cool." She looked thoughtful. "A warning—that makes sense. But why would he put any kind of spell on that list?"

Spike shrugged. "What kind of list was it?"

"I told you, a book list."

He rolled his eyes. "Yeah, pet, I heard you, but what was it *for*?"

Willow blushed. "Oh. Oh, it was a list of books he wanted me to find so I could do an annotated bibliography."

Spike pulled his smokes out of his duster pocket and started to light up again. Willow frowned at him, glancing over at a poster plastered on the wall opposite the door, which read NO SMOKING IN THE STAIRWELL! He laughed. "You've got to be kidding, Red," he said as he flicked the lighter out. "Evil, here."

"Oh. Right." To Spike's chagrin, she looked a little embarrassed, as though she'd forgotten. *Sodding chip* . . .

He leaned against the wall, looking at her through the smoke he blew out in a long stream. "What kind of books?"

Willow shrugged. "Stuff about the origins of magick and ritual in the theater. Nothing really exciting. Although some of them did have some cool stuff about . . ."

Spike pushed off the cinderblock wall, frowning. "Wait, you found these books?"

"Yeah. It's weird. The library didn't have any of them, but between our stuff and Giles's and the Magic Box, I found every one of them."

"Bloody buggering hell! He's still looking for that

bleeding incantation!" His hands clenched into fists, and for a second his eyes flashed gold. "Willow. Where are the books now? You didn't give them to Addams, did you?"

"No, they're in my room. I haven't done the paper yet."

Spike thought for a minute, gnawing at his lower lip. If Red still had the books, Addams would be trying to get them from her soon enough. Spike wasn't sure exactly what the incantation did, but Addams had been looking for it for over a hundred years. It must be important, and likely dangerous. Anything that was hidden that well couldn't be anything minor. It was probably another damned apocalypse, this being the Hellmouth and all. *Buffy's been through enough of those,* he thought. *She's got enough on her mind with all of the other beasties she fights. Best I take care of this before she has to.*

"Come on," he said, grabbing Willow's wrist. "I think I know what he's up to. We need to get those books somewhere he can't find them."

Chapter Eighteen

London, England, 1880

Number 14 Whiteside Street looked from the outside just like any other building in the street, neglected and dirty. But that was only the outside.

Inside, the wood paneled walls gleamed with polish, the furniture was fashionably uncomfortable, and the champagne was not quite what you'd expect to find at an ambassador's dinner table, but ran a close second.

Albert Addams handed his hat and gloves to the butler, who ushered him into the parlor. Peggy Dover, the Madam, sat at a ridiculously small desk, writing letters.

"Pardon, Mrs. Dover," the butler said, "But Mister Addams would like a word."

"Peggy, my dear!" Addams said, giving her a kiss on the cheek, followed by a very serious look. "I'm afraid I've been having a problem with one of your girls. Might you be good enough to send Darabont up to Laurette's room in, say, fifteen minutes' time?"

He shoved open the polished walnut burl door so hard that it crashed into the wall behind, rattling the pictures hanging there and sending a decorative china plate crashing from its hanger to smash on the floor.

Before he could even step into the room, he was pinned against the doorframe.

"That plate was over a hundred years old. It belonged to my mother." The vampire's tone was mild, but she didn't let her face change back to human right away. Nor did she let him go.

"You never knew your mother." The words, pushed through a throat nearly closed off by the steel grip of her fingers, nevertheless carried a placating tone, and she shook off her vamp face with a grunt of laughter.

"Bertie, it isn't Thursday, or had you forgotten?" she said. She went back to the chair she'd been sitting in and picked up her knitting, wound the tail around both ball and work, and tossed the bundle into the basket beside the chair. "Or are you here for vengeance, like that fellow from your club last month?"

"Laurette, I don't have time for this." Addams rubbed at the marks that were already purpling to bruises under his collar. "I'm looking for vampires. Two of them. One is only a few weeks old, the other . . . I think the other one is old."

Laurette's dark eyebrows vanished underneath her fringe, and she laughed.

"What, Bertie, I'm suddenly not enough for you anymore?" She came to him and rested her cold fingers on the bruises on his neck. "You think you could handle three of us?"

Addams reached into his pocket and pulled out a gold crucifix. She laughed again, making as if to slap his hand away, but he caught her arm, pressing the cross to her wrist, where the flesh began to sizzle and smoke. She screamed and snatched her arm out of his grasp, vamping out as she cradled her wounded hand.

"You'll be sorry for that," she hissed at him.

"I do daresay," he said dryly. "Now, before you go breaking one of Peggy's extremely strict rules about draining her customers, perhaps you'll tell me what I want to know?" He took a roll of pound notes out of his other pocket, held them up between two fingers. "For our standard fee, of course."

The vampire cast a look toward the door, which still hung open. For a moment, she rubbed at the wound on her wrist, making him no answer. Then she reached forward and snatched the cash out of his hand. "You'll have to tell me more," she said sullenly. "One old, one young, that's not much to go on."

"The older one, he's tall," Addams said. "Quite tall."

"Spaniard? Lots of hair? Eyes to drown in?"

Addams shook his head. "No, I believe he's Irish."

Laurette stared at him for a long moment, her mouth twitching, and finally she broke into laughter again. "Angelus?" she said, gasping for air between spasms, "You're looking for *Angelus*? You poor bastard." She tucked the roll of bills down the front of her corset.

"You know this vampire?"

She shook her head. "I know of him, though. And you don't want nothing to do with *him*. He never played by anyone's rules but his own, and he'd kill you just as soon as step on you. Wouldn't even eat you, most likely. Just kill you." She gave him a predator's grin, all sharp white teeth.

"Where can I find him?"

Laurette shrugged. "I don't move in those circles, Bertie," she said. "Bit beneath those Aurelians, I am. You'll have to ask some other vampire." She gave him the predator's grin again. "If you can find one that won't eat you first and ask questions later." Before he could move, she had one hand around his throat again and the other around the hand holding the cross. "You shouldn't have used this on me, Bertie. Ruined a perfectly good working relationship, you did. Peggy won't let me drain you completely, but that doesn't mean I can't make you wish I would."

She pulled his arm outward until the joints groaned, pushed his head back. Just as her teeth met his throat, she gave a gasp, and, eyes wide, crumbled into dust.

Addams sneezed. "Thank you, Darabont," he said, and took the hand of the spiny-faced green Bracken demon who had stepped in to keep him from falling. "Damn shame. Laurette was my favorite." He brushed at his clothes, making a face at the amount of vampire dust.

Darabont gave him back a bland servant's look.

"Indeed, sir. A shame," he said. "Mrs. Dover would like a word with you before you go, sir, if you would." He waited until Addams had crossed the threshold before he began sweeping up the pile of dust.

The next evening the demon underworld was buzzing with the news that vampires had kidnapped a human girl. Darla found it quite amusing that Addams had not only used every demon contact he had to get the word out that he was offering a reward for Cecily's safe return, but he had also taken out several different ads in the agony columns of the evening newspapers.

Angelus didn't find it so amusing.

"We've got to get back to the house," he said grimly after he'd staked the third vampire of the night to waylay them and demand that he turn over "that human girl." "Spike isn't experienced enough to hold off a crowd, and Drusilla's just as liable to kill the girl as intruders."

"Well, then, let her," Darla said. "Really, Angelus, I don't see what's so important about this girl. Why you don't just have Spike kill her and be done with it is beyond me." She shook her head, making the green feather on her hat wobble.

"He wanted to make her suffer," Angelus said. "Which, actually, I heartily approve of." Darla rolled her eyes.

"Of course you do, darling. Torture is your element, after all. I'm just not so sure it's Spike's."

"He'll learn. Look who's teaching him." Angelus smirked down at her, and she patted his arm.

"If you say so, Angelus. Here, if you're that worried about getting back, do let's take a cab." She removed one of her gloves, put her fingers to her mouth, and let out a piercing whistle at a passing cab. By the time the driver pulled up to the curb, she had her glove back on and a perfectly innocent expression on her face.

"It's only a matter of time until he finds us." Angelus spread the newspaper out on the table in the breakfast room and tapped one of the circled ads that Addams had placed. "If he's not already on his way. We haven't exactly made a huge secret of where we're staying, and some of the demon population of this town would love to see us dust." He sighed.

"Is there somewhere else we could go?" Spike asked. He had not so far seen Angelus this worried over anything.

"Carrying a screaming female in a ball gown under your arm? Hardly." Darla's tone dripped contempt, and Angelus nodded.

"Exactly," he said. "It'll be much easier if we can get him to come here on our terms. On our schedule."

"And how exactly do you propose to do that?"

Angelus looked at Darla, a huge grin splitting his face. "Ah, darling, that's where you come in."

She set her feet on the floor with a thump and stood. "Oh, no, you don't," she said, crossing her arms firmly. "Don't even try to involve me in this scheme."

"But we need you to go and dangle the bait under his nose."

"Dangle your own damn bait." Darla's foot began to tap, making the hem of her skirt shimmy. "The last time you wanted me to dangle bait, I ended up stranded on an ice floe for a month. Do you have any idea how *horrible* seal blood is?" She shuddered. "I still have nightmares."

Angelus gave her a shrewd look. "It'll have to be Drusilla, then," he said. Indicating Spike, he went on, "Addams won't let either of us in, that's for certain." He leaned closer to Darla. "Of course, you know how she is," he whispered, with a sideways glance at Dru. "She'll like as not get distracted by some pretty vision and forget about us." Dru whipped her head up and gave him a sharp look. Angelus turned so that Darla couldn't see and winked at her. Turning back to Darla, he continued. "They'll come and stake us in our beds."

Darla rolled her eyes and huffed out a sigh. "Oh, all *right*," she said. "I'll go." She put her hands on her hips and gave him a baleful glare. "But you're going to owe me for this."

Angelus laughed. "That's my girl!" he said. "Now, here's what you do. . . ."

It was nearly midnight when Darla rang the Addamses' bell, but the butler answered the door promptly, looking down at her standing on the step with a deep distrust in his eyes.

"Yes?"

"I've information about young Miss Addams," she said. The man's eyes widened. "Indeed," he said, stepping back from the door. "Please wait a moment." He disappeared toward the back of the house at what, for a butler, was quite an unseemly pace.

Darla snickered to herself. "Smart man," she said, then cocked her head as she heard footsteps down a side passage.

A short, plump woman appeared at the end of the hallway, poking her head out from the passage. She had a heavy woolen robe wrapped about her shoulders and there was a dark glint in her eye when she saw the front door standing open.

"Mary, Joseph, and all the saints," she muttered savagely as she stumped down the hall and past the stairs. "Drat that Mister Clermont. How many times today have I told him to shut the front door? We'll all wake up murdered in our beds one day, you mark my . . ."

She broke off when she saw Darla standing on the step.

"Oh!"

Darla pulled her cape about her and gave the woman a wan smile. "Hello," she said, and shivered. "I've come about Miss Addams. . . ."

"And Mister Clermont just left you standing there on the step?" The woman clucked her tongue and shook her head. "I don't know what that man has been thinking today. Come in, dear. You look well nigh frozen." She held her hand out to Darla, who took it. "Lord have mercy, child!" the woman cried. "You're cold as death. Here, come into the kitchen where there's a fire."

The clatter of footsteps coming to an abrupt halt behind her made her turn. Clermont, eyes wide, nostrils flaring, stood beside Albert Addams, whose face bore an equally surprised expression.

"Cook!" Clermont's tone was stern, and Addams laid a hand on the butler's shoulder.

"Never mind, Clermont," he said. "The damage is done. Bring her to my office." He turned and walked back along the passage, disappearing through a dark, heavy door.

"This way, madam," Clermont said, in the same tone he might have used to a duchess, and indicated that she should follow him. "I'll deal with you later," he hissed at Cook as he passed her. She only pursed her mouth at him.

Darla knew from the sweet tang of fear in the butler's scent that he knew what she was, but he never so much as tensed his shoulders all the while she walked behind him, and when he stopped in front of the door to Addams's office, he bowed and held the door for her. As she passed through into the small room, Addams gave the butler a speaking look, and he gave the slightest of nods in reply.

"Oh, don't trouble yourself," Darla said, giving Clermont her most engaging smile. "I'm only here for business, and I'm sure Mister Addams here knows plenty of people who will be able to uninvite me once I've gone." Clermont said nothing. He merely flicked a glance at Addams, nodded, and stepped out of the room.

"You will forgive me for taking precautions," Addams said dryly as he reached into his desk drawer and brought out a large silver cross and a wickedly sharp wooden stake. The stake he laid on the desk, but he kept hold of the cross, resting it against his chest as he leaned back in his chair.

"Perfectly understandable," Darla answered with a businesslike smile. "Now, I hear you've misplaced your only child."

Addams's face suffused with blood and his jaw clenched so hard that the muscles in his temples jumped like galvanized frogs' legs. "Where is she?" he spat, standing up from the desk.

"Calm down," Darla said, showing more of her teeth than was strictly necessary. "You mustn't give yourself apoplexy. That's so bad for my digestion."

He growled and held up the cross. She shifted uncomfortably, taking a step back from the desk. "Where is my daughter?" he said, each word so particularly enunciated that Darla felt every sound strike her in the face.

"She's safe . . . for now."

"What does Angelus want with her?"

"To eat her, like as not," Darla said carelessly, and smirked at Addams's sudden loss of color. "But it's not Angelus you have to worry about."

"William." Addams sat heavily in the chair and passed a shaking hand over his mustache.

"Yes."

"What have you to do with any of this?" Addams's thumb moved over the cross he held, tracing the lines of the rose design in the center. He looked quite weak and harmless, sunken in on himself in despair, but Darla hadn't survived for nearly three hundred years by trusting appearances. She watched his eyes carefully, noticed the flick of his glance toward the stake, the slight hesitation of his thumb on the cross.

"You're offering a reward for information, aren't you?" She stepped forward, ran a finger over the edge of the mahogany desk, positioned herself so that she had a better angle on the tall window behind the desk. "I've found that I'm running short on cash. I thought we could come to a . . . mutually agreeable arrangement." She tilted her head and smiled at him, biting her lower lip, and fluttered her eyelashes. She hadn't been around for nearly three hundred years by failing to use all her assets, either.

Addams, affected in spite of himself, ran his tongue over his bottom lip. When he realized what he was doing, he snapped his mouth shut and blinked rapidly, tightening his fingers and lifting the cross toward her.

"You don't care that I'm going to kill Angelus?"

She waved her gloved hand. "Pfft, why should I care about that? As long as you pay me, you can run him up the flagpole at noon for all I care."

"What about William?"

"I care even less what happens to him." Darla made a face. "Wretched boy, he's been nothing but trouble."

"But . . ."

She leaned forward, bracing her hands on the top of the desk. "Look, Mister Addams," she said directly, "I'm not interested in you or your daughter or"—she gave a delicate sniff, and fixed her gaze on his throat, where dark bruises and old bite scars were just visible underneath his collar— "or any of the twisted vampire games you obviously play. If you want my information, pay me. If not, I'll go." She straightened up, and her hand brushed against a large book lying open in front of Addams. His eyes flickered toward it, and he closed it with a thud, laying his hand over it protectively. It was bound in battered red Moroccan leather, and the title was picked out in gold.

"Very well," Addams said. He took a large leather wallet from his coat pocket and removed a hundred pounds in notes. "Will that do?" he said.

A sudden shout from the front of the house made him jump.

"It's fine," Darla said, holding out her hand. More shouts and the pounding of feet echoed down the passage. Clermont had apparently gone for reinforcements after all.

"Where are they?" Addams held out the money, just out of her reach. She closed her fingers on the bills, but he did not let go.

"All right." She sighed, and gave him the address. He let go of the notes, and she folded them neatly and tucked them inside the back of her glove. The uproar from the front of the house was growing louder, and Addams gave a very pointed look toward the door.

"Oh, you go ahead," Darla said. "I'll just let myself out." She waved a casual hand and moved backward a couple of steps, mentally calculating the distance to the window if she used the desk as a springboard.

"Oh, no," Addams said, picking up the stake. He came around the side of the desk, brandishing the cross, and Darla moved, countering him. "I'm afraid I can't leave you here to wreak havoc on my household."

He leaped forward, the cross held high, and when she flinched from it, he grabbed her hand and stripped off the glove where she had hidden the money. At the same time he plunged forward with the stake.

Darla roared into her vampire face, ducked her shoulder, and drove it into Addams's middle. He dropped the stake, but managed to hold onto the cross.

"Did you really think I wouldn't see that coming?" she said, gloating around her fangs. "You moron." She threw an uppercut at his jaw that sent him crashing backward into a bookcase. As the shouting in the corridor drew closer, she scrambled up on the desk. "And since you've taken back your money, perhaps there's something of value you'd rather I take instead." She nudged the large red book with one kid-booted toe. "This looks valuable." She bent to pick it up, and Addams, with a cry, maneuvered himself out of the welter of leather-bound quartos, flinging books aside with abandon as he launched himself at Darla.

Just as he jumped, the door opened and Clermont burst in. Addams, unable to stop himself, crashed into the butler and they both went down in a tangled, groaning heap.

"Well, I see I made a good choice," Darla said brightly. She tucked her head, clutched the book to her chest, and pushed off the desk, left shoulder leading, to smash through the window. She laughed as she picked herself up, brushing shattered glass from her shoulders and absently licking the blood from her fingers when some of the shards cut her. "Ta!" she called through the window as Addams and Clermont both swore and struggled to get up. "I'll be back later to eat the scullery maids." She ran to the garden wall, leaped to the top of it, then dropped down onto the pavement on the other side.

"That was fun," she said to herself as she strolled down the mostly-deserted street. "Maybe I *will* come back later and eat the scullery maids." She began to whistle as she headed back toward Milbury Court.

"For God's sake, man, sit down!" Angelus sat with his head lolling on the back of the settee, his eyes closed, as Spike paced from the window to the fireplace and back.

"She should have been here hours ago," Spike said, worrying his thumb between his teeth.

Angelus lifted an arm into the air, pointed a finger unerringly at Spike, following him as he moved. "And that changes the fact that she's not here how, precisely?"

Spike growled, but made no further answer. From upstairs, Cecily, voice thin from hunger and thirst, called out pitifully for William. Her cries were accompanied by a weak banging on the door, then the sound of sobs.

"God, I wish she'd stop that!" Spike's pace sped up, his bootheels making distinct, if muffled, thuds on the carpet.

Angelus waited until Spike was right in front of him, then sprang up, catching the younger vampire by his lapels.

In a deceptively mild voice, which the amber flash in his eyes belied, he said, "I told you to sit . . . down."

He flung Spike into the wing chair beside the settee and then sat back down himself.

Spike straightened his cravat and smoothed out his lapels. "Where the bloody hell is she?"

"Didn't your mother ever tell you patience was a virtue, boy?" Angelus had flung his arm over his face; the words were slightly muffled.

"I thought 'virtue' and 'vampire' were antithetical," William snapped. Angelus gave a short bark of laughter.

"Keep using those big words, Spike. That's really the way to frighten your victims."

"Sod off." Spike pushed himself out of the chair and resumed pacing.

"Tsk. From one extreme to another," Angelus said, then sat up, alert, as the front door slammed open.

"It's Darla," he said, and Spike stopped in midstep.

"Angelus!" Darla was clearly furious. The front door slammed again, closing, and Darla stalked down the hall and into the parlor.

Angelus gave another bark of laughter when he saw her. Her hat was half off her head, the feather broken and dangling down to her chin. The curl had come out of her hair, and it lay in draggled locks over her shoulder. Her dress was torn in half-a-dozen places, and the bottom of her skirts was filthy with mud and manure and several other equally unpleasant substances.

"I thought," Darla said icily, "that you said he would come straight here once I told him the address."

Angelus, wise enough not to say anything when she used that tone of voice, put his hand up to his mouth and chewed on his knuckles to hide his smile.

"Well, he didn't." Darla stamped her foot, causing the broken feather to tickle her chin. With a muffled oath, she tried to brush it out of her face, but only succeeded in getting it into her mouth. She snatched the hat off and, with a snarl of rage, tore it in two and flung the pieces to the corners of the room. She pushed her now completely ruined coiffure away from her face.

"I doubled back, like you told me," she went on, "and waited for them to head here. But they followed me instead. I tried to lose them, but the bastards were persistent, I'll give them that. I have a feeling it has something to do with this." She hurled the red leather book, now damp and stained and with several of the pages seemingly pulled out at random and then stuffed back in the same way, straight at Angelus's head. He caught it awkwardly, and several of the loose pages fluttered to the floor.

"What the devil is this, then?" he said, turning it over.

"That's where he's hiding. That's where the stoat-man went." Drusilla, drawn downstairs by the shouting, clapped her hands with glee and hurried forward to take the book from Angelus. She took it to the sofa and began flipping through the pages, looking for something, and seemed not even to remember that anyone else was there at all. "There'll be fire and pain and lovely sweet blood," she said in a sing-song, "and we'll all be happy, even though we're dead."

Darla rolled her eyes heavenward. "I have no idea what it is," she said, rubbing a spot between her eyebrows. "That man seemed to value it, so I took it when I left." She slumped tiredly into the wing chair and rested her head on the back of it.

Spike stepped forward, pushing past Angelus and giving Dru an absent caress on the arm as he passed her. "So where is he?" he demanded, leaning over the chair, one hand resting on the top of the wing.

"He's on his way." Darla did not move, but something in her demeanor made Spike back up a step. "It took me hours, but I finally managed to convince the old fool that I really was headed here. I'd suggest you get your playing pieces into position."

"Where?" Angelus lifted an eyebrow at Darla, who shrugged.

"You're the tactician, darling," she said.

Angelus thought for a moment. "The breakfast room," he said finally, with a look at Spike.

Spike nodded. "Yes, I think that will do nicely."

"All right, then. Spike, you bring her down to the breakfast room. She's going to try to get you to let her go. Eventually she'll offer herself as an inducement, and you'll pretend to go along with that." He grinned at Spike. "So, when her father arrives, he'll find the two of you in . . ."

Spike grinned back, seeing where Angelus was going. "A compromising position," he said. "Brilliant. Too bad I'll kill them both before word could get out. I'd love to have seen Cecily's face when some baronet's third son told her she was beneath *him*."

"Right, then," Angelus said. He nodded to Spike. "Be off with you. And let her think she's escaping before you corner her. They taste so much sweeter when they realize there never really was any hope after all." He turned to Darla. "If he brings any help, you and I will take care of them." She nodded, then sighed.

"I don't suppose there's time for me to change first," she said, and sighed when Angelus shook his head. She combed her fingers through her hair, and, after finding several hairpins that had somehow remained in place, twisted the straggling locks up out of her face and secured them.

"What about Dru?" Spike said, nodding to the settee, where Drusilla was absorbed in the large book. She was rocking and humming to herself, and it was quite plain that she neither knew nor cared that there was anyone else in the room.

Angelus hunched his shoulders. "Leave her. If it comes to a fight, the smell of blood will rouse her. Otherwise, it's not worth trying to snap her out of it." He'd obviously dealt with this kind of deep focus on more than one occasion, for his voice bore a distinct note of grim resignation. He settled himself next to Drusilla on the settee, waiting. Darla, brushing half-heartedly at her skirts, took the chair.

* * *

Spike stood outside the door to the room they'd locked Cecily in, listening. She seemed to be sitting on the floor, from the sounds of her sobbing. He turned the key in the lock and opened the door.

She was leaning against the chiffarobe, her hands

slack in her lap. Her gown was crushed and stained with blood, and her elegant coiffure was drooping but not quite ruined. She'd made some attempt to wipe off the blood from her bite wound; her innermost petticoats were stained rusty brown with it. The bite itself was healing, but the surrounding flesh was a deep blackish purple, fading to yellowish brown in spots.

She looked up at him, eyes wide and red. Her face was stained with the salt of dried tears.

"William," she said, lifting one lax hand from her lap. "Please, William . . ."

"Please, what?" he said, the sneer plain in his voice. "Please let you go? I think not." He approached her and hunkered down beside her, and she shrank from him, pressing herself into the chiffarobe. He reached out and stroked the back of a finger down her cheek. She closed her eyes and shuddered, and he gave a low laugh.

"Afraid of me now?" he said.

She opened her eyes and looked into his. "Why are you doing this?" she whispered.

"Because I can. Because you deserve it, you bitch."

The word made two spots of color flame in her cheeks, and she pushed away from the wall.

"How dare you speak to me that way!" she said, mortal affront snapping in her eyes. "Whatever you were before, you were at least a gentleman."

"How would you know? You never saw me as anything but *beneath* you."

She looked down, twining her fingers together in her lap. "William, I . . ." She looked up at him from underneath her lashes, and he leaned forward, letting himself wobble just enough for her to notice that he wasn't quite perfectly balanced.

She was a smart girl; the second she realized it, she shoved him. He sprawled onto his back, letting his head bounce on the floor at the same time as he thumped sharply with his bootheel. She was up in a flash, skirts flying as she made a dash for the door. He let her get completely through it before he got up.

She tore down the stairs, her soft dancing shoes making scarcely any noise on the bare wood. Spike followed her, thumping loudly, and at the bottom of the staircase he put on a burst of vampire speed and passed her, getting between her and the front door. "Tsk," he said, and changed into his demon face. "That wasn't very smart of you, Cecily."

She made a frustrated noise deep in her throat, and looked around, seeking another way out. He took a step toward her, stamping hard on the carpet, grinning, and she bolted down the passage that led to the breakfast room. Spike laughed softly.

"Stupid bint," he said, and followed her again.

It was simplicity itself to drive her where he wanted her to go, and when she was safely in the breakfast room, he closed the door behind him and stalked her to the edge of the room.

She backed away from him until the wall brought her up short. She pressed against it, and he took one more step, bracing a hand on the wall beside her head, looking down at her with a half-smile on his lips.

"William . . ."

"Shhh." Her eyes flicked to the side, and he put his other hand on the wall, trapping her between his arms. She looked up at him, her eyes huge. There was fear in them, but there was also a certain amount of fascination. Her heartbeat sped up and she began to breathe in quick, shallow gasps. Her tongue crept out, resting on the point of her upper lip. She smelled deliciously afraid.

"Well," he said, his voice low, "I believe we are at an impasse." He tilted his head, let his eyelids droop, and moved one hand a fraction of an inch closer to her head.

She swallowed. "William," she whispered, her gaze flicking from his eyes to his mouth and back to his eyes. "I . . . You're right. I never . . ." She swallowed again, biting her lower lip, fixing her eyes on the top button of his shirt. "I never really looked at you. At the . . . the man you really are." She looked up at him again, regret filling her face, moistening her eyes. "You said that you're a good man, and I realize now that you were right. I never gave you a real chance." She dropped her head, and a tear rolled down her cheek. "I'm sorry," she whispered.

Spike dropped one arm and leaned back. "That's a load of rubbish," he said with a snort, and her head snapped up.

"It's not. I . . ."

"Cecily. Please." He tucked a finger underneath

her chin, and, caught in his eyes, she went completely still. "Even as a human, I knew you were completely serious about me being beneath you." His thumb stroked over her chin, pausing for a moment in the slight cleft there. "Do you know I left your party and ran right into Drusilla? She killed me."

Cecily's eyes widened. "K . . . killed you? But . . ."

"Vampire. I told you earlier, do you remember? She killed me and made me into a vampire. And now I'm not precisely alive, but not precisely dead, either."

She put her hands up to cover her trembling lips. "Killed you? Oh, God, you did die because of me." She pressed her hands to her face, hiding it from him. "William, I'm so sorry. I didn't mean for you to die. I . . ."

He took her hands and gently tugged them away from her face.

"Don't be sorry," he said. "Before Dru turned me, I was exactly what you thought me: a weak, callow boy who wasn't worthy of you. But now . . ." He grinned fiercely. "Being a vampire is so much better. I should thank you, really. I'm so much stronger than that pathetic excuse for a human being I was." Leaning closer, he sniffed at her skin. "And I can do all sorts of things that pitiful boy couldn't do. For instance, I can tell how much this frightens you." He pressed his body closer and brushed his cheek along hers, and she gasped and held very still, though her heart was pounding hard enough for him to feel the vibration through the air. He put his mouth near her ear. "I can also tell how much it excites you," he whispered, drawing out the words so that the movement of his breath stirred the hair at her temple.

He pulled back enough to see her face. Her eyes were dark, and the scent of her fear and desire rose up to him, suddenly much stronger than before.

"Yes," she said, and if he had been human still, he wouldn't have heard the word. "You're . . ." Her hand came up, as though of its own volition, and she rested her fingers lightly against his lower lip. Once, he would have fainted dead away at such boldness from her, but now fierce joy sang through him and he flicked out his tongue to taste her.

She was delicious, and he growled, deep in his chest. He remembered her hot blood in his mouth and struggled to keep his face human. It was too soon; if he changed now, she'd be too afraid to take the next step.

"Cecily," he whispered against her fingers, letting his lips make the word a caress, and she whimpered. He laid a hand on her throat, let his fingers trail down over the bite wound, over her collarbone, down to the top of her dress. "What do you want, Cecily?" he said, his voice a seductive purr. "Shall I let you go, or kiss you?"

"I . . ."

But she'd already decided, for she slid her hand behind his neck and pressed him close, reaching for his mouth with her own.

She wasn't like Dru. She was warm, and comfortably padded in all the right places, and Spike found that the warmth had a certain charm of its own. He pulled her away from the wall, wrapped his arm around her back, and hauled her as close as her voluminous skirts would allow, and she put both arms about his neck and clung to him.

Her kisses were hungry, and quite a bit more thorough than Spike was expecting. He stumbled backward, knocking over the wrought-iron candlestand that stood at the end of the table, then righted them both and, picking her up bodily, turned around and set her down on the table, which, fortunately, was bare. Not that either of them would have noticed if it were not.

He caught her face in his hands and pulled back to look at her. Her mouth was swollen with his kisses, and she was gasping for breath so that her breasts strained against the fabric of her gown. Spike growled and buried his face in her neck, his tongue coming out to lap at the wound he'd already made there.

She gave a sharp cry and buried her fingers in his hair, her breathing grown suddenly harsh, and trembled underneath him.

He pushed her flat on her back on the table and bit down on the wound with his blunt human teeth, and she cried out again as the flesh, just starting to heal, parted. He sucked eagerly at the small trickle of blood, letting his face change.

Chapter Nineteen

Sunnydale, California, Fall semester, 2000

Spike, unable to take the direct route to Willow's dormitory in the middle of a typically sunny Sunnydale afternoon, knocked on Willow's door several minutes after she'd come in to find the books missing. She'd had just enough time to work up a really good panic by the time he arrived.

"They're gone," she said as soon as she opened the door. "I can't find them anywhere." Her eyes were wide, her bottom lip trembling. "Giles is going to kill me; some of those books were hugely valuable." She began to pace the room, wringing her hands and biting her lip. "I didn't exactly tell him I was taking them. Oh, my God. I'm so dead."

She turned a panicked face toward Spike—who

still stood outside the door. He was slouched against the invisible barrier that was keeping him out.

"Take a breath, Red," he said. "And if you want my help, you might invite me in. Be a lot easier to figure things out if I don't have to shout it to the whole dormitory." He sniffed, then grinned. "Not that some of them would notice, hey?"

She stared at him, uncomprehending, for long seconds, her mouth hanging open. All thought of the missing books evaporated in the face of the wrongness of Spike's request. "Invite you . . . in?" she said at last. *Oh, that is such a bad idea . . .*

Spike sighed. "Uh, yeah." He straightened from his slouch. "Unless you don't need any help figuring this out. . . ." He turned, and Willow squeaked.

"No, wait, come in," she said, all in a rush. He gave her a saucy grin and stepped into the room, closing the door behind him.

She remembered the last time he'd been alone in a dorm room with her, and frowned.

"Don't worry, witch," he said. He was grinning, as though he knew exactly what she was thinking. "I learned my lesson last time. Won't try to bite you again." His grin widened. "At least not until I get this chip out of my head. Here now, kidding, kidding," he said, as she felt the blood drain from her face, but she was pretty sure he hadn't been.

Vampire, Rosenberg. Remember that.

"You may not be able to bite me," she said, glad to find her voice coming out strong and level, "but that doesn't mean you can't get someone else to hurt me."

"Well," Spike said with a pleased grin. "'Bout time somebody remembered I'm still the Big Bad. But don't worry, Red." His expression settled into one of chilling malice, and Willow shuddered. "I'd promise never to bite you as long as you live if it means I can cock up Albert Addams's plans."

"How do you know him, anyway?" Willow, to distract herself from the frightening look on his face, busied herself with making tea at the hot plate. She took down the blue willowware tea service that had been a gift from Tara, and turned to Spike. "Would you like some tea?"

"I don't suppose you have anything stronger, do you?" She shook her head, trying not to smile. Spike sighed. "Tea'll do, then."

Life on the Hellmouth is so weird, Willow thought as she measured out the tea leaves into the teapot. *Here I am, making tea for a vampire who tried to kill me last year.* She shook her head, smiling. *And he's being pretty polite . . . for Spike.*

"So," she said. "You. Professor Addams. You two have obviously met."

Spike gave a bitter laugh. "Yeah. We have." He didn't continue, and Willow sighed.

"Animal, Vegetable, or Mineral?"

Spike's eyes flew wide. "What . . . ?"

"Well, you're obviously going to make me play Twenty Questions to find out the answer, so I thought I'd begin with the traditional question."

"You're not going to leave this alone, are you?"

Willow gave him a cheeky grin. "Nope."

"Wonderful." Spike flopped into the chair near the desk. "I knew his daughter when I was still alive."

Willow's mouth opened, but no sound came out. She'd never heard Spike talk about his human self, and from the tone of his voice, it wasn't a happy memory. Then the sense of what he'd said penetrated. "Wait, wait, he's over a hundred years old?" She gave a little squeak. "He's not a vampire, is he? Oh, swell, I've been taking a class from a vamp. Well, I guess that explains how he knows so much about theater history." The water boiled, and she poured it into the pot with the tea leaves and put the lid on. "Wait until Buffy hears about this. She'll freak."

"He's not a vampire." Spike was almost snarling. "He's human enough. Probably used some deep, dark mojo to keep himself alive all these years."

"Oh, great," Willow said, and slumped on her bed. "He's a wizard. Probably a powerful one. I so love living on the Hellmouth. Not." She looked at Spike, who was staring at the desk, a faraway look on his face.

"So," Willow tried hard for casual. "What happened with you and the daughter?" Had they been lovers? Had he ruined her reputation or stolen her away from her father's house? Willow smiled a little, thinking of what a rake Spike must have been as a human.

"She died." The grim, flat tone of his voice precluded any further questions; clearly she would get nowhere with the subject. Spike could be stubborn when he set his mind to it. Willow sighed, got up, and poured the tea.

"Cream? Sugar?" she said. He looked up at her

blankly. "For your tea." She held up the blue and white cup, lifting her eyebrows, and his face cleared.

"Just give it to me straight, love," he said, and she handed him the cup.

"So," he said, taking a sip of the tea, "the books are gone, are they?"

Willow, just pouring her own cup of tea, nearly dropped the teapot. "What am I going to do?" She set her cup down and began to pace again.

"I suppose you've looked everywhere?" Spike said, pushing back his chair and propping his Doc Martens on the desk. "They've not got tossed under the bed or in the closet?"

Willow stopped, shot him a withering glare.

"Of *course* they're not under the bed or in the closet. I checked. I also checked under Tara's bed and in her closet, and no books. Besides, I had them all on that desk—which you're cleaning, by the way, if you get crypt mud on my textbooks—just before I did the spell on the list."

"You sure you didn't take them to Addams?" Spike shifted his feet to a more comfortable position, right on top of a paperbound copy of *Physics for Dummies*.

"No, I didn't take them to him. I haven't even started on the paper yet." Willow's voice was plaintive. "Dammit."

Spike lifted an eyebrow. "Tsk," he said, "I'd never have pegged you for swearing, Red." But he quirked up the corner of his mouth, apparently teasing.

"You know any spells that will tell you if you've had a spell put on you in the last day?"

Willow looked thoughtful. "I think there may have been something in one of Tara's books that might do that." She went to Tara's bookshelf and sat cross-legged on the floor in front of it, running her finger along the spines of the books.

"Let's see," she said, her voice taking on what Xander called *research ecstasy*. "I think it was in the Egan. Or maybe the Hillerup." She pulled two volumes off the shelf and began flipping through them. "Thank goodness they weren't on Professor Addams's list."

The books were fascinating, and several times she let the cool things she was coming across take her attention away from her search. Spike, who seemed to know the signs, brought her back to her purpose more than once.

After a few minutes she closed the first book and went on to the other, but she had no success with that one, either. She put them both back on the shelf, sighing. "Okay, maybe it was the Chenanceou." She scooted over to the other bookshelf and pulled a leather-bound quarto from it.

"A-ha!" she cried, after several minutes spent muttering to herself and flipping pages. She looked up at Spike, her face glowing. "Found it!"

"Have you got the stuff to cast it?" Spike took his feet off the desk, setting them on the floor with a thump that made Willow wince. Her downstairs neighbor was going to turn her in to House Council again. He was such a wuss about noise. . . .

She looked back at the book, skimming over the ingredient list, which was, mercifully, short. "I think so," she said, bouncing a little where she sat.

"Right, then," Spike said. "Let's get started."

Willow gathered the ingredients while Spike set up the candles in a circle on the floor. There was a bad moment when she couldn't find the sage, but then she remembered that Tara had stashed a bundle in her closet for emergencies, since they were always running out. *Have to remember to replace that,* Willow told herself as she pulled the brown-paper-wrapped packet off the shelf.

When everything was laid out properly, she motioned Spike out of the circle and sat down in front of the burning bowl. He leaned against the wall, fiddling with his cigarettes as though he wanted to smoke. "If I suddenly develop a funky orange aura, we'll know that I've been bespelled."

She set about combining the ingredients into the burning bowl, then took a couple of branches of sage and wound a strand of her hair around them. *"Let this purify; let this reveal; let this expose the hidden power brought against me."* She lit the sage from the candle to her left, then dropped the herb into the burning bowl. The rest of the ingredients burst into flame and burned away rapidly, leaving the sage smoldering at the bottom of the bowl.

The smoke from the combustion wreathed Willow's body, seeming to settle on her skin. Where it touched, it began to glow a rich golden orange, and soon Willow looked as though she'd been dipped in saffron.

"Uh-oh. . . ."

"Bloody hell."

Willow sighed. "Okay, now what?"

Spike shrugged. "Know any spells to get your memory back?"

"Hmmm." Willow put out the candles and got up. "Not exactly. But I have something that might work. It's usually for clearing the residual magick out of your cells. Maybe it'll get rid of the effects of a forgetty spell."

She went to her dresser and opened a drawer. Reaching underneath the clothes, she took out a silk bag. It contained a long, cloudy crystal. She sat down on the bed and drew it through her closed fist in a way that made Spike grin, and said, *"Cleanse!"*

Beginning where Willow's fingers touched it, streaks of purple spread out into the crystal until the entire length had changed color. Currents swirled inside the quartz, and after a moment faded away.

"Oh!" Willow jumped up. "Oh, that jerk!" She turned to Spike, dark eyes snapping with anger. "He told me I'd already done my extra-credit paper! And that I got an *A*!" Color burned in her cheeks and she huffed out a breath. "I would *so* have gotten an *A+*!"

"That all he did, love?" Spike drawled.

Willow's brows drew down, her lips thinned. "No," she said. "I brought him a bunch of books, the ones on the list for the bibliography. He told me to remember that I'd taken them back to where they're supposed to be." She sat down on the bed again with a plop that sent pillows flying. "Oh, great, now I can't do the bibliography. No extra credit, then. Shoot. And then he told me to forget and to be at the theater tonight."

Spike straightened from his slouch against the wall. "Bloody hell," he said. "What's he want you there for?"

Willow shook her head. "He didn't say. But it can't be anything good, can it?"

"Probably right about that, ducks," Spike said dryly. Then he gasped; he seemed to have remembered something important. "One of those books wasn't a great huge red thing, was it?"

Willow gave him a measuring look. "Yeah," she said, "as a matter of fact. . . ."

Spike groaned. "Damn. We'd better make sure we're in the theater tonight, then. He may have just found what he's been looking for."

"And that would be . . . ?"

Spike glared at her, nostrils flaring. "I don't give a bloody damn what it would be. I just know the blighter has been looking for some incantation for the last hundred years or so, and whatever it does, it won't make the world safe for kittens and puppies." He paused, his lips drawing back over his teeth in a cold smile, and his eyes focused on something Willow couldn't see. "And even if it did," Spike went on softly, "I'd try to stop it, just because he's a bastard of the first water. It should have been me. It was mine to do, and he took that away from me."

"Took what?" Willow said. Spike's attitude was freaking her on so many different levels.

Spike came back abruptly from wherever he'd

been. "Never you mind that, witch. Just help me stop him, right?"

"Jeez, Spike, you're just a fount of information today," Willow said, crankiness sharpening her tone. "And thank you so much for being concerned about my welfare, too. Do you happen to have any idea what the incantation he's looking for does, so maybe we can be prepared?"

"I dunno exactly. It has something to do with old plays, and a ritual he thought he'd find hidden in them. I heard him talking about it at *A Midsummer Night's Dream*."

"Oh, gosh!" Willow said. "And those books were all about how ritual turned into theater." She went to the desk and began shuffling through her notebooks. "The Fates! Remember what the theater ghosts said? That whoever was destroying them was looking to summon the Fates."

"That bastard," Spike said quietly. "It's Addams."

Willow's eyes grew wide. "That makes sense," she said. "He knows way a lot about the older plays and ritual and stuff." She found the notebook she'd used to research the Greek gods, the Fates, and the Furies, and began turning the pages, but she hadn't gotten far when she remembered something else the ghosts had said. "Oh, dear. If Addams is trying to summon the Fates, we could be looking at another apocalypse."

"And we haven't had one of those in weeks," Spike said sardonically. "I knew I was missing something. . . ."

"Well, we'd better get hold of Buffy and Giles and the others," Willow said, reaching for the telephone.

Before she could lift the receiver from the cradle, Spike was beside her, gripping her wrist.

"No," he said. "I don't want the Slayer involved in this."

"What?" Willow shook his hand off. "Are you nuts? Wait, of course you are. I retract the question." Spike rolled his eyes, but Willow ignored him. "Buffy will be extremely unhappy if she misses something apocalypsy," she went on. "Giles, too."

Spike stared at her, his gaze hard. "We are not telling the bloody Slayer, and that's that," he said. "She won't kill him; he's human. And I won't risk him killing her. Because," he went on at her lifted eyebrow, "if anyone's going to be killing the Slayer, it's going to be me." Did he sound the tiniest bit too defensive? Willow shook her head. She must be imagining that.

He was right, of course; Buffy wouldn't kill a human. And if he were as powerful a wizard as she thought he was, that might be the only way to stop him. And with Spike chipped . . . "But neither of us can do it, either."

Spike's mouth fell into grim lines. "Wouldn't bet on that, Red," he said, very low. "I'd put up with a lot to get my own back from that man."

Willow gulped. He was completely serious.

"Well, let's try to find something else. Killing is . . . just too icky."

Spike sighed and ran a hand through his pale hair, making it stick up in a very endearing way. *Wait,* Willow thought quickly. *Did I just call Spike endearing?*

"Think you're strong enough to go against him?" He seemed a bit skeptical of her ability.

She straightened her spine and stuck out her chin. "I'll just have to be, won't I?"

He stared at her for a moment. "Yeah," he said at last, and there was grudging respect in his voice. "I guess you will."

She nodded. "Good. Glad that's settled." She turned back to the bookshelves. "Here, help me research." She pulled a copy of Fraser's *Grimorum Defensor* from the bottom shelf and tossed it to him. Grumbling a little, he sat down on the floor with his back propped against the bed and began to page through the volume.

Chapter Twenty

London, England, 1880

Drusilla suddenly broke off her humming and snapped the heavy red book shut. Angelus looked up and cocked an ear toward the breakfast room. What he heard made him grin.

Drusilla stood up. "Naughty girl," she said, her brows drawn together in a scowl. "He's mine, and I never said she could share." She took a step forward, but Angelus caught hold of her before she could take another.

"Now, Dru," he said, his voice low and calm. "She's not sharing. He's just . . ." His head whipped around at a sound from outside—footsteps, coming up the walk.

"Darla." He let go of Drusilla and, laying his finger over his lips, indicated the door.

"He's here," he whispered. Darla nodded and Drusilla's eyes grew bright with excitement.

"All right," Angelus said, still whispering. "He's got a couple of men with him. Maybe as many as three. Dru, you see if you can lead him to Spike and the girl. Darla and I will take care of the extras." Drusilla nodded mutely, and skipped over to wait at the front door.

Several sets of footsteps came slowly up the porch steps, but the men stopped outside the door to hold a whispered conversation about tactics, which the vampires could hear quite plainly. Drusilla, growing impatient, put her hand on the doorknob and looked a question at Angelus, who shook his head vehemently. She heaved a huge silent sigh and nodded.

Then one of them shouldered the door open, and the four men rushed into the house. Outside, the sky was beginning to lighten; dawn was very near.

Addams, brandishing a large cross, advanced into the room, striding purposefully toward Drusilla.

"Where is my daughter?" he demanded. The other three men spread out, one on each side of him, with Clermont at his back.

Drusilla looked sadly at the cross Addams held, stretching out her hand toward it. "I used to sleep under a cross like that once," she said, her voice hollow. "But it couldn't protect me." She shifted into her vampire face. "It won't protect you, either," she said, backing away as Addams advanced on her.

"It seems to be working so far," he said, the trace of a gloating smile on his lips.

Drusilla smiled at him, her eyes blazing. "Not everything is as it seems," she said, and, whirling, dashed down the passageway. Addams followed her, cursing, and the other men leaped after them.

As they passed by the parlor, Angelus and Darla sprang on them from the shadows, carrying two of the men to the floor. Angelus reached up as he landed and snapped one fellow's neck, and Darla pulled the other one down on top of her and, holding him with her legs, drained him in a matter of seconds. Clermont, still on his feet, lifted his hands and backed slowly toward the door, his face drawn and white. Angelus flipped himself upright, reached out, and seized the taller man by the throat.

"Sorry, m'lad," he said, "but you don't get off that easily." Then he tore out Clermont's throat.

"Well," he said, dropping the limp body and wiping his mouth, "that was fun. Shall we check on Dru and Spike?"

Darla shoved the body off her and stood, tidying her hair. "Oh, why not?" she said, and, taking Angelus's arm, they strolled down the passage.

Drusilla skipped ahead of Addams, darting into rooms and out of them, until she came to the breakfast room. She ducked through the door, and this time, did not come out. Addams, advancing cautiously, his stake at the ready, peered through the door. What he saw made him blanch.

Cecily was sprawled on the long table that ran down the middle of the room, her head thrown back, her skirts above her knees, and she was making the most appallingly abandoned sounds as William bent over her. With a roar, Addams flew across the room and, with a strength he would never have credited to himself at his age, jerked the boy off his daughter and flung him aside.

Spike landed on a toppled iron candlestand, screaming as one of the sconces punched through his chest.

"Spike!" Drusilla was by his side in a flash. She wrenched off the cup end of the sconce, and he screamed again, and again when she lifted him off the candlestand. Holding his bleeding body to her with one arm, she turned carefully to Addams.

"You hurt my knight," she said, her voice like the north wind, and she reached out and seized him by the throat, shaking him like a cat with a mouse. "Don't *ever* do that again." With a snarl, she flung him away from her. He flew through the air to land skull-first against the far wall, and the last thing he heard before everything went black was Cecily calling out to him.

The pain in Spike's chest was vicious, but he could feel it starting to abate even as Drusilla sank to the floor, holding him against her, stroking his hair with gentle fingers.

Cecily, who had leaped up as soon as Dru seized her father, cried out and ran to where he lay crumpled on the floor between two of the tall windows.

"Papa! Papa!" she said frantically, shaking his shoulder, and he groaned. Spike tried to sit up, but Drusilla held him tightly.

"Shhh," she said. "Don't try to move yet. Watch."

She smiled down at him, her eyes alight with some secret knowledge, her smile terrible. "He cannot see, cannot hear." The pain in his chest persuaded Spike not to argue with her.

Addams groaned again and tried to push himself upright. Cecily reached forward to help him, but when he saw the wound on her throat, he struck her hands away, his expression grief-stricken. "Oh, God, it's too late, too late," he said, and dropped his head into his hands.

Cecily reached out and touched his arm. "Papa . . ."

"Get away from me," he said roughly, scrabbling on the floor for the cross. He snagged it with the tips of his fingers, and pulled it to him.

Cecily sat back on her heels. "Papa!" she said. "I just want to help you!" She leaned forward again, but Addams waved her off, dragging the cross onto his lap.

"I said get away, you foul thing!" His chin trembled, and he scrubbed at his mouth with the back of his hand, blinking hard.

Cecily slumped, her throat working. "Papa," she said, her voice thick with tears, "I know it looks awful, I know I was . . ." She broke off, looking down at her fingers writhing together in her lap. "But nothing really happened, Papa. You must believe me." She looked up at him, eyes pleading. "No one in society need know. If you don't tell, how will anyone find out?"

Spike barked out a laugh, which turned instantly into a groan. "I could tell them, you stupid cow."

Cecily shot him a venomous glare. "Not if you're dead," she said, "and you will be, soon enough."

Addams drew in a shuddering breath and shook his head sadly. "God would know," he said. "And this . . . You couldn't keep this a secret. You're different now. You're not my daughter anymore, and people are bound to notice, no matter how you try to hide it."

"No!" Cecily buried her face in her hands for a moment, and her shoulders shook. When she lifted her face to her father again, tears dripped down her cheeks. "Please, Papa, couldn't we at least try?" She reached for him, leaning forward. He held the cross up between them and lifted the stake so that it was pointed directly at her heart. She flinched back from the unexpected threat, and Spike, seeing the last hope die in the old man's eyes, gave a terrible, cold laugh.

"You're a thing," Addams said, his voice broken. "You're a filthy, soulless creature, and I won't have it. Do you hear?" His voice rose as anger and grief warred in his eyes. "I won't have my daughter become one of those loathsome monsters."

Spike saw Addams's arm tense, saw his eyes shift to Cecily's chest. "No!" he shouted, struggling to get up, to stop what was coming, but Drusilla held onto him tightly. "Dru! Don't let him!" he said fiercely as he strained against her strength. "She's mine, mine to . . ."

With a strangled sob, Addams drew his arm back and thrust the stake straight into Cecily's heart. When he pulled the stake out, blood spurted outward in a three-foot stream, soaking Addams with gore.

For a moment she stared at him, shocked. And then she tried to scream, but the sound had scarcely begun before it died in a gurgle of blood that gushed from her mouth. She slumped, her weight slowly dragging her to the floor as Addams stared, open-mouthed, at the blood pouring from the gaping hole in her chest. Inside the wound, her ruined heart gave one final, weak pulse, and then was still.

Spike slumped back against Drusilla. "She was mine to kill," he whispered, looking up at her with haunted eyes. "Mine." For a brief moment, he recalled Cecily's smile, her laugh, how he had loved her when he was a man. How she had crushed him with her cruel words. "I should have killed her. . . ." If he'd killed her, he could have silenced those awful words forever in the taste of her blood.

Addams, at last realizing that the body before him was not going to crumble into dust, let both cross and stake fall from his hands. They landed on the carpet beside him with muffled thuds. Addams looked down at his hands, covered with Cecily's blood, and an anguished scream rose in his throat.

"Didn't see, didn't hear," Drusilla crooned into Spike's ear. The pain in his chest was lessening by the minute as his wound knit itself together, but it was still agony to move, so he held himself still until Addams's scream suddenly broke off.

He looked up to find the older man staring at him, his face a mask of fury and grief.

"You did this," Addams said. "You made me kill her." Tears streamed down his face, unnoticed, and he got to his feet.

Spike carefully pushed Dru's arms away and

struggled to stand, one hand to his chest, swaying like a sapling in a strong wind.

Drusilla stepped in front of him, her hands raised and her fingers crooked at Addams. "Ah-ah-ah," she said. "I warned you about hurting my knight again." She began to advance on Addams, her eyes boring into his, her fingers twitching, humming a little to herself.

From the doorway, Spike heard a sigh.

"Think she needs any help?" Angelus, who was leaning on one side of the door, quirked an eyebrow at Darla on the other side, who gave him a long-suffering roll of her eyes.

"He *is* family now," Angelus said.

"Since when do you care about family, darling?" Darla's tone was mocking.

"Oh, come on. It'll be fun."

Darla considered this. "You're right, it will," she said, smiling. "Besides, this bastard made me ruin one of my brand-new Madame Verdi gowns. And he owes me a hundred pounds." Ridges rose on her forehead and her eyes blazed gold as she showed her fangs.

As though they had practiced the move countless times, Angelus and Darla vaulted over the table, landing between Drusilla and Addams. They waited a moment for Drusilla to step forward and then, as one, the three vampires stalked toward Addams.

He backed away, trying to watch all three of them at once, until his back was against the wall. He put his hands out beside him, trying to flatten himself against it, and when his hand touched the heavy draperies of one of the windows, Spike saw the sudden flare of hope in Addams's eyes.

Spike shouted a warning as Addams's hand clenched in the deep pile of the velvet curtains. He gave a powerful yank, and the thick cloth, ripped from its moorings, billowed out and floated to the floor.

The first beams of dawn spilled into the room, and the vampires snarled, scrabbling away from the deadly light and into the welcoming shadows.

"Never think this is the end!" Addams shouted at them, spittle flying from his lips. "Never!" He looked directly at Spike, pointing an accusing finger at him. "You. I'll find you again, no matter how long it takes me. And I'll make you pay for Cecily. It's your fault she's dead." His wide, mad eyes swept the other three vampires. "And if you get in my way, try to protect him again, I'll kill you all."

Backing slowly to the window, he stepped up onto the wide sill and, covering his face with one arm, smashed the plate glass with his other elbow.

"You can't hide from me forever," he said, and leaped down onto the lawn.

Darla got to her feet and looked at Angelus. "What is it, do you think," she said lightly, brushing splinters and shards of glass from her skirt for the second time that night, "that makes them all say the very same thing?" She sighed dramatically. "I suppose this means we're moving again."

"Ooooh," Drusilla crowed. "We could go to someplace warm. Someplace where the children are sweet."

"Or we could go to Paris," Darla said, and Angelus laughed.

"Girls, girls, I think since Spike is the one who got the, er, spike through the chest, he should get to decide." He held out a hand to Spike, who took it and allowed Angelus to pull him to his feet.

Pressing a hand to his chest with a groan, he said, "I bloody well don't care *where* we go, mate, as long as it's far away from this sodding place." He limped away from them, supporting himself on the table, and left them in the sunlit room to discuss their travel plans.

Chapter Twenty-One

Sunnydale, California, Fall semester, 2000

She was summoned. Supposed to be here.

> *Gather ye*
> *Gather ye*
> *Summon ye*
> *To the beginning*
> *To the beginning*
> *The origin*

Willow Rosenberg could hear the words from the stage even in the very back of the dressing rooms. The acoustics of the old theater were amazing.

> *Spin*
> *Weave*
> *Measure*
> *Call on thee*

She had spent all afternoon wrestling with whether or not Spike was right about not asking Giles and the rest of the Scooby Gang to come with them to the theater tonight. She'd decided very quickly not to involve Tara; after all, they were just going to find out who was troubling the characters, right?

The trouble was, if that argument worked for Tara, Spike was right, and it worked for Giles and the Scoobies, too. After the conversation with Spike in her room—(and she was still a little wigged that she'd invited him in)—she was pretty sure she already knew who was behind the troubles in the theater. Tara was going to be really mad that Willow didn't tell her.

Ancient Ones, gather ye

There. From the shadows of the wings, between the first and second sets of curtains, she could see an angle of the stage and part of the audience. She chewed on her lower lip and faded back, tiptoeing around to the side door that led from the backstage area to the orchestra, and slipped out, closing it softly behind her.

No one else had been called to this place the way she had been. Nobody else seemed to feel as connected to the place as she did. She was *supposed* to be here, in this place, at this time. Even if Addams hadn't commanded her, even if he weren't calling her now, she would have come.

The words from the stage now were no longer in English, but in what she guessed was some ancient Attic dialect. She could feel the fine hairs on her arms and the back of her neck rising in response to the immediate buildup of power in response to the change in ritual language.

And in the middle of the stage, in the center, was the same tall thin figure that had held that place earlier in the day. Only now, instead of a brown wool suit and expensive angora sweater, he was wearing a loose gown with broad sleeves that slipped down his raised arms, and she glimpsed bare feet slapping against the plywood that covered the planks of the wooden floor. His hood had fallen back, and the stage lights were reflecting off the lenses of his glasses.

Lights? The house lights were down, and the stage was brightening, as if in response to the power. She so hoped it was something—someone—else. She couldn't see anything up in the tech booth, but Spike was supposed to be up there. He'd agreed. He was going to provide a sound-and-light show for a distraction. She wasn't seeing it.

What she *was* seeing, though, were the characters. They were in the audience, the way they'd been before, but instead of sitting and chatting with each other, they were all focused on the man on the stage. And they were leaning forward, almost as intensely as Spike had been, only they didn't look hungry, they looked scared. And Sherlock Holmes just was *not* supposed to look scared.

They were beginning to arrange themselves by era, she noticed. Oedipus, Lysistrata, Medea, the whole early classical bunch were down in front, and they were beginning to move toward the stage. Not bothering to go sideways along the aisle, they were moving directly through the seats, obviously resisting the pull of the figure on the stage but unable to deny the call of the ancient words. Medea's murdered children wept, and she wept with them as she gathered them in her arms and answered the same summons that Willow did.

Behind them came the characters created by the Romans, the mystery players, the dancers and taletellers, ones she had never seen before and would never have recognized, characters she was certain had never been created on the UC Sunnydale stage: characters created by Maori storytellers, Zulu, Yanomamo, Inuit, Iroquois, Celts, Finns. The audience was packed, and still they came, flowing like a massive silent river up to the stage in response to the chanting command.

And as they came they flowed around the figure in the center, forming a semicircle around him.

The stage shouldn't be big enough to hold them all, she thought. *There are too many of them.*

But as they flowed onto the stage and into the circle, they blurred. She studied the mass of characters frantically, looking particularly for Medea, seeing the image sharpen and fade. And Medea saw her in return and lifted up her children, beseechingly. And then she was gone.

Willow searched for Midge, the sharp, three-dimensional aliveness of him, and watched as he grew thinner, more indistinct, more transparent, until he suddenly popped out of sight as if he had never been there.

The man on the stage extended a hand to her, and she began to feel something tug at her, very faintly.

Above the milling blur of characters on the stage

three images began to form. As the characters disappeared, the images began to solidify, almost as though they were consuming the characters.

The stage itself, the very building, began to shift. Willow glanced down to see the wooden railing under her hand twist and change, along with the steps under her feet, until she was no longer standing in a theater, on the steps that led from the wings of backstage to the safe warm audience on a university campus, but in a forest glade, on the slope of a hill leading down to a hollow, a grassy basin rimmed with olive trees, where a chorus stood entreating the powers, the gods.

They were being led by her Introduction to Drama professor.

And he was sucking the life out of every character on the stage and using them to create . . . something . . . in the air over the chorus.

If whatever it was took shape, the characters would be gone.

He looked up, saw her still standing where she had been, stretched his other hand out to her. She could feel the power thrumming through the air, and the tug became a pull.

Well, there didn't seem to be a sound-and-light show on deck to distract things. There was just Willow Rosenberg, junior witch, not at all sure about the idea of people staring at her, not at all sure of her lines, and with no chance at all to rehearse. Only this time she was the audience, and everyone else was on stage and slowly fading into oblivion.

And Willow Rosenberg was not going to let them

fade into the background. It was time to take a step into the spotlight.

Willow began a chant of her own.

Clotho! Lachesis! Atropos!
You spinner of life, who spins these lives,
You measurer of life, who measures these lives,
You ender of life, who ends these lives?
You spin them not!
You measure them not!
You end them not!

The three gigantic figures took up most of the sky overhead. They barely seemed to notice the activity going on below them. Willow couldn't see their faces, and all things considered she was glad of it; she was too busy seeking words and power of her own. This wasn't the kind of spell one found in the average book of shadows, and she and Spike had been luckier than they probably deserved to find it.

One of the powers made visible reached to the stuff of the stars, gathered it on her fingertips, stretched it out, twisted it.

The next took it from her sister and measured out its length.

The last took it and sliced it clean.

Clotho. Lachesis. Atropos.

Fates.

Older than the gods themselves.

Addams's voice rose into a scream, and incredibly, the Fates paused.

The spinner, the measurer, and the cutter paused and looked down at the little human at their feet, and for that moment no new lives were spun, measured, or ended.

> *These live which you did not spin, O Clotho!*
> *These live and you cannot measure, Lachesis!*
> *These live and you cannot end them, even you,*
> *Atropos!*

The three Fates looked at each other and at the blur of power that were the characters on the stage, and Willow redoubled her petition. But they weren't looking at her.

> *Undo what you have done and I give you what*
> *you have not done!*
> *I offer you this!*
> *Give me what I desire!*

The grass at his feet was beginning to glow pink. In the distance, Willow could hear the sound of trumpets.

Smoke began to billow in rainbow colors from the boles of the olive trees. *Do olive trees have boles?* Willow wondered. *And why is the grass yellow now?*

Oh, *now* Spike decided to show up. Maybe vampires couldn't see the Fates when they leaned down to pluck at the images of dreams and stories?

Where was he? She looked around and realized she had lost track of her spell, lost track of where she was and what she was doing. It didn't matter where Spike was and what he was doing, she decided, even as curtains dropped out of nowhere across the grassy glade, showers of glitter appeared out of nowhere, spotlights cycled through every color of the rainbow, and every sound effect in the repertoire thundered in her ears.

The Fates were lifting something out of the characters, shaping it, placing it on the stage in front of Addams.

No, please, Willow petitioned. *Atropos, Lady of Endings, hear my will, take my will, know my will, that you should not end at the command of one whose thread your sister measures—*

"That ought to keep the bastard busy," Spike snarled in her ear. She noticed he'd gotten one of the swords from the prop room, one that had a red ribbon wound around its hilt. *Well, at least he's prepared,* she thought, *even if it's not going to do much good against gods. . . .*

She ignored him and stepped forward to confront Addams face to face, pulled into the arena by the twisting of threads in the massive glowing hands above her.

"What's he doing?" she heard Spike saying behind her.

"I give you this as well," Addams said triumphantly, catching sight of her and holding out his hand. "This life for the life I ask in return, an even exchange! Give her to me!"

Again the Fates paused, and the world stopped.

A third figure began to form on the stage between Willow and Dr. Addams.

"Cecily!" Addams cried out triumphantly.

"Cecily!" Spike roared.

The figure forming before her was a young woman her own age, dressed in a lilac Victorian walking dress, and Willow could feel magick sucking at her bones even as it sucked at the remaining essence of the characters before her. Whoever Cecily was—and Willow was fairly sure she must be Addams's daughter—she had mad Medea's eyes.

"*No*," Willow Rosenberg said. Cecily shook her head and looked around uncertainly.

Willow's eyes grew wide as she saw the glowing starry fingers of Atropos reaching down for her.

"*No!*" Spike echoed. "Damn you. You died once, and you'll *stay* dead!"

The man on the stage heard him, and the chant abruptly changed from an invocation of the Fates to an invocation of something else.

Alecto, Tisiphone, Megaera! I command you to my call, O Furies, O Hounds of Vengeance! Come claim what is yours!

From far overhead, the scream of a raven answered him, and the images of the Fates paused.

Phantoms began rising among the characters. *I,* Willow thought, *have their monsters.* There one snapped poor Nat's neck, and there another hunted down Medea's screaming children, and there another came out from the wings bearing lighted torches and danced along the curtains, along the scraps of oily ply-wood lying on the floor, and clutched the support beams and pulled at them until they buckled—

And still Addams held out a hand to her, demand-ingly, and she could feel the compulsion to climb up on that stage and submit her will to him, her power to him, to let him take her and use her to race the flames up the allegedly fireproof curtains, to give herself over, to add her own substance, as the characters were adding their own substance, to the one shape taking form in front of her teacher.

And then she went sprawling as a maddened Spike knocked her aside in his drive to get to Addams. The vampire's shriek of pain blended with the scream from Cecily, and he staggered, pulled himself back to his feet, and then in full vampire form he went for Addams again.

He didn't make it this time, either. But the form of Cecily did. With a rushing sound, as of many wings, the Furies appeared, fully formed. They swooped down and surrounded the girl, touching her, and the still figure lifted her head, terribly, and looked around, and there was death in that gaze.

"You killed her!" Addams screamed. "You made me kill her! But I've brought her back! I've won! I've won and I've got her back!"

The Fates withdrew to watch, with silvery threads running back and forth in Lachesis's fingers as Willow watched. Those threads were her life, she realized, hers and Addams's.

And the proper spell came to her, and she raised her hands in appeal to Clotho, and the Fate turned and held her in its terrible regard as the winds rose, and the sounds and the lights and the trees and the stones and the very foundations of the grassy glade shuddered and twisted in the release of power.

And Clotho smiled and turned to the blur of characters and raised her hand as she had raised them to the stars, as Willow raised her own hands, and threads of life began to rise from the mass of imagination behind Addams.

The figure of Cecily, cut free from it all, turned to look at Spike, who lay gasping in agony and laughing up at the Furies, saying, "Not I, you bitch. Remember? They go by the rules. I didn't get to kill you. Daddy got to you first."

The Furies shrieked.

Willow could barely see now, through the smoke and dust from the fire and the collapse of parts of the ceiling. The whole building was trembling. The phantoms raced each other through the walls. The electrical system had shorted out and was sparking in the light cables overhead; she could hear the cracking and snapping of ripped wiring.

Lachesis caught up the threads, not silver but rainbow colors, and instead of measuring them out wove them together. With each separate thread an individual character came free from the blur, and because of the individual colors the character did not lose its individuality in the reweaving.

As more and more threads came out of the blur, the mass of inchoate character shrank, and as it shrank, the Fates receded. Willow stared after them, trying to see what became of the cloth they created, if Atropos would cut it to pieces once it was woven.

She couldn't tell, but she thought she saw the three fling it wide around their shoulders before they faded into nothing, and sweet Cecily turned to regard her loving father, and the theater around Willow Rosenberg exploded.

* * *

"Only in Sunnydale," Rupert Giles observed dryly,

"could one have an earthquake which would totally destroy a single building, without so much as breaking a window in the buildings next door."

"Well, it was due for renovation anyway," Xander said. "Guess they'll be moving up the new building contract."

"It is a shame they'll be looking for a new professor in the middle of the semester."

"Yeah, Will, what's that going to do to finals?" Buffy chirped. "Are they going to bring in somebody new? Are you going to have to do a new paper?"

Willow looked around at the circle of her friends. If she looked hard enough, she thought, she could almost see the silver threads of their lives.

She really could, she realized with a small shock, if she wanted to. She was really that strong. She would never have known that, if not for Addams.

"I don't know if they're going to hire someone or not," she answered, completely avoiding the subject of term papers. "What do you think, Giles? Would you be interested in the job?"

"Oh, absolutely not," he said, turning back to re-shelving some books. "I'm not the dramatic type. Not at all."

Elsewhere, in the midst of the ruins of what had once been a theater, Spike the vampire who was William the Bloody and who had once been someone else and was now a demon glared up at the starry sky. "Fates," he said. "Furies. Bloody hell. *I'm* the only Fate the bloody bint ever needed. And we'll bloody

well keep it that way, got it? It's poetic justice, got it?"
He showed his teeth—human teeth. "And *that's* the
kind of poetry I'm good at, understand?"

The universe did not attempt to contradict him.

ABOUT THE AUTHORS

Ashley McConnell is the author of more than sixteen fantasy, horror, and media novels, all produced while working full-time for a national laboratory.

Her first book, *Unearthed*, was a finalist for the Bram Stoker Award. She lives in Albuquerque, New Mexico, with three cats, two dogs, and two Morgan horses, all of whom want dinner at exactly the same time.

Dori Koogler lives on a farm in the Shenandoah Valley with her husband and two teenage children. She is currently working toward a Master of Fine Arts in Shakespeare and Renaissance Literature in Performance at Mary Baldwin College. She is active in community theater. When she isn't reading Shakespeare or seeing *Hamlet* at the newly opened Blackfriars theater, she works on her yarn collection and helps make costumes for the shows.